MW01169856

N.O. JUSTICE

An Alex Shepherd Novel

C.W. LEMOINE

This book is a work of fiction. Names, characters, places, and incidents are either products of the author's imagination or used fictitiously. Any resemblance to actual events or locales or persons living or dead is entirely coincidental. The views in this book do not represent those of the United States Air Force Reserve or United States Navy Reserve. All units, descriptions, and details related to the military are used solely to enhance the story's realism and credibility.

Cover artwork by EBook Launch

eBook Version

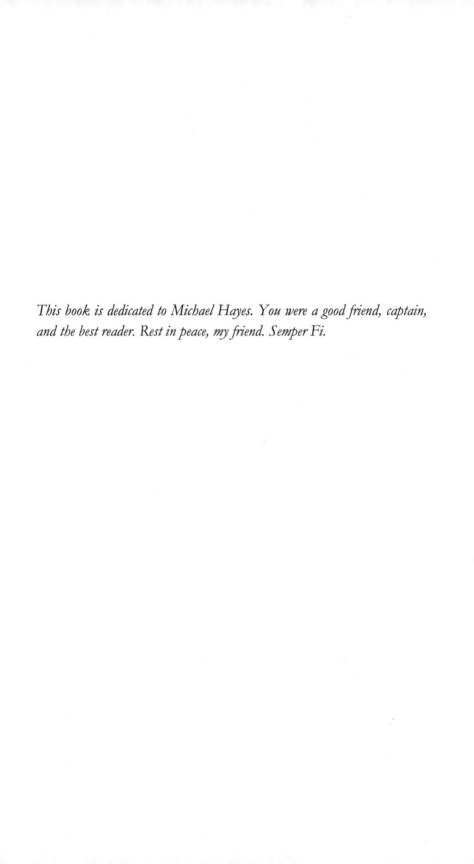

This book is dedicated to Michael Hayes. You were a good friend, captain, and the best reader. Rest in peace, my friend. Semper Fi.

"Revenge is an act of passion; vengeance of justice. Injuries are revenged; crimes are avenged."

— Samuel Johnson

THE *ALEX SHEPHERD* SERIES:

ABSOLUTE VENGEANCE: THE ALEX SHEPHERD STORY (BOOK 1)

THE HELIOS CONSPIRACY *(SPECTRE SERIES BOOK 7)*

I AM THE SHEEPDOG. (ALEX SHEPHERD BOOK 2)

Visit www.cwlemoine.com and subscribe to C.W. Lemoine's Newsletter for exclusive offers, updates, and event announcements.

PROLOGUE

Trooper Darryl Simmons had only been out of the academy for just over a year. He had joined the Louisiana State Police at the age of twenty-six after two tours in Afghanistan with the Army and earned his degree in Criminal Justice at Southeastern Louisiana University. It was his dream job.

He had quickly proven himself in his new profession, earning the Aggressive Criminal Enforcement (ACE) Award after recovering six stolen vehicles with arrests in twelve months. It was the reason he had been hand-selected to DUI enforcement and trusted to work his own flexible hours.

It was an assignment he enjoyed immensely. He had become a Drug Recognition Expert and Standardized Field Sobriety Test (SFST) Instructor with a conviction rate just shy of 100%. The only case that had been thrown out was due to a local jurisdiction's handling of the suspect at the scene of an accident, so the evidence was not admissible in court.

But that was all behind him, and Simmons was sure tonight's shift would bring his numbers up to appease his superiors. He had already made two arrests that were slam dunks, and he still had three hours left to go in his shift. Simmons was confident he would at least get another drunk or ticket to finish out the evening, maintaining his place in the lead for stats in his small DUI unit.

It was just after 3 a.m. and Simmons was sitting in his unit parked in a church parking lot on a narrow stretch of two-lane highway between the small towns of Folsom and Sun in Southeast Louisiana. Simmons was just finishing up his report when he looked up and saw a small sedan with only one headlight approaching from the south on Highway 25.

The car passed by the lighted church parking lot, and Simmons saw a black Honda Civic with partially lowered, dark-tinted windows, and a broken license plate light. Having enough equipment violations to reasonably make a traffic stop, Simmons turned on his headlights and pulled out onto the highway behind the car.

As he accelerated to catch up with the car, he observed the vehicle slowly cross the centerline and then weave back toward the shoulder. When he was within a few car lengths, the driver apparently noticed him and brake-checked Simmons in an attempt to get him to back off.

Simmons called in the stop to dispatch and activated the blue emergency lights on his fully-marked Chevrolet Tahoe. The vehicle once again hit his brakes, but this time more gently, and pulled onto the shoulder.

Simmons pulled up behind the car and angled the nose of his vehicle to the left, giving him both cover in case the driver started shooting and protection against a vehicle rear-ending his Tahoe while he was conducting his roadside investigation. He called the driver out of the vehicle using the unit's PA system as he grabbed his hat and killed the front emergency lights. He left his lightbar's takedown lights and spotlight on the vehicle. His rear emergency lights remained on to warn any approaching motorists or potential backup of the traffic stop.

The driver stumbled out of the car, squinting and shielding his eyes with his right hand as he turned to face the bright LED lights. He left the door open as he pulled up his pants and staggered to meet Simmons at the rear of the vehicle. He was a black man with a shaved head who appeared to be in his mid to late thirties. Simmons estimated he was at least 6'4" and over three hundred pounds, nearly half a foot taller than the 5'9" state trooper.

"Step over here," Simmons said, directing him away from the highway to the right rear corner of the Civic.

Simmons immediately noted the distinct odor of an alcoholic beverage and marijuana on the man's breath and clothes as he neared. Simmons knew this would lead to another arrest, but he was careful not to let his guard down. He was alone on this stretch of highway, and backup from the local sheriff's office could be anywhere from 10-20 minutes away since he was so close to the parish line.

"Man, why the fuck you hasslin' me?" the man asked as he reluctantly complied.

"I'm Trooper Simmons with the Louisiana State Police. The reason I pulled you over tonight is your headlight was out, and you crossed the double-yellow line back there. Have you had anything to drink this evening, sir?" Simmons asked, maintaining a bladed stance with his right leg slightly back in case the man lunged toward the Glock 17 on his right hip.

"You pulled me over for a fucking headlight?" the man asked angrily as his right hand went into his pocket.

"Sir, keep your hands out of your pockets," Simmons warned.

The man stopped and stared at Simmons. "I need a cigarette."

"You can get a cigarette later. For your safety and mine, I need you to keep your hands out of your pockets."

"Man, shit. This is bullshit," the man said as he slowly removed his hand from his pockets. "I'm just trying to go home, and you are just harassin' me."

"What's your name, sir?" Simmons asked as he observed the man's dilated pupils.

"Terry," he replied, leaning against the trunk of his car.

"Terry. Okay, what's your last name?"

"Haynes," Terry replied with a look of disgust.

"Okay, Mr. Haynes, where are you coming from this evening? Have you had anything to drink tonight?"

Terry shifted, still leaning against the car. "Man, I ain't answering shit. I didn't do nothin' wrong."

Simmons took his pen from his pocket and rested his finger on the top. "Okay, Mr. Haynes, I'm going to need you to stand up straight and look at the tip of my pen."

Terry lazily stood, swaying slightly. "Follow the tip of my pen with your eyes and your eyes only. Do not move your head, do you understand?"

"Yeah," Terry mumbled.

Simmons held the pen a few inches from Terry's face. He then moved it from side to side, looking for the involuntary jerking of the eyes known as horizontal gaze nystagmus. As he moved the pen, Terry tracked it by moving his entire head.

"Keep your head still, Mr. Haynes," Simmons warned.

"Man, fuck this," Terry snapped.

Having established enough probable cause to make the DWI arrest, Simmons put the pen back in his shirt pocket. As he did, a car sped by, and Terry lunged toward Simmons.

Simmons, stepped back, dodging Terry's first punch but stumbled and tripped on a pothole on the shoulder. Terry connected with a right cross, and Simmons fell back into the grass by the ditch.

Simmons was dazed by the massive man's hit but was determined to stay in the fight. As he reached for the Taser on his belt, he accidentally knocked the body-worn camera out of its holder, causing it to fall into the grass. He drew the Taser and fired as he scrambled to his feet.

One of the prongs connected and stuck in Terry's shoulder, but the other missed, causing the Taser to be ineffective. Simmons started to rip the cartridge out to install a new one, but there was no time. His NFL lineman-sized attacker was surprisingly quick and already within striking distance.

Simmons managed to hit the red panic button on his radio, sending out a tone to alert dispatchers and other units that he was in the fight of his life. "Stop resisting!" he yelled.

Terry once again swung but, this time, Simmons surged toward him and bear-hugged him, staying inside Terry's massive wingspan and taking him to the ground as his collar mic fell from his shirt.

As they went back to the ground, Terry grabbed Simmons and turned his body, landing on top of Simmons as the two hit the asphalt. Terry started pummeling Simmons as the much smaller trooper did his best to block the blows.

Simmons did his best to fight back, but he was no match for the much larger man who had the upper hand. As he started to feel himself losing consciousness, he felt Terry reaching for the Glock 17 in his holster.

Using his last bit of strength, Simmons punched Terry in the throat as hard as he could, causing him to choke and fall backward momentarily.

As Terry recovered and started back toward him, Simmons drew his weapon and fired rapidly from the hip, hitting Terry six times in the chest and abdomen until the man fell face down into the grass next to the shoulder.

Simmons struggled to his feet and grabbed the collar mic that was now swinging by its cord. “Shots fired! Shots fired!”

CHAPTER ONE

It was only June, but it had already been a long, hot summer. And tempers, much like the temperatures, were on the rise.

At least, that's what the nightly news told us every night before bed. I personally hadn't seen any of the rioting, violence, or negative attitudes against police yet. For the most part, Fredericksburg was a sleepy Texas town and people seemed to be happy staying inside to avoid the heat.

And the ones that were out seemed to appreciate and support law enforcement. Although I was a School Resource Officer (SRO) for the Gillespie County Sheriff's Office, I spent summers assisting various shifts in criminal patrol with my K-9 partner, Kruger. Almost everyone we encountered on the road told us how grateful they were that we were out there every night. We hardly ever paid for a meal in public. It was almost too much.

But on the opposite end of the spectrum, the rest of the country seemed to be in disarray. The shooting death of Terry Haynes by a Louisiana State Trooper near my old home in St. Tammany Parish had ignited riots and violent protests against law enforcement across the country. It was a war against law enforcement, and "Justice for Terry" was their battle cry.

It was a hotly debated topic among friends and family alike. My co-workers with the sheriff's office were almost unanimously in support of Trooper Simmons's actions. Terry Haynes had been solely responsible for his own death. Had he not decided to fight a state trooper on the side of the road while both drunk and high, he might still be alive.

But others, including the more liberal side of my fiancée's family, felt that Haynes had been stripped of his right to due process and that this was more of the systematic racism present in law enforcement. They tended to side with the protesters, and although they didn't believe Haynes had been executed in cold blood as some of the more radical rioters suggested, they did feel that Haynes was clearly a victim.

The Louisiana State Police was still investigating but had released the dashcam footage to try to ease tensions. Instead, it only seemed to make matters worse. The angle that Simmons had parked his unit made it hard to see what was going on, and as the fight progressed, the two were off-screen. All that could be heard was the sound of the two men scuffling. During the struggle, Trooper Simmons's radio toned out before he yelled for Haynes to stop resisting and then shot him.

To make matters even worse, the media had discovered that Simmons had been wearing a body camera, but officials had yet to release the footage. The Louisiana State Police had explained that it wouldn't have done any good in the incident because it had been knocked off during the fight, but of course, that didn't seem to matter to anyone.

To the people protesting, none of the circumstances surrounding the death of Terry Haynes really mattered. Their reality was that another unarmed black man had been gunned down by police in cold blood for the simple crime of having a burned-out headlight. Enough was enough.

A few years ago, I might've been passionate about this issue. I probably would've been just like my co-workers, getting into debates with friends or family that sided with Haynes and explaining that law enforcement was a dangerous job without the benefit of perfect 20/20 hindsight.

I had felt passionate about that when I was a shift corporal with the St. Tammany Parish Sheriff's Office. Working the streets was hard, and even when you did everything right, sometimes the best you could do was break even. The thin blue line of law enforcement was all that separated the innocent from the criminal element in the world, and some people just didn't get it.

But that was Alex Shepherd – a part of me that had been buried with my family, only to be resurrected for a short time when my new friends in Fredericksburg found themselves in danger. But after the threat had passed, that part of me was once again dead and gone. After nearly losing everything yet again, I had locked it away in the depths of my soul and thrown away the key.

I had replaced it with a new identity, an identity I had created named Troy Wilson, or more formally, Deputy First Class Troy Wilson. Unlike the late Alex Shepherd, Troy Wilson was actually happy.

Despite a rocky start with my new identity, I had managed to bury my past and find true, lasting happiness as Troy Wilson. I loved my job as the SRO for Fredericksburg High School (FHS). I loved the people I worked for and with. And most importantly, I loved my new fiancée, Jenny Jenkins.

Jenny was a teacher at FHS, and although I had saved her life from some really bad guys, I credited her with saving mine. She had taught me how to love again and showed me it was okay to be happy again. She knew about my past, and it didn't bother her one bit. It was like she could see right into my soul, as broken as I thought it was.

So, it was hard to care about the rest of the world's politics and drama when everything in my life was finally back on track. Jenny and I were planning a fall wedding and using the summer slowdown to relax and just enjoy being in love. The rest of the world simply did not matter to me.

And why would it? I found myself in bed with my arms wrapped around the woman I loved in post-coital bliss. My best friend and K-9 partner, Kruger, was curled up at the foot of our bed next to Jenny's miniature dachshund, Bear. It was exactly what I needed after a long day on duty.

I'm not sure why, with all of that going for me, I decided to turn on the evening news that night, but I did. The breaking news story was enough to jolt me back to reality like a cold bucket of water being dumped on me.

I shot upright in the bed as I read the headline and turned up the volume. Startled, Bear yelped and jumped off the bed, scrambling for cover while Kruger gave me a confused look.

"What's wrong?" Jenny asked as she slowly sat up next to me and put her arm on my shoulder. "Are you okay?"

I said nothing as I turned the volume up. The station cut to a female reporter standing in front of a hospital.

"Thanks, John. What we know so far is that earlier this afternoon, at around 2 p.m., Corporal Cindy Parker was dispatched to a medical emergency involving a small child just outside of Covington, Louisiana. When she arrived at the address, she was ambushed by two armed men who, police say, fled before deputies arrived," the reporter said.

"Is that your old department?" Jenny asked.

I said nothing as footage from Sheriff Leon's press conference started. I had worked for him as a corporal in St.

Tammany Parish. He was a good man who really cared about his people. I could see the pain and anguish in his eyes as he stood in front of the crowd of reporters on screen.

"We are working with state and federal authorities to bring the men responsible for this heinous act to justice," Sheriff Leon said. "Corporal Parker has been with this agency for ten years and was responding with lights and siren, risking her life to get to the scene of what she thought was an unresponsive child. The call was apparently fake, and the suspects were able to use the element of surprise to ambush Corporal Parker."

"Jesus," I mumbled.

Sheriff Leon looked right into the camera and said, "Regardless of the political climate, these acts of violence against our deputies cannot, and will not, stand. I will do everything in my power to bring these thugs to justice. Dead or alive. Thank you, and good night."

The screen cut back to the reporter, "Corporal Parker is currently undergoing surgery for her injuries. We'll have more updates as we get them. This is Taylor Downing, reporting."

I turned off the TV. My hands were shaking. Jenny stroked the back of my head.

"Talk to me, babe," she said softly.

"Cindy was on my shift. I was her corporal," I said.

"You were pretty close to her, huh?"

I nodded, holding back tears. "Everyone on my shift was like my second family. We had each other's back. Cindy was there almost every day at the hospital when I was in a coma. She helped pull me back from the edge when I had lost all reason for living."

"I'm so sorry. Do you want to go there?"

I shook my head. "I can't. They'll recognize me. For all they know, Alex Shepherd died in Syria three years ago."

"I'm sorry, babe."

"Cindy is tough. She'll make it," I said as Jenny grabbed my shaking hand and squeezed. "She has to."

"She will, sweetie," Jenny said as she gently stroked my head.

"*She has to*," I said softly.

CHAPTER TWO

I didn't sleep much that night. I tossed and turned until, finally, I gave up and got up at 3 a.m. to get ready early for my 6 a.m. shift. I started a pot of coffee for Jenny and, by 4 a.m., I was out the door and headed to the sheriff's office substation.

One of the cable news channels played in the squad room as I sat down at the computer. Kruger curled up in a bed I had left in the corner of the room for her as I grabbed the remote and turned up the volume. I had hoped to get an update on Cindy's condition.

Instead, I was blasted by a constant stream of nonsense. Reporters droned on about celebrity gossip, the latest gaffe by the president, and a scandal by some politician I had never heard of. They couldn't bother to report the condition of a real hero like Cindy Parker.

After twenty minutes of feeling like I was losing IQ points, I muted the TV. As I did, I saw the Louisiana State Trooper's service photo that had been involved in the shooting of Terry Haynes. I turned up the volume, hoping they would give some clue as to who had ambushed Cindy and maybe update us on her condition.

I was once again disappointed as the panel of "experts" began dissecting the recently released dashcam footage from Trooper Simmons's unit. One panelist argued that Haynes momentarily crossed the yellow line and then touched the white line on the highway which did not constitute sufficient probable cause for the stop.

The former cop, outnumbered as he was, tried to explain that reasonable articulable suspicion was all that was required and not PC, but the distinction fell on deaf ears. The others at the roundtable talked over him, arguing that it was more evidence of systemic racism in America's justice system.

I turned off the TV and tapped my thigh for Kruger to follow. We loaded up in my Tahoe and called dispatch to let them know we were 10-8, on duty, and available for calls. I needed to drive around a bit to clear my head.

There weren't many cars on the highway as the sun started to rise. I couldn't stop thinking about Cindy and her husband, Mark. He worked for Covington PD, a local city in St. Tammany Parish near the ambush location. I wondered if he had been on duty when the call came out that she had been shot—w*hat a horrible feeling.*

It was something I was all too familiar with. I had lost my family while working a shift as a corporal with the sheriff's office. A group of terrorists had stolen a school bus that my wife and daughter had taken to the local elementary school. It was my daughter's first day and my wife's second year as a teacher.

When we discovered that their bus was missing after finding the school bus driver's body next to an abandoned vehicle near the school, we had initiated a school lockdown of the nearby Mandeville Elementary and started a desperate search. Our air unit found it after what seemed like an eternity, and the chase was on.

I joined the chase just as the bus reached Slidell, Louisiana. The terrorists took the bus and its occupants to an empty movie theater parking lot. I did everything to get to my wife and daughter, despite several fellow SWAT deputies trying to hold me back. I managed to kill a couple of the terrorists, but I was too late to save my family. They had executed my wife shortly after taking the bus and rigged it with explosives that detonated just as I reached the lead terrorist.

It was the worst day of my life. Cindy and the rest of my team had been there to help me through it as I woke up from my coma nearly two months later. She didn't deserve to be ambushed by cowards, and I was sure her family was devastated over the thought of losing her.

I drove around for a bit as I tried to clear my head. Kruger and I responded to a few calls for service, backing patrol deputies on a false house alarm and a suspicious vehicle report in a ritzy neighborhood. The van turned out to be someone's landscaper, and the call was quickly cleared.

After that call, I met Jenny at the school for breakfast. Although summer school was in session, the county had decided that keeping an SRO on duty was not cost -effective, so we only worked there during the regular school year. Kruger and I did a quick walk -through to make sure everything was okay and then met Jenny in the cafeteria.

"You look tired, babe," Jenny said as she hugged me and gave me a kiss on the cheek. "What time did you leave?"

"Too early," I said as I grabbed a tray. "I couldn't sleep."

"I know," she said. "I was there."

"Sorry."

Jenny smiled. "You know I'm just kidding."

I grabbed a full plate of eggs and bacon with a little extra for Kruger and a cup of coffee, and we headed to a table in the corner of the cafeteria. As we sat down, Jenny scrolled through her phone.

"Have you heard anything about your friend?" Jenny asked.

Realizing we were in public, I said, "Not so loud."

Jenny's eyes widened. "Oh. Right. Sorry."

"No, I haven't," I said, handing Kruger a strip of bacon under the table. She nearly took my hand off with her titanium incisors as she immediately inhaled the strip.

"I'll look it up," Jenny said, staring at her phone.

I picked up a bacon strip as Jenny suddenly gasped. "Oh, Troy…"

"What is it?" I asked nervously. "Don't tell me."

"I'm so sorry," she said softly.

"Goddammit," I said. "What happened?"

"Corporal Parker succumbed to her injuries just after 2 a.m.," Jenny said as she read the article on her phone.

The news hit hard. I felt like I was processing it in slow motion as the words hung in the air. *Cindy was dead.*

Jenny put the phone down and looked up at me. I was staring off into space as she grabbed my hand. "I'm so sorry, sweetheart."

"She didn't deserve this," I mumbled.

"I know, babe," Jenny said.

I pushed aside my breakfast. I didn't have much of an appetite that morning to begin with, but the news of Cindy's death made me sick to my stomach.

"You should go to the funeral," Jenny said softly. "*We* should go."

I considered her proposal for a minute and then quickly brushed it off. There was no way I could show my face there without someone recognizing me and realizing that Alex Shepherd wasn't dead after all. We had already been through that drama once before, and I had almost lost Jenny as a result. There was no way I was risking that again.

"I can't. You know that."

"You don't have to talk to anyone," Jenny said. "But I'm sure there will be a big event, and lots of cops will be there. You could blend in and pay your respects."

"I shouldn't go anywhere near that place. It's not safe. Remember the last time someone figured out who I was?"

"This is different."

"How?"

"She was your friend, Troy. You need closure."

"And if someone recognizes me? Then what?"

"They won't," Jenny said, gently stroking my beard. "It's been years, they think you're dead, and they've never seen you with this beard, right? Besides, we'll stay in the background just in case."

"It's not a good idea," I said.

"Yes, it is," Jenny said. "I'll be there with you. And so will Kruger."

"I'd have to get permission to take her out of the county."

"Then do it," Jenny said. "You need your girls there with you."

I sighed softly. "I'll talk to the boss."

"Thank you," Jenny said, stroking my arm. "This will be good for you."

CHAPTER THREE

Surprisingly, the sheriff's office was totally on board with me taking a few days off and taking Kruger with me to Louisiana for the funeral. They even encouraged it.

I told my boss that Cindy Parker had been a family friend, which wasn't a lie, but he didn't question it. I had plenty of leave built up, and after everything I had done for the department in working both as an SRO and supporting the road deputies when called upon, he felt I had earned it. School was out of session anyway, so no worries at all.

Although it was only Tuesday and the services weren't until Friday, Jenny and I decided to head down early and spend some time across Lake Pontchartrain in New Orleans. She had never been and thought some time away might be good for us while taking my mind off things.

That night, I found a pet-friendly bed and breakfast in Uptown New Orleans near Loyola University and made reservations. Before dawn on Wednesday morning, we loaded up my truck and headed east. I drove while Bear and Jenny rode shotgun, and Kruger slept in her crate behind my seat.

We stopped for lunch in Lake Charles. As we went through the drive-thru of a local po-boy place, the local radio station DJ went through the day's headlines. Protests were still ongoing in various locations across the state. Some had even turned violent, but police had been able to deescalate before anyone had gotten hurt. Tensions were high as protestors called for the arrest of Trooper Simmons. No one even mentioned Cindy's ambush.

After picking up food, we stopped at a nearby gas station for fuel and to let Kruger and Bear stretch their legs for a minute. Jenny took them while I filled up my truck. As I did, a teenage male approached me.

"You a cop?" he asked.

I kept pumping gas while slowly moving my hand toward my holstered Glock 43 near my appendix. "Why do you ask?" I replied.

"I saw your dog. You look like a cop. Except for the beard."

"That a problem?"

"Nobody likes cops anymore. They say y'all keep killing unarmed people."

"Sorry you feel that way," I said, watching the kid's hands.

"Be careful. I support y'all," the kid said with a big smile. "I'm gonna join one day too. I want to be a K9 officer. Anyway, take it easy. Be safe."

The kid waved shyly and then kept walking toward the exit of the gas station parking lot. Jenny returned, eyeing the boy as she helped Kruger and Bear back into the truck and gave them water.

"What was that all about?" Jenny asked.

"I have no idea," I replied. "That was weird."

Jenny shrugged and then gave me a kiss. We got back into my truck and continued driving east toward New Orleans.

"What did that kid tell you?" Jenny finally asked as we got back onto the interstate.

"He knew I was a cop. I thought he was looking to get into something, but then he just told me he supported cops and wanted to be one someday. Told me to be safe."

"Aww…that's sweet."

"Just weird," I said.

"How are you holding up?" Jenny asked, stroking the back of my neck.

"I'm fine."

"Are you sure?"

"Yes." I didn't want to talk about it. Cindy was dead for no good reason. There was nothing I could do to change that. I had no intentions of dwelling on it.

Jenny fell asleep a few minutes after taking the hint that I didn't want to talk about any of it. I flipped through the stations, careful to avoid the local newscasts. I was sick of hearing about the protests and updates about the Simmons shooting. It had become a media circus.

We arrived in New Orleans just after 5 p.m., in time to sit in rush hour traffic. Students protested in front of Tulane and Loyola as we passed, causing traffic to back up even further as campus police attempted to deal with them. I had never seen anything like it.

Just before 6, we checked in at the bed and breakfast. I was exhausted from driving all day. I took a shower while Jenny fed the dogs. When I stepped out to get dressed for dinner, I saw Jenny sitting on the bed watching TV.

"Nothing good ever comes from watching that junk," I said as I dried off.

"You need to see this." Jenny turned up the volume.

I stood there in stunned silence as I realized what was going on. A service photo of a New Orleans Police Department officer that had been with the department for fifteen years was on the screen as the reporter went over what they knew so far.

"At just after 2 p.m. this afternoon, Sergeant Ronaldo Higgens was alone in his police car when an unknown male suspect approached and opened fire," an NOPD spokesperson said. "Higgens was transported to University Medical Center where he succumbed to his injuries."

"Turn it off," I growled.

"Troy-"

"Turn it off."

Jenny complied and turned to face me. "What is happening? Why are they doing this?"

I shook my head. "I don't know."

"Maybe we should just go back home," Jenny said as she looked into my eyes.

"You pushed for us to come here," I said, confused by her sudden reversal. "To risk it."

"I don't know, Troy," Jenny said. "I just have a bad feeling about this. It's too dangerous."

"For the men and women that put on the badge right now, it is. But we're just going to the funeral."

"I don't know. It just doesn't feel right. Maybe this was a bad idea."

"No," I said. "We're here to honor Cindy. That's what we'll do."

"I love you," Jenny said before kissing me.

"I love you too," I said before shaking off the anger of another murdered officer. "Now, let's get ready. I know a great little seafood place right down the street. I think you'll love it."

"This state is going to make me gain fifty pounds," Jenny said, clutching her stomach.

"That's what we're famous for," I said with a grin.

CHAPTER FOUR

Law enforcement officers from agencies all over the state showed up in full uniform to pay their respects to Cindy. It was a touching tribute to a hero that had died serving her community. But as beautiful as the service was, the loss of Cindy just sucked. She was far too young and too good of a deputy to be taken so soon.

I wore a suit and tie, careful to blend in with the crowd as Jenny and I stood in the back of the packed multimillion dollar church. Bagpipes played as deputies wearing dark blue dress uniforms with white gloves carried Cindy's flag-draped coffin to the stage. Her husband followed the procession in his Covington Police Department uniform, escorting their young son in his suit and tie. Jenny clutched my arm as a tear rolled down my cheek.

I saw my former shift lieutenant, Dan Jacobson, and my former shift sergeant, Sean Taylor, walking with the procession. I noticed that Jacobson had made captain and Taylor had made lieutenant. They had both been huge parts of my life when I worked for the sheriff's department there and even more significant in keeping me alive after my family had been killed.

They took their seats behind Cindy's husband and son as the preacher approached the podium. After he finished with the various prayers and said a few words about Cindy's service to the community, Jacobson stood and walked to the stage.

Jacobson was a big man, pushing 6'4" and solid muscle. He had served in the Army in Afghanistan. He was burly and rough, but the best leader I had ever worked for. He was a good soldier but an even better cop. Sometimes I wished I could just sit down with him for a few minutes and tell him all the stuff I had seen since leaving my home state. I was sure we could tell war stories over beer until we were both blacked-out drunk. I respected the hell out of that man.

He walked up slowly but deliberately. He thanked the preacher as he took the podium and then paused. The look on his face was exactly what I had expected. The tough-as-nails cop standing at the podium was on the verge of breaking down. Because, as quickly as he could snap your neck with his meaty hands, he cared about his people more than anything. He looked like a father that had just lost his only daughter. It was a look I knew all too well.

Jacobson's booming voice echoed through the PA over the massive church's theater seating. I was convinced that we would've been able to hear him clearly even from the back row without the assistance of a microphone, but the sound system made his thunderous voice sound all the more impressive. It was as if God himself was delivering the eulogy.

He said his own prayer and then talked about Cindy's time with the St. Tammany Parish Sheriff's Office. He began with the story of how she had started as a dispatcher and then moved her way through corrections until finally getting a coveted slot with the academy. She had worked tirelessly and without complaint until she eventually earned her spot on the road and criminal patrol. He had been so proud to call her with the news.

He told a few funny stories from her time on criminal patrol and then talked about her promotion to corporal. She had always had great attention to detail, and the reports her team wrote the best in the district. His only regret was that she didn't get promoted sooner.

When he was finished, Cindy's husband took the podium. He thanked everyone for coming out and then spoke of Cindy not as a cop but as a wife and mother. I looked down to see Jenny standing next to me, bawling her eyes out as she listened to him speak. I unhooked my arm from hers and wrapped it around her, pulling her close as she buried her face in my shoulder.

Cindy's husband finished, and "Amazing Grace" began playing. The honor guard ceremoniously retrieved her casket and escorted it down the aisle. We stayed behind the crowd as people followed the casket outside to the waiting hearse.

A loudspeaker had been set up outside. One of the department's dispatchers came over the radio, calling Cindy's radio number several times before announcing her end of watch date. Hundreds of officers saluted as "Taps" played, and the honor guard folded the flag. They presented it to Cindy's husband and saluted him.

With the ceremony concluded, an official announced that the procession would be proceeding to the burial site. Friends, family, and law enforcement guests were welcome to attend, but he asked that the media please respect the family's wishes for a private burial.

Motorcycles from the St. Tammany Parish Sheriff's Office traffic division and other agencies led the way as procession left the parking lot. Jenny and I went back to my truck and waited as the long line of cars filed out of the parking lot behind the police cars and hearse.

"Are you still going to go to the burial?" Jenny asked as she grabbed my hand.

"We need to go back to Kruger and Bear," I replied. We had left them both in our room at the bed and breakfast to not stand out since I was going as a civilian and not a K-9 deputy from Texas.

"They will be fine," Jenny said. "We should go."

"They are burying her in a small cemetery in the woods on the north side of the parish," I replied. "I don't think it will be as easy to hide without someone recognizing me."

Jenny turned her entire body in the seat to face me. "You don't want to go at all, do you?"

"What do you mean?"

"When we left, you said you wanted to be there. Now, you're making every excuse you can think of to not go."

"I just don't think it's a good idea," I said.

I didn't want to admit it, but she was right. Not only had Cindy's death hit me like a ton of bricks, but the entire event was starting to bring back memories of losing my family. The crowds, the police processions – all of it – reminded me of the day I got out of the hospital after the attack. I didn't want to admit it, but I was starting to feel sick to my stomach.

Jenny seemed to study me for a bit and then said, "You don't have to go, sweetie."

"No, you're right," I said as I put the truck in gear. "That's what we came here for. I need to face this."

CHAPTER FIVE

We waited until the last car and escort unit left the church parking lot and then filed in behind them. We didn't turn our hazards on or act as part of the procession. We were just following at a comfortable distance. I wanted to remain in the background as much as possible.

Jenny and I didn't say much as we followed the funeral procession to the gravesite. A light rain started just as we neared the turnoff to the narrow asphalt road leading to the cemetery. I didn't want to tell Jenny, but I was struggling. It felt like a knife had been jabbed into my chest, and someone was twisting it ever so slowly.

I didn't know how to tell Jenny that we were traveling down the same road that I had driven before leaving for the Middle East. It was the same cemetery where my wife and young daughter had been buried while I was in a coma. It was the place that had driven me to a murderous rage that had taken me across the world. I was sure Jenny wouldn't recognize or love the man I had become that day.

The memory of seeing my young daughter's headstone for the first time came rushing back. I remembered falling to my knees as I contemplated taking my own life to join them.

"Are you okay?" Jenny asked, snapping me out of the flashback. She was staring at my hands on the steering wheel.

I looked down to see that my knuckles were white as I held a death grip on the wheel.

"Huh?"

We turned onto the narrow road toward the cemetery just as I looked at Jenny, not knowing what to say.

"I just…"

Before I could get the words out, Jenny's eyes widened, and she suddenly pointed to the car in front of us. "Look out!"

I slammed on the brakes as I turned to see the car in front of us doing a panic stop and swerving into the ditch. We stopped just inches from the car's rear bumper as it came to a rest in the shallow trench.

I started to get out of the car and heard a rapid succession of *POP-POP-POP*. At first, I thought it was a car backfiring until the cadence change, and I realized it was return fire. There was a gunfight happening a quarter of a mile in front of us at the front of the convoy.

I ran back to my truck and grabbed my Glock 19 from the holster under the seat. "Get down!" I yelled.

"What's going on?" Jenny asked as she reluctantly complied.

"Shots fired!"

I reached in and tried to push her head down. "Get as small as you can."

"Where are you going?" Jenny asked.

"To see if I can help," I said as I grabbed a spare, full-size magazine from under the seat and stuffed it in my pocket.

"Troy, be careful!" she yelled as I closed the door.

I brought my Glock 19 up to the low ready and started toward the sound of gunfire. Cars in front of me began turning around to get out of the ambush zone as I ran past them.

I moved toward the tree line to flank where I thought the ambush was coming from. The gunfire was deafening. I had no idea if I was hearing both sides firing at each other or just the cops returning fire, but it sounded like a war zone.

Two cars ran into each other and blocked the road as they desperately tried to escape the kill zone. I ran back toward them, keeping my weapon out of sight as I made sure both drivers were okay, and then headed back toward the gunfire.

As I got closer, I could hear people yelling. Some were cops trying to coordinate fire and movements. Others were trying to yell loud verbal commands at the suspects. But others were screaming for help. Their pleas were haunting.

I moved out into the woods slowly, trying not to draw the shooters' attention or the officers and deputies returning fire. I nearly tripped over a body as I reached the ambush area. He was dressed in all black and had a MAC-10 machine pistol lying next to his body in the grass. I noticed a tattoo on his neck but couldn't make out what it was. It looked like a spider or scorpion or something similar, but I didn't have time to examine it since there was a gunfight still going on.

I could see movement deeper in the woods and continued moving toward it. The gunfire subsided as I came across another body. It was clear the suspect was dead, so I moved his handgun out of the way and moved on.

As I stood, I heard movement to my left and looked to see three officers moving toward me with their patrol rifles raised. A bullet zipped past my head and hit the tree next to me, splintering the wood.

I ducked down and yelled back toward the approaching officers. "Get down! I'm a friendly! We're taking fire!"

The officers took cover as I looked to find the suspect. I saw a man running in the woods and realized it was the man who had just taken a shot at my head. He was running and blindly firing behind him. I started to take the shot but thought better of it.

Instead, I pulled out my badge from my pocket and held it out with my left hand so the other officers could see. "Friendly! Suspect is running east! This one is down."

The three officers continued moving past me in pursuit of the suspect. I turned back toward the scene of the ambush to see if I could render aid. As I got closer, I saw the bodies of officers lying on the road and in the ditch next to the vehicles. A tree had fallen in the roadway and created the roadblock that had allowed the shooters to ambush the procession.

Some officers had set up a defensive perimeter while others tended to the wounded and dead. I tucked my Glock into my waistband at the small of my back and went for the nearest unattended downed officer.

I rolled him over and saw that he had been hit with a headshot. I didn't recognize the officer, but that didn't make it any easier. I moved on to the next one near the hearse as I heard sirens approaching. The cavalry was on its way – too late to do anything but collect the dead and wounded.

The next victim was leaning against the front of the hearse. As I realized who it was, my heart sank. The big, burly combat veteran I had looked up to for so long was leaning against the front bumper, clutching his abdomen as he sat in a pool of his own blood.

I pulled out the small individual first aid kit I always kept in my pocket and unzipped it as I dropped to my knees next to Captain Jacobson.

"Alex?" he called out weakly as I tried to assess his wounds.

"Try not to talk, Dan. It's going to be okay," I said as I franticly moved his hand and poured the QuikClot into the wound.

"You're alive," he said, moving his bloodied hand up to touch my arm.

I pulled out the bandaging and packed the wound as best I could. "Apply pressure here," I said as I moved his hands.

"I'm not going to make it," Jacobson said. "Don't waste your time."

"Bullshit," I said, moving to his leg as I retrieved the tourniquet from the first aid kit. He had been shot in the thigh, just above the knee. It looked like it had nicked his femoral artery. I had to stop the bleeding.

"I like the beard," Jacobson said weakly. "You look like a Green Beret."

"We can talk more when you get better, buddy, don't worry," I said as I wrapped the tourniquet around his leg.

"I'm so sorry about your family. I know you went over there because we didn't do enough."

"You did all you could. Don't worry about that."

"You're a ghost," Jacobson said, laughing. "I'm already dead, aren't I?"

"No," I said as I twisted the tourniquet. "I'm not dead, and neither are you. And you *won't* die, do you understand me?"

I finished securing the tourniquet to see Jacobson staring off in the distance. It was the cold, blank stare of a man who had just crossed into the afterlife.

"Dan!" I yelled as I tried to shake him.

I pushed him down onto the asphalt and started CPR. As paramedics arrived to relieve me, I realized he was gone. I stumbled backward, blood-soaked hands shaking as the scene became even more chaotic.

An EMT tried to see to me, but I pushed past them as I stumbled back toward my truck. I was shell-shocked. Jenny leapt out of the truck and ran to me as she saw me, bloodied and shaken, approaching her.

"Troy!" she yelled as I collapsed to my knees.

CHAPTER SIX

The Louisiana State Trooper that took our statement was professional and courteous. I told him that I was a K-9 deputy from Texas and had run to render aid as soon as I realized there was an ambush. After we finished writing our statements, he made copies of my credentials and driver's license as well as Jenny's ID, and we were on our way.

The scene was a chaotic mess. The sheriff's office had been overwhelmed since so many deputies had been a part of the procession. State Troopers had come in to assist, and I even saw a few FBI agents show up in unmarked Tahoes. It would take days and possibly weeks to process the crime scene.

The initial victim count was staggering. I didn't know the names besides Cindy's husband and my former lieutenant, Dan Jacobson, but I overheard one of the troopers say there were at least five killed and fifteen wounded. Most of the dead were likely traffic deputies on motorcycles that had been escorting the hearse near the front of the procession, and I was sure some of them were people I had known while working at the St. Tammany Parish Sheriff's Office.

I didn't talk about what happened on the drive back to the bed and breakfast, and Jenny didn't ask. We were both shell - shocked. And there was really nothing left to say. A good man had been murdered, just as Cindy and the other victims of these animals had been.

Animals. That was the only word I could think of to describe them. They were sub-human, the scum of the earth. No decent human beings would do what they did. I couldn't even imagine someone thinking up a plan to ambush a funeral. It was beyond comprehension.

It took almost two hours to get to the bed and breakfast with traffic. We let Kruger and Bear out to stretch their legs and do their business. After that, we changed clothes, and then all four of us crashed on the bed. Kruger could tell something was wrong and snuggled her head under my arm to get as close as she could to me.

"What do we do now?" Jenny asked softly.

"You and Bear are going home," I replied, still staring at the ceiling fan as it slowly rotated above us.

Jenny sat up in the bed, causing Bear to groan as she moved him from her chest. "What do you mean *me and Bear*? What are you going to do?"

"I'm going to stay for Dan's funeral."

"Then I'll stay with you."

"You have to go back to work on Monday," I said.

"I have plenty of leave built up."

"Did you not see what just happened?" I asked, making no effort to mask my frustration. "They're targeting cops and their families. They just shot up a *fucking funeral*."

"And?" Jenny shot back.

"*And* you don't need to be here with all of that going on."

"And you do?"

"Dan Jacobson was my friend," I said.

"Troy, look at me," Jenny said.

I slowly sat up and faced Jenny. "Before you say what I think you're going to say, I'm going to tell you now, I'm not changing my mind."

"It's not up to you," Jenny said. "I'm a big girl. I can decide for myself."

"You need to go home," I said. "It's not safe here."

"Well, then, so do you. If it's not safe for me, it's surely not safe for you."

"You don't understand…"

"Well, then talk to me, Troy. Make me understand," Jenny replied. "What's going on in that head of yours."

I felt a flood of emotion rushing over me and pushed Kruger aside as I got out of bed. My hands were shaking as I started pacing around the room. "You have to go," I mumbled.

"Troy, why?" Jenny asked. She got out of bed and walked over to meet me. She saw my hands and grabbed them. "Talk to me."

"I can't lose you too," I said, my voice quivering. "I won't."

"You're not going to, sweetheart, I promise."

"They're attacking police. They're attacking us. They could have killed you. And it happened *there*."

"There?"

I said nothing as I wrestled free of Jenny's grip.

"Troy, *where*? What are you talking about?"

"I didn't want to go there," I muttered as a tear rolled down my face. "I didn't want to go back."

Jenny rushed to me as I paced away. She wasn't going to let it go. I didn't want to tell her anymore.

"Troy, where? The cemetery?"

As soon as she said it, her eyes widened as the realization hit her. "Oh my God, Troy."

She grabbed me and hugged me tightly as she started to cry with me. "I am so sorry, sweetheart. I am so, so sorry."

I broke down. I couldn't bite my lip any longer. It was all just too much for me to handle.

"Is that where your girls were buried?" Jenny asked as she wiped away a tear from my cheek.

I nodded, avoiding eye contact – embarrassed that I couldn't keep it together in front of her.

I pulled her away from me, looking into Jenny's eyes. "If we had left earlier with the procession, we could've been in the middle of that. I could have lost you too."

"Troy, you're not going to lose me," Jenny said.

"Please go back," I said. "Don't make me beg."

"Okay, Troy, I'll go home," Jenny replied reluctantly. "But promise me you will stay out of trouble and come home safe."

"I will," I said. "I just think saying goodbye to an old friend is the right thing to do. And if there's another attack, I don't want you here for it. That's all. I would much rather have you by my side, but I can't lose you too."

"You don't have to explain anymore," Jenny said. "I understand now. It's okay."

"You're not mad?" I asked cautiously.

Jenny shook her head. "No…but I just wish you would talk to me and not bottle everything up like this."

"I'm sorry. This place just brings back so many memories of a life I thought I had left behind."

"I know, sweetie," Jenny said before changing the subject. "So can you at least take me to dinner before you ship poor Bear and me back to Texas?"

"Yes, ma'am," I said before kissing her.

CHAPTER SEVEN

I bought Jenny and Bear a ticket back to San Antonio and brought them to the airport the next morning. I walked her into the terminal, and we had a tearful goodbye near security.

"Be safe," she said as she hugged me one last time. "I mean it."

"Yes, ma'am," I replied.

"Please come home to me safely, Troy," she pleaded. "I know what you're thinking…"

"Really?" I asked. "Because I don't."

"Just be safe," Jenny said. "That's all I'm saying."

"Okay," I said as I kissed her. I unzipped Bear's carrier slightly and scratched his ears before zipping it back up and kissing Jenny again.

"Have a good flight," I said.

"Call you as soon as I land," she replied as she turned to enter the line.

I walked back to the parking garage, watching the other travelers as they entered the terminal. They seemed oblivious to the war raging just outside the terminal. To them, the ambushes and assassinations were just headlines to be ignored.

But to me, it was personal. I had lost two very close friends from my former life. And in the ambush, four more had been killed – two deputies, one officer from a nearby city, and Cindy's husband. Her child had been orphaned in an act of senseless violence. It was deeply personal for me.

I went back to my truck and exited the parking garage. As I turned onto Airline Highway and headed back to the B&B to pick up Kruger, I turned the radio on. It was still tuned to a local AM talk radio station, and they seemed to be talking about the ambushes.

"...I'm just saying," the male caller said, "if the police wouldn't be out there killing unarmed black men, none of this would be happening."

"So, you're saying what happened yesterday is justified in your eyes?" the female host asked.

"I ain't saying that, but...all I'm saying is I understand why it's happening. Enough is enough."

"Okay, thank you for your call," the woman said. "Let's take the next caller. Hello, Tony? You're on with 'Helen in the Morning'."

"Good morning, Helen, I just wanted to say that I think it's a damned shame what's happening right now. The police are afraid, and they're being targeted. They deserve to come home just like anyone else."

"Do you think we need law enforcement reforms to make this stop, as a previous caller suggested?" Helen asked.

"No, I think the media needs to stop lying about what's happening, and y'all need to start reporting the truth!"

"Tony, we only report the news as we are given the information. Why do you say it's a lie?"

"You know as well as I do that the media blows things out of proportion to get ratings. Headlines like 'unarmed black man killed by police.' You know that's a lie."

"I'm not sure I understand how that is a lie, Tony. Can you give me a specific example?"

"Like the Terry Haynes shooting. I watched that video. That was a big man who decided to fight with that trooper. He wasn't innocent."

"I understand that, Tony, but Terry Haynes was, in fact, an unarmed black man."

"So?"

"So, I don't see how you can say we're lying when we reported the facts. The headlines did not say he was innocent."

"You know damned well what I mean! Y'all frame it that way just to make people mad. Actin' like cops go out there every night looking for young black men to execute. I'm a black man, and my father was with NOPD for twenty-three years. I know that's not true!"

"Okay, Tony, thank you for the call. We have to go to commercial break now, but…"

I turned off the radio. The politics of it didn't matter. Nothing would change no matter who won the political debate. There was no justifying what happened to Cindy or the funeral procession.

I picked up Kruger, let her go to the bathroom outside, and then we loaded up and headed north. We crossed the Causeway Bridge and then turned onto I-12. I couldn't help but think about the school bus attack and the deaths of my wife and daughter. It was the same stretch of highway I had sped down trying to intercept the hijacked school bus. I could still hear the blaring siren and radio calls from Air One. It felt like a bad dream.

I exited the interstate and took the back roads to the scene of the ambush. As we reached the site, I saw that the road was open, but crime scene tape and small fences had been set up on the shoulder and into the wooded area. The vehicles had all been removed, but crime scene technicians from both the Sheriff's Office and FBI still appeared to be processing the scene.

One of the techs made eye contact with me as I slowly drove by. I quickly looked away, afraid that the FBI technician would somehow recognize me. I continued along the winding single-lane road until we reached the cemetery.

I pulled off to the side and put my truck in park as I took a deep breath and exhaled slowly. I hadn't been there since making the decision to avenge my family's death. It was a decision that had taken me on a path of bloody vengeance from Mississippi to Georgia, and finally, the Middle East.

There, I would join the Kurdish militia group known as the *Lions of Rojava* in their fight against ISIS. Using my skills as a SWAT sniper, I helped them take back cities in Northern Iraq and Syria, until the bloody reality of war came front and center. I soon learned that I wasn't the only one who had suffered in the fight against evil, and watched a good friend brutally murdered by an ISIS executioner.

It was where my former life as Alex Shepherd had officially died. I was rescued by a paramilitary group known Odin, who trained me and eventually gave me my new identity. I never thought I'd find myself back at the place that started it all.

I let Kruger out of the truck, and we walked down the path between the headstones. I could see the fresh grave plot a few rows down and turned toward it as Kruger paced me on my right side.

She nudged her head up under my hand for me to pet her as we got closer. She obviously could sense my pain and was doing her best to calm me down. I scratched her ears, and she looked up at me. Her doggy charm had a calming effect.

I stopped at Cindy's headstone. I thought about Cindy sitting next to my bedside in the hospital after the attack and how she kept checking in on me when I finally went home. My eyes watered as I thought about all the good times we had on shift together.

"I'm so sorry," I mumbled as I turned away.

Kruger followed me across the cemetery. I was expecting to see two headstones exactly where I had left them nearly two years ago, but instead, I found a third. As I got closer, I realized that it was my own.

"Alex Shepherd," I said to myself as I read the inscription. When Julio "Coolio" Meeks, Odin's cyber analyst and computer whiz, faked my death, he had apparently gone all out. I wondered if there was an actual body in the grave as well.

Small American flags had been planted next to my headstone, and fresh flowers had been placed on the graves of Lindsey and Chelsea. I walked around my grave to Chelsea's little headstone and found the stuffed bear I had placed on it. It was in pretty rough shape from the weather and elements, but the faded bear was still intact.

Kruger sat next to me as I clutched the little bear. I bit my lip and tried to hold back the tears but couldn't. I started sobbing as I stared at the three headstones. It was a fitting tribute to the beautiful family I had lost and a man that had died with his two girls one sunny summer day.

I started to put the bear back on Chelsea's grave but held onto it instead. I don't know why, but I just couldn't let go. I wiped away the tears and whispered, "I love you," to my girls and then headed back to the truck.

Kruger and I went back to my truck, and I opened the door for her. She hopped in, and I closed the back door.

As I started to open the driver's door, I suddenly heard someone behind me.

"Alex?"

CHAPTER EIGHT

Justin Hyatt had barely been out of the academy a year when he was assigned to my shift. He was smart and motivated, a former Marine who had been to Afghanistan twice. He had a Purple Heart and had earned the Navy Cross. He was a war hero by every definition of the term.

But you wouldn't know it just talking to him. I only knew it because I had read his personnel file. He didn't talk about his service at all. Instead, he just seemed like your average cop in his late twenties – complete with a highly inappropriate sense of humor while maintaining the ability to be serious when necessary.

Hyatt had been the deputy that discovered the body of the school bus driver near the school that my wife and daughter were on their way to. It was a radio call that haunted me to this day. He knew something very bad was happening even before we realized that a group of terrorists had hijacked the bus.

I wasn't surprised that he was standing in front of me, wearing a suit and tie and a detective's badge. He had always been meticulous in his reports and investigations, making him a highly qualified candidate for such a promotion.

But despite all of that, I was surprised that he had recognized me. Not because I thought my beard held magical powers of disguise, but because I had subconsciously fallen into the trap of believing that Alex Shepherd truly was dead. Troy Wilson was all that left, so it had become almost inconceivable that anyone would recognize me. I had gotten careless.

"We buried you, man," Hyatt said as he tried to make sense of my presence. "I carried your…*A*…body and buried you right over there."

I said nothing as Hyatt pointed in the direction I had just been. I honestly didn't know what to say. I never expected to run into anyone there, and I didn't really have a plan.

"I'm sorry," I said finally.

"That's it? You're fucking *sorry*?" Hyatt asked angrily.

Before I could answer, Hyatt suddenly hugged me. "Jesus, man, I'm glad you're alive."

I looked around nervously, hoping no one else was nearby. "You have to promise me you won't tell anyone."

Hyatt released his bear hug and stepped back with a look of confusion.

"What? Why?"

"There's a diner down the road. I'll buy you lunch and tell you all about it," I said, still nervously scanning the cemetery for others.

Hyatt looked around, not sure what to say. "Okay, but…"

"I'll drive," I said before he had a chance to question it further.

We got in my truck, and I put Chelsea's stuffed bear on the dash before slowly backing out of the cemetery. As we turned onto the narrow road back to civilization, I started my story.

I left out everything that happened in the states – the Imam, the terrorist financier, and the trail of bodies I left in my wake. I told him about the Lions of Rojava recruitment video I had watched on the internet and how angry I was that ISIS had taken everything from me.

Hyatt listened intently as I recounted my journey into Iraq and feeling like I had landed on an alien planet. I told him about the recruits I met from all over the world and the tryouts I had gone through.

"That actually sounds kind of fun," Hyatt interjected.

"It wasn't," I said. I continued, telling him about the field hospital where we watched a wounded Brit lose his leg and my first realization that I was in the middle of a war zone.

"I remember that feeling," Hyatt said.

I told him about the Kurdish warrior I met named Zirek. His story was not unlike mine, having lost everything when his village was overrun by ISIS. I talked about how he took me under his wing and taught me how to survive in his country.

I talked about the convoy and my first experience in battle – how everyone was speaking a language I didn't understand, but my training kicked in, and I managed to save a guy's life. By the time we reached the little diner, I had told Hyatt all about the secondary training I had received, the impromptu sniper tests, and the Kurdish scout/recon team with whom I had been assigned to fight.

We walked into the diner and picked a booth at the far back corner, away from the windows. The older waitress took our order, and Hyatt pressed me to continue.

"So, what was it like fighting with them? I did several ops with the Afghanis. It was hit or miss. Sometimes they'd fight, sometimes they'd run, and the worst was when they'd flip and fight with the Taliban against us," Hyatt said.

"The Lions of Rojava were all very brave," I said. "But pushing into Ma Shuq was eye-opening. So many different factions. No one was wearing uniforms. It was hard to tell who the good guys and bad guys were, and their culture often got in the way of tactics."

"Sounds exactly like Afghanistan," Hyatt said. "You'd think they'd be a lot better at fighting since they've been at war for a few thousand years."

I told him the rest of the story of my time in Syria as the food arrived. I didn't directly mention Odin, but I did tell him I had been recruited by a private military contractor. It was a decision I partially regretted, given the fallout I endured in Texas, but it was also the reason I had been able to start over. And it was that group that had convinced the world that I had died on the battlefield in Syria.

"It was closed casket," Hyatt said. "They said you had been killed by an IED. Whatever body they used for you was pretty heavy."

"I'm sorry you had to go through that," I said. "I was just trying to move on."

"So, should I call you Troy now?"

"That would probably be best," I said. "Just to be safe."

"And you're a school resource officer in Texas now?" Hyatt said as he chewed on the information.

"Yes, sir."

"And she's your partner?" Hyatt asked, nodding to Kruger, who was lying under the table next to my foot.

"She is," I said as I bent down to scratch behind her ears.

"And no one else knows you're here?"

"Just you."

"I'm surprised I didn't see you at Cindy's funeral."

"My plan was to stay out of sight. We stayed near the back and were at the tail end of the procession."

"So, you were there for the attack?"

I nodded. "Jacobson died in my arms."

"Jesus," Hyatt said, shaking his head as he looked away. "He was a good man."

"The best."

"He interviewed me for my detective position. He spoke at your funeral. He really loved you, man," Hyatt said.

"Any idea who's behind the ambush on Cindy and the procession?" I asked, trying to change the subject before it got emotional.

"The bodies we've found have all had significant criminal histories. We're working right now to put together a connection between them all."

"I saw a tattoo on a dead guy's neck. Looked like a gang sign," I replied.

"A lot of the guys we found had tattoos. They were all from different gangs – 610 Boyz, Young Blood Mafia, 13th Ward Killers, you name it. Some of these gangs are even at war with each other. There's no immediate connection."

"What about Cindy's killers?"

"We're stretched thin right now, man. We had a person of interest in Mid City, but NOPD just had their own officer ambushed, so they haven't been all that helpful," Hyatt said. "And then there's the FBI…"

"What about the FBI?"

"They're in the middle of a civil rights investigation on the shooting with the trooper. If they've found anything, they're not sharing it with us."

"What's the person of interest's name?"

"You know I can't give you that information," Hyatt said.

"Can't or won't?"

"Both," Hyatt said. "It's an active investigation, and you're no longer with the agency. I could get fired. Besides, what are you going to do – go find this guy and question him?"

"I'll do what needs to be done. For Cindy. For Captain Jacobson."

Hyatt looked around the diner to make sure no one was watching as he seemed to consider what I was saying. He hesitated and then pulled a pen from his pocket and wrote something on one of the napkins on the table. He slid it to me and then stood.

"I'll get lunch," he said as he tossed a twenty and a ten onto the table. "It was nice meeting you, *Troy*."

CHAPTER NINE

LeShawn Revis had the kind of criminal record you'd expect from a man suspected of ambushing a law enforcement funeral. He had been in and out of jail for aggravated battery, weapons charges, drug possession and distribution, and resisting arrest. The tattoo on his neck pledged his allegiance to the Young Blood Mafia, and his '86 Chevy Monte Carlo with 22" wheels and illegally tinted windows screamed probable cause.

But you'd never know he was a hardened criminal after following him for a day. In fact, after almost thirteen hours of surveillance, I was beginning to wonder if I even had the right guy. The only thing that kept me going – besides the coffee and Red Bull – was that tattoo. Everything else about the man's behavior and demeanor seemed to point to a man who turned his life around and left a life of crime in the past.

In fact, Revis seemed to have a normal job and family. I started following him early the morning after my chat with Hyatt, using the address I found on Revis through a Spokeo search. He hugged his toddler son in the driveway at just after 7 a.m., kissed his girlfriend, and headed to his job as a car washer at a low-budget rental car place in Mid City.

Kruger and I watched Revis all day as he worked diligently washing and detailing cars. He seemed to get along well with his fellow employees, and at lunch, he shared part of his sack lunch with one of his fellow washers. By the end of the day, I was ready to move on and look for another lead. Kruger and I were both starting to get restless.

I stuck it out to the end of his shift, following him at a safe distance as he left the rental car place. I expected him to head back home – it would've made sense given what I had seen so far. But when he kept going after passing his street, my interest was piqued.

Revis continued out of Mid City and into the lower 7th Ward. He stopped at a liquor store and parked next to a group of men standing by their cars. He got out and hugged one of them before initiating a hand-to-hand transaction of some sort. It looked like Revis put a brown paper bag into his pants pocket, but I couldn't be sure as I watched through my binoculars.

The two exchanged a few more words, and then Revis got back into his car. He turned right out of the parking lot and continued toward the 9th Ward. I followed him into a neighborhood where he stopped momentarily in front of a house.

A twenty-something-year-old kid in a white wife-beater hurried from the front porch into the front seat. It was hard to tell from the distance, but it looked like he was carrying a handgun in his left hand. Revis's status as a person of interest suddenly made sense, despite the mild-mannered daytime evidence to the contrary. There was no doubt in my mind that those two were looking for trouble.

Revis and his new friend continued down the street and then made a hard right. They doubled-back and headed toward downtown New Orleans. Traffic was light as they bounced along the pothole-filled streets with rap music blaring and smoke billowing from the passenger side window.

It started to rain as we reached Canal Street, and they turned onto Loyola Avenue toward the Central Business District. It didn't really make any sense, but then, none of what I had seen made all that much sense while following Revis.

At the intersection of Loyola and Poydras Avenue, the passenger door suddenly opened and the passenger got out as we waited at the red light. I was close enough this time that I could clearly see him stick his handgun into his waistband and cover it with his shirt.

Revis continued down Loyola as the light turned green. His armed passenger walked quickly down Poydras toward the Superdome and Smoothie King Center, where a concert was playing. I had to decide quickly whether to follow Revis or pursue his associate.

There was no hope of pursuing the armed associate on foot without leaving my truck in the middle of the road, but I couldn't let him head toward a public venue with a weapon and bad intentions. I turned right onto Poydras and followed. Luckily traffic was heavy enough due to the game that I was able to stay behind him as he continued down the sidewalk toward the Superdome.

He reached a crosswalk to cross over to the Superdome parking lot at the next red light. I changed lanes into the left lane, but traffic was stopped. He did his best to stay hidden within the crowd of people as the group crossed the four-lane road.

As he made it across, he made a hard left. I watched his hand reach under his shirt and go for his weapon as he appeared to be heading toward two NOPD officers that were directing cars as they went into the parking garage.

Traffic was stopped in both directions. I could get out and run, but I knew I wouldn't make it there in time. I thought about sending my fur-missile in the back seat after him, but there was no guarantee she'd make it there in time either or recognize the threat before he fired. I had to act immediately. I cut the wheel hard left and jumped the concrete median, heading straight toward the parking garage.

I swerved and narrowly missed a car exiting the structure as I punched it and aimed at the armed menace. I saw the two officers turn to face me as they suddenly realized I was barreling for them.

As I ran over another curb, the would-be assassin raised his gun toward the officers. I hit him with the front grill and slammed on the brakes just as the officers drew down on me. My truck skidded to a stop a few feet from where the gunman landed. His weapon had flown clear of his hand as he had been launched twenty feet from his point of attack.

I put the truck in park and put both hands on the wheel as I saw the officers approaching with guns drawn off to my left. They had no idea I had just saved their lives, and I wasn't planning on getting shot, so I just stayed still as they opened the door and pulled me out of the truck.

As they slammed my face down onto the asphalt and cuffed me, I saw the medics reach the gunman. It was too late, however. The officers stood me up, and I could clearly see that his neck had snapped, and his eyes were staring off into oblivion.

"What the fuck are you doing?" the officer asked angrily as he frisked me. "Are you drunk?"

"You're welcome," I replied calmly. "Please don't hurt my dog. She's a police K-9."

CHAPTER TEN

"Alright, Mr. Wilson, let's go over this one more time," Detective Mark Jackson said as he handed me a cup of coffee and sat down across from me in the interrogation room. "Walk me through what happened."

I accepted the cup of coffee and slowly took a sip as I gathered my thoughts. "I was sitting at the red light, and a man drawing a gun from his waistband caught my eye. He appeared to be heading toward two officers standing near the parking garage, so I took action."

"Why did you think he was heading toward the officers?" Detective Jackson asked while scribbling notes on his legal pad.

"Because he had a gun and was walking in that direction. Haven't law enforcement officers been ambushed lately?"

"You're in law enforcement, right?" Detective Jackson said as he looked in his notes. "School Resource Officer, K-9 with the Gillespie County Sheriff's Office?"

"Yes, and where is my dog?" I asked. In the confusion and chaos, while being pulled from the truck, I had done my best to let them know that I was a K-9 deputy, and Kruger wasn't just my pet as she barked furiously at them. The last thing I wanted was for something to happen to her.

"She is safe. Animal control has her."

"Animal control! Are you fucking serious?" I yelled.

"Calm down, Troy," Detective Jackson said.

"Calm down? I saved your officers' lives, and you sent my dog to animal control?"

"They know she's a police K-9, Troy. And your agency has been contacted. She's going to be well taken care of until we clear this matter up."

Agency has been contacted. It was something I hadn't yet considered. No matter the outcome, I knew I would soon be getting a call from my sergeant demanding that I return home with Kruger. Or, worse yet, they would send someone to go get her out of dog jail and suspend me until this blew over.

"Okay," I said as I tried to calm myself down. "What else do you need from me to clear this up?"

"What were you doing in the area?" the detective asked.

"What do you mean?"

"You said you were in town for a funeral on the Northshore. So, what were you doing by the Superdome in the late evening?"

"What difference does it make?"

"I'm just trying to establish why you were there. You obviously weren't going to the concert."

"I hadn't been to New Orleans in many years and was out for a drive," I replied. It wasn't a lie, but I also wasn't going to give up my lead on Revis. I didn't want to open that can of worms of following a person of interest in an active investigation and how I had come to learn about him.

"When you just happened to see Carl Thomas pull a gun and attempt to ambush those officers?" he asked, using the suspect's name for the first time since we had been chatting.

"If that's his name, then yes," I said. "Did you find the weapon?"

"Yes, we did," Detective Jackson replied.

"And did it have his fingerprints on it?"

"The Crime Lab is working on that right now."

"So, I've been cooperating, you have a weapon, and I was well within the law in using deadly force to prevent a forcible felony upon another. When will you release me?"

"That's for the DA to decide, Mr. Wilson," Detective Jackson said.

"Oh, come on! I saved those officers' lives!"

"You have a history of being at the right place at the right time, don't you, Troy?" Detective Jackson asked as he thumbed through his notes.

"What's that supposed to mean?

"When we contacted your agency, they were also kind enough to provide your service record. This isn't your first lethal force encounter."

"So?"

"So, I'm just saying it's quite the coincidence that these things keep happening to you."

"I think we're done here," I said. "Am I free to leave?"

"Just one more question. If you don't mind."

"What?" I snapped.

"LeShawn Revis, does that name ring any bells?"

I did my best to hide any tells as I pretended to mull the name over. "Should it?"

"Carl Thomas was last seen in LeShawn's car before the incident this evening," Detective Jackson replied.

"Have you tried talking to him?"

"We sure did, but that may prove difficult to do," Detective Jackson replied, grimacing.

"Why is that?"

"His car and body were found in the canal near Pumping Station Six in Metairie an hour ago. JPSO is working on recovering his body right now," Detective Jackson said.

"Jesus," I said softly. My mind raced as I tried to figure out the timeline. By my estimate, it had been almost five hours since I had been taken into custody. That was an eternity when it came to homicide investigations. Anything could have happened to Revis after dropping off Carl Thomas.

"So, you know him?" Detective Jackson pressed.

"If he dropped Thomas off, and you're just now finding his body with me in custody this entire time, it's highly unlikely that I had anything to do with it, don't you think?"

Detective Jackson's left eyebrow suddenly raised. "I didn't say Revis dropped him off."

"It doesn't matter," I said dismissively. "Thomas was about to kill two more of your officers. I stopped him. End of story."

Detective Jackson placed his pen on the legal pad and smiled. "You're right. You stopped a potential ambush. You almost killed two pedestrians in the process, but you did stop an ambush. Thank you. Thank you for your service."

I stood. I had had enough of his "bad cop" routine. "At this point, I would like to either be released or to speak with legal counsel. This interview is over."

"Of course," Detective Jackson said. "You are free to leave. Just make sure we have a way to contact you if we have any further questions."

He reached out to shake my hand. I stared at his hand for a second and then looked him in the eye as we shook.

"Look, I know you're just doing your job, but I'm not a bad guy. I did what I thought was right, given the information I had available to me at the time. I couldn't watch another innocent officer die."

"I know, Deputy Wilson," Detective Jackson said. "And that's what I've been trying to find out – what information you had available to you at the time. I think it's more than you're letting on. I'll have one of my officers escort you to get your truck from impound and your dog from animal control. I'll be in touch."

CHAPTER ELEVEN

It took an hour after my discussion with Detective Jackson for NOPD to give me back my belongings and process me out of their custody. I was finally free to go just after 1 a.m. The impound lot and SPCA where they were holding Kruger were both closed.

I begrudgingly took an Uber back to the B & B and slept until my alarm went off at 7 a.m. I was exhausted from a full day of surveillance and the adrenaline high from the incident. It was the only reason I slept at all despite being worried about Kruger.

When my alarm went off, I got up and took a shower. I ate a protein bar as I waited for the Uber driver to arrive. The nice older lady in a brand-new Honda CR-V drove me to the Almonaster Avenue Impound Lot, where my truck had been taken after investigators had finished with it.

She dropped me off just as the attendant was opening the front gate. I thanked her for the ride and paid using my cell phone as I got out of the car.

"I'm still getting set up. Just give me a minute," the portly lot attendant said as he waddled toward the nearest of the three buildings to my right.

There were rows of cars lined up as far as I could see. Some were in good condition, while others were anything from completely totaled to torn apart. They were all marked with the dates they had arrived in white shoe polish on the windshield.

I followed the attendant into the building. The floors creaked as he waddled toward his desk and put the keys he had used to unlock the gate in the drawer. He sat down at his computer, let out an exhaustive sigh, and looked up at me.

"How can I help you?"

I pulled the folded piece of paper out of my pocket that the NOPD clerk had given me to retrieve my truck. I handed it to him and then pulled my driver's license out of my wallet and placed it on the desk. "Just trying to get my truck back."

He took the piece of paper and studied it. "Yeah, I remember that truck. You're the guy that hit that kid by the Dome."

"He wasn't a kid, but yeah," I said.

"No, no, don't get me wrong," the attendant said, holding up his hands. "I ain't judging you. From what I hear, you saved those officers' lives. You're a hero in my book."

"So, about my truck…"

"It's safe," the attendant said. "We made sure you were taken care of once we heard the story."

He pulled out a piece of paper and handed it to me. "Here's the inventory log they did on the scene, signed by the tow truck driver. You'll need to verify it's all there before you leave or make a claim with the city. Your firearms are in evidence at the precinct that processed you. You'll have to get those back from them."

I had been so preoccupied with getting Kruger out of dog jail, I had forgotten about the firearms I had locked up in the truck. It would pose a serious problem if I intended to continue my investigation.

"But they usually hold them for a few days, so you might have to wait unless that badge in your wallet can convince them," he said, pointing to my wallet still in my hand. "Saw it when you got your ID."

"Thanks, but first, I'll need my truck."

"Of course," he replied as he used the desk to help himself stand.

I waited as he shuffled into the back office. He opened a lockbox on the wall and scanned the paper tags on the keys as he cross-referenced the paper I had given him. After a few seconds of searching, he found my keys and closed the lockbox.

"Let's get you on your way," he said as he motioned for me to follow him out the side door.

I followed him out into the lot. The humidity had to be nearing 100% already. We were both sweating as we walked to where the tow truck company had dropped off my truck.

As we passed through a row of cars with fresh dates, I suddenly stopped. I immediately recognized the '88 Monte Carlo of LeShawn Revis and turned to look at it.

"That was brought in last night," the attendant said as he noticed me turn toward it. "Fella killed himself and ended up in the canal."

"Killed himself?" I asked as I looked in the passenger side window. The driver's side window had been broken and replaced with a black garbage bag duct-taped in place.

"That's what I heard anyway. I wasn't here when it was brought in."

I cupped my hands on the glass and looked inside. There were bloodstains on the cloth seats and there was still water pooled near the floormats.

"He shot himself and then drove into the canal?"

"What do you mean?'

"The headrest has a bloodstain on it," I pointed out. "If he shot himself as he was driving, it stained pretty quickly."

"I don't know, that's just what they said," the attendant replied. "It's open if you wanna look inside. I won't say nothin.' Crime scene techs have already been through by the time it gets here."

I carefully opened the door and water spilled onto the ground. The car smelled awful – a mix of marijuana, Swisher Sweets, and stale water. I did my best to hold my breath as I inspected the interior of the car.

As expected, there wasn't much to find in the car. The crime scene techs had done a good job removing anything of interest. I bent down and looked underneath the seat, hoping to find something.

"Why's this car so interesting to you?" the attendant asked.

"The guy that tried to kill those cops was riding in it," I replied.

"No shit?"

"No shit," I said as I turned and opened the glove box.

"I said you could look, not dig through it," the attendant said. He appeared to be getting anxious as I looked up and saw him nervously looking back toward the main building.

I thumbed through the papers in the glovebox. They were mostly receipts and parking tickets, but as I dug through them, I felt a business card. I turned it over in the light and saw a name and address scribbled on the back.

"You need to get out of there and come on," the attendant warned.

I grabbed the card and quickly closed the glovebox. I discretely placed the card in my pocket and gently closed the door. "Sorry," I said.

"Your truck's over here," the attendant said.

CHAPTER TWELVE

After picking up my truck, I drove straight to the humane society and bailed Kruger out of dog jail. She was happy to see me and in good health. The volunteers working the shelter said she had been a perfect angel and a sweetheart throughout her short incarceration.

I called Jenny on my way out to the truck to tell her what had happened since we last spoke after she landed in San Antonio.

"You did *what*?"

"I think there's a lot more going on here than just gangbangers shooting up cops. Someone is behind this," I replied.

"What happened to agreeing that you wouldn't get involved?"

"My friends were killed, Jenny," I replied. "You know I can't sit this one out."

"So, what are you going to do?"

"I'm going to find out who's behind this," I said.

Jenny sighed softly on the other end. "Please be careful. I can't lose you."

"I will. I love you."

"I love you too."

As we hung up, my phone rang again. I put Kruger in the truck, got in, and cranked the engine as I looked at the caller ID and answered.

"Hey, sarge," I said, wincing for the inevitable ass-chewing that was about to commence.

"Troy! Jesus, man, are you okay?"

"I'm fine," I said.

"What the hell happened over there?! NOPD tells me you saved one of theirs by ramming some asshole with your truck. They wanted us to come get your dog."

"We're both free."

"Good. I didn't want to have to drive all the way over there just to kick your ass and take your dog. Now tell me what's really going on."

I paused momentarily as I gathered my thoughts. I thought about feeding him the same story I had given NOPD, but I knew that wouldn't fly. My sergeant's bullshit meter was finely tuned. He knew me and trusted me. I decided that I needed to keep it that way.

"Another good friend of mine was killed in the funeral procession ambush, so I decided to help the detective with the case. I was following a perp when I saw his passenger exit the vehicle with a weapon and head toward those cops. I had no choice."

"You did a good job, Troy, but you're hanging your ass out there by doing anything. You know that, right? We can't help you if you get rolled up. You're a Texas deputy, not a New Orleans cop."

"I know," I said. "I was just doing a little surveillance as a private citizen. I had no intention of interacting with them until they made an obvious attempt to ambush two cops."

It wasn't a lie, but it wasn't exactly the truth either. Honestly, I had no idea what I intended to do to these people if I caught them. I was still processing the rage and sadness from the deaths of Jacobson and Cindy.

"When are you planning on coming back?"

"When do you need me?"

"Orientation for the next school year is next Friday. I'd like you to be there. Otherwise, as long as you keep your ass out of jail, you have enough leave on the books to stay until then. Would that help you?"

"Yes, sir. Thank you."

"Don't thank me," he said, suddenly becoming gruff. "Anyone else would have their ass in a sling right now, Troy. I'm only doing this because of what you did last year. Don't make me look like an asshole."

"10-4, sir," I said.

"Alright, be safe, and remember, you're on your own out there."

"Understood."

"Alright, I'll tell Michaels he can stay home. But if you end up in jail again, I'm sending him to get the dog and your badge. Got it?"

"Yes, sir," I replied meekly. *There* was the boss I had learned to know and love. It was good to see he hadn't gone soft suddenly.

I hung up with my sergeant and then headed to the NOPD precinct that had booked me. I put Kruger's working harness on her to identify her as a law enforcement working dog and then brought her into the building with me.

The clerk made me provide my identification and law enforcement credentials and returned my weapons to me. They had taken my department-issued Glock 17 and the Daniel Defense MK18 rifle I kept under the rear seat.

As I finished inspecting the condition of the weapons, Detective Jackson noticed me as he walked down the hall and came over to talk to me.

"Listen, I hope there's no hard feelings," he said. "You know those interviews are filmed, and the media sometimes gets ahold of them. We've been under fire before for going easy on cops, and I couldn't make it look like I agreed with what you did...because, well, I did. And you were well within your legal rights to do so."

"Okay," I said, unsure of his tactics.

He reached down to pet Kruger, and I stopped him. "She's a working dog. No petting."

"I'm curious, why didn't you send her instead?" he asked as he quickly withdrew his hand.

"Too many people, and I don't have a door popper on my truck. I did what I did because it was the only way without firing off rounds at a moving target from my truck with a crowd of people."

"Yeah, that makes sense."

Jackson reached into his coat pocket and pulled out his wallet. He opened it, took a business card out, and handed it to me.

"Here's my card. I know you're not a fan, but we're both on the same team here. You saved our boys' lives. If you need anything at all, please don't hesitate to call me."

I took it and studied the card for a minute. "Did you find out anything about Revis?"

"All the evidence points to a suicide."

"A suicide? So, he drops off his buddy and then offs himself while driving into the canal?"

Jackson shrugged. "The evidence is heavily in favor of a suicide. He owed a lot of bad people money, and he had a pretty big insurance policy in his name that would go to his family."

"Seems like an awfully big coincidence."

"Not really. If he knew what his friend had planned and was somehow coerced into being the wheelman, he may have seen no other way out."

"Maybe," I said. "You ever heard of Jeremiah Sharp?"

"You mean *Reverend* Jeremiah Sharp?"

"Sure."

"Yeah, who doesn't know him? He's the most influential preacher in the 9th Ward. He has a mega church that gives back millions to the community. The guy is a rags to riches fairytale story. Why?"

"Just heard the name mentioned. Thought it might be relevant," I said, deciding not to share the card I had found in the car.

"No way," Jackson said, shaking his head dismissively. "Sharp is a hero in the hood. He had nothing to do with any of this."

"I see," I said as I looked down at Kruger. Neither of us had eaten since the day prior, and we both needed some rest. "Well, I'd better get going. Thanks for your time. No hard feelings."

"Call if you need anything," Jackson said, shaking my hand.

CHAPTER THIRTEEN

Reverend Jeremiah Sharp's church stood out amongst the run-down houses in the impoverished New Orleans neighborhood. It wasn't a huge building like some of the televangelist churches I had seen on TV had, but it was brand new construction and appeared to have been recently remodeled. There were also high definition security cameras at every corner and a couple of large men acting as security near the front and side entrances.

After recovering my weapons and rescuing Kruger from dog jail, we had gone back to the bed and breakfast to recharge with food and a nap. After, I fired up my laptop and started doing research on the card I had found in LeShawn Revis's recovered Monte Carlo.

On the surface, Reverend Sharp's "Church of The Glorious Savior" appeared to be a very positive influence in the local community. I found multiple articles documenting the work they had done helping people find jobs, rebuilding houses after a recent tropical storm, and even offering free daycare so that single mothers could work. I couldn't find a single article that might tie Sharp to anything nefarious.

With nothing more than a business card and a hunch, Kruger and I loaded up and drove over to the reverend's church. It was just after lunch, and the only activity seemed to be associated with the small daycare.

Kruger slept in the back of my truck as I watched a younger woman escort four children to the nearby playground. It also appeared to be brand new with freshly painted equipment and a well-maintained yard. Money was apparently no issue for this church, which was in stark contrast to its surroundings.

We were parked across the street in between another truck and an old minivan. I struggled to stay awake as I watched the woman sit down on a park bench and pull out her cell phone. She appeared to look around nervously as she started texting.

Moments later, a man emerged from the church with two large men wearing black t-shirts. They appeared to be his bodyguards as they shadowed him to where the woman was sitting. She seemed startled as she looked up and saw him approaching.

The woman quickly put away the phone and then called out to the children. They turned toward her and froze when they saw the man approaching. She stood to face him as he entered the playground, leaving the bodyguards behind.

The kids stayed where they were as they watched the man walk up to the woman and hold out his hand. She shook her head and looked away, but the man seemed to insist. She reluctantly pulled out the phone and handed it to him.

As they stood there, I took out my phone and zoomed in as best I could before the image went grainy. I snapped a few pictures, just in case either of the two was important to the case.

The man looked at the phone as the woman cowered before him. He scrolled through it for a few minutes, presumably reading the text conversation she was having before he arrived, and then tossed the phone to one of his men.

Kruger perked up in the back seat as she sensed me getting tense. I was sure that the man was about to get violent with the obviously scared woman. She started crying and shaking uncontrollably as she stared at the ground with her arms folded. I debated whether to cause a distraction to spare the poor woman the inevitable abuse.

Time seemed to stand still as the man moved toward her. My stomach turned as I saw the man raise his right arm. There was nothing I could do to stop it, but I had already calculated my next move.

As I put the truck in gear to drive over there and stop what I thought to be a battery in progress, I saw the man instead wrap his arms around the woman in a full embrace. I put the truck back in park as the woman buried her head in the man's shoulder.

He patted her head as he held her in his arms. It had been a very weird interaction. I was a little ashamed of myself for being so wrong in reading the situation. I was more tired than I had originally thought.

The man kept his arm around the woman as he escorted her inside. One of his bodyguards stayed behind and made the children follow them in single file while the other went ahead to open the door for the duo. It all seemed very strange and cult-like, or I was very tired. Or both.

I had been so fixated with the scene unfolding outside the church, I had completely missed the NOPD Ford Explorer pull up next to the car behind me. Kruger suddenly started barking, causing me to nearly go through the roof.

I looked up and saw an officer standing near the rear of my truck, calling in my license plate on her collar mic. I turned back left, and a male officer knocked on my window. I gave Kruger a command to stop barking and then put both hands on the wheel.

"Turn the vehicle off and step out, please, sir," the officer said before I could lower the window.

I did as he instructed, placing the keys on top of the dash as I slowly exited the vehicle with my hands visible.

"Do you have any weapons on you today?" the officer asked as he grabbed my left wrist. "Any guns, knives, bombs, bazookas?"

"My off-duty weapon is holstered near my appendix," I said. "I'm an off-duty twenty-six."

The officer ignored the fact that I had just told him I'm a police officer using the code *twenty-six*. Instead, he grabbed my right hand and placed it behind my back with my left.

"For your safety and mine, I am detaining you until we figure this out," the officer said as he clicked the handcuffs. "Is your dog aggressive?"

"She's a police K9," I said. "What's going on?"

"I'll get to that in a second," the officer said as he turned me around and lifted up my shirt, revealing the holstered Glock 19.

The female officer joined us, and the male officer handed her the weapon. She cleared it, placing the chambered round on the driver's seat of my truck along with the magazine. She walked back to the rear of the truck and keyed her collar mic, presumably to run the serial number of the weapon to check if it was stolen.

"Any other weapons on you?" the male officer asked as he put on a pair of black gloves.

"Just my knife in my left front pocket. Mind telling me why you're detaining me?"

The officer did a pat-down, once again ignoring my questions. He removed my wallet from my front right pocket and opened it, revealing my commission and badge. He took out my driver's license as the other officer came back and shook her head as she placed my Glock in the bed of the truck. The male officer nodded and handed her my ID before ordering me to sit on the curb.

"Troy Wilson?" he asked.

"That's me."

"Before she runs your information, do you have any warrants or anything we should know about? Ever been in trouble?"

"You have my commission and badge in your hand; what do you think?"

"I think you're a long way from Texas, so you should probably lose the attitude."

"Maybe," I said as I grew increasingly more annoyed. "But we're still in America, right? Constitution is still a thing, yeah?"

"Well, if you're really a cop, you should know that everything we've done so far is perfectly within the limits of the Constitution. You are being detained and are not under arrest. You're in handcuffs for your safety and mine because you were armed."

"Okay, first of all, you didn't know that before I told you. And second, being armed is perfectly legal in the State of Louisiana. So, why don't you save us the bullshit and tell me what's really going on here."

"How long have you been sitting here?"

"I don't know," I said as I rolled my eyes. "You just made me sit down. Maybe a minute."

"Now, you see, when you're evasive like that, it doesn't really help your case."

"What case? Is it illegal to sit in a parked car in New Orleans?"

The officer shook his head. "No, but it *is* illegal to sit in a parked car masturbating to kids on a playground, you sick fuck."

"Have you lost your goddamned mind? Who called that in?" I asked angrily. *Masturbating?* I couldn't believe it.

"Ten fifty both ways," the female officer said as she walked back and handed the male officer my driver's license.

"See!" I said as I tried to calm myself. "I told you who I am. Now, this is bullshit!"

"What are you doing here?" the male officer asked again. "Why are you watching this church and playground, then?"

"It doesn't matter," I said as I finally calmed myself. "Public street. Do you have any witnesses?"

The officer hesitated for a minute before looking at his partner. *Of course!* The security team must have seen me and called it in. It was the only logical explanation.

"Tell you what," I said as they seemed to suddenly be confused by my question. "Look in my wallet and pull out the first business card. Call Detective Jackson. He'll vouch for me because I've already been through this with him after I saved two of *your* boys last night."

"Saved our boys?" the female officer asked.

"Yeah, at the Super Dome."

"The *dog*," I heard her mumble as she looked at Kruger, who was sitting patiently staring back at her. "That was you two."

"What?" the male officer asked her.

"Last night. The guy with the dog who hit that kid with the gun," she said before nodding toward me.

The male officer opened my wallet and found Detective Jackson's business card. "Ah, fuck," he said as he flicked it. "Stand up, my man, I'm sorry."

I complied and turned around as he pulled a cuff key out of his shirt pocket.

"Okay, now how about you tell me what's really going on here?" I asked as I turned to face him.

I caught him nervously glancing back at the church.

"Alright," he said, "but not here. We can talk somewhere else."

"Lead the way," I said.

"No," he said, shaking his head. "I'll give you an address. You meet us there."

CHAPTER FOURTEEN

The address the officer had given me was a strip mall a few miles away. He told me his name was Officer Dan Hodgins, and his partner was Wanda Fraisure. He asked me to leave first, and they would meet me later so as not to arouse suspicion, but wouldn't tell me whose suspicion they were concerned with.

I drove to the strip mall and did a quick lap around it. The parking lot was mostly empty, but there were a few cars in front of the liquor store. There was an area in the back where I guessed the officers "parked up" to finish their reports while on shift to stay out of sight.

I stayed out in the open in a spot at the corner of the lot near the street as I waited for the officers to arrive. My Glock was safely back in its concealed holster in my waistband, and my patrol rifle was within reach in the back seat area with Kruger if things went sideways and we were ambushed again.

I clipped a leash to Kruger's collar and let her stretch her legs in a grassy area near the parking spot I had chosen. As she finished doing her business, I saw the NOPD Ford Explorer with Fraisure and Hodgins arrive. Hodgins stuck his hand out the window and waved for me to follow him to the area in the back that I had scoped out earlier.

I loaded Kruger back into the truck and gave her a treat. As I got in the driver's seat, I saw a blue Ford Fusion turn in the parking lot and follow the Ford Explorer. I could see light bars in the back rear by the third brake light, indicating it was a detective or supervisor, but it had driven by too quickly for me to get an idea of who was driving.

When I reached the park up area, I saw Detective Jackson standing next to the driver's side window chatting with Officer Hodgins. They had backed their Explorer up to the fence line, and Jackson had parked on the other side. He turned and looked at me as I pulled up next to the Explorer with Jackson between us.

"We meet again," I said as I lowered the window and put the truck in park.

Jackson frowned and then turned back to Hodgins. He said something to the officer and then tapped the roof. Hodgins exchanged a look with his partner and drove off, leaving Jackson standing by my window.

"The old bait and switch," I said as I watched them drive off.

"I thought we had an understanding," Jackson said as he turned and put both hands on my door. "*Masturbating in public?*"

"Let me guess, the church's security called that in, and y'all are on his payroll."

"Jesus Christ, Troy, *everyone* is on his payroll," Jackson said, shaking his head. "That man spends hundreds of thousands of dollars on details every year."

"So, they were on a detail?"

"Twenty-four hours." Jackson nodded.

"Who called it in?"

"What difference does it make, Troy? You stand out like a sore thumb in that neighborhood. What did you think was going to happen?"

"Hey, now, I'm offended," I replied.

Jackson rolled his eyes. "You're playing with fire if you think you'll get anything out of shaking that tree."

"Why don't you explain it to me, then?"

"That church does a lot of good for the local community. More than you could ever imagine."

"But…"

"*But* nothing. The good reverend has been a staple in this community for thirty years."

"Okay, I get it," I said. I could tell by his tone that he clearly had a personal interest in Reverend Sharp and his church.

"So, what's with all the security?" I asked.

"Did it look like a safe neighborhood to you?"

"If he's done so much for the community, I can't see why he'd be so worried."

"Until you've lived it, you have no idea, my friend. You'll never understand."

"Okay, fair enough. But who was the other guy with all the security?"

"What other guy?"

"When I was minding my own business, rubbing one out in my truck," I said, pausing to see if he'd react and break the tension.

"Not funny," he said with a half-grin.

"Anyway, I saw a man surrounded by security walk up to a younger woman who was watching the kids. She had been texting someone and he took her phone. He looked pretty important."

"Had to be Deacon Emmanuel Carter," Jackson said. "Everyone calls him Deacon."

"Is he a saint too?"

Jackson shrugged. "It's best to not ask questions when it comes to that entire church."

"Why not?"

"Money."

"They seem to have lots of it."

"And very powerful friends, including most of the City Council and the Mayor."

"So, it's political."

"Isn't everything?"

I reached into the center console and pulled out the card I had found in the car in the junkyard. I handed it to Jackson and gave him a minute to look it over.

"I found that in Revis's car in the impound lot."

Jackson's eyes widened. "You were digging through an impounded vehicle?"

"Cut the crap," I said. "Don't give me that holier than thou bullshit."

"This doesn't mean anything," Jackson said as he studied the card.

"You don't even think it's worth looking into?"

Jackson glanced back toward the strip mall and then said, "Not if I want to keep my job."

"*Your job*?" I snapped. "Didn't you just have an officer get ambushed too? What about that? What about the ones I saved last night? You're not the least bit fucking curious about that?"

"Fuck you," Jackson snarled. "I'm going to do my job and we will find the people responsible for this. And I don't need *your* help."

"Look, man, I'm sorry. I'm just trying to find answers."

Jackson leaned in. "Consider this professional courtesy. Look elsewhere."

"Seriously?"

"As a heart attack," Jackson replied before returning to his car and driving off.

CHAPTER FIFTEEN

"If this is your idea of laying low, it's not working," Detective Jason Hyatt said as he sat down across from me at the small coffee shop in Metairie. "People are starting to ask questions."

"Like what?" I asked as I smiled at the waitress approaching our table.

"Service dog?" the woman asked as she pulled a notepad from her apron and stopped beside me.

"Law enforcement," I replied as I reached down under the table to scratch behind Kruger's ears.

"I feel for y'all," she said, shaking her head. "Ain't a good time to be a cop around here."

"Thank you, ma'am," Hyatt replied.

"What can I get for y'all? It's on the house."

I ordered a black coffee and Hyatt ordered some concoction that amounted to little more than milk, sugar, and a hint of coffee. After the waitress delivered our order, Hyatt pulled a folded-up piece of paper out of his shirt pocket.

He opened the paper and placed it on the table before sliding it to me.

"Her name is Cynthia Haynes, younger sister of Terry Haynes," Hyatt said in a low voice.

I looked at the paper, seeing a mugshot of the woman from the park staring back at me. It was a printout from the National Crime Information Center database listing the information on file for Ms. Haynes, including what appeared to be a very minor criminal record for drug charges and her current address.

I folded the paper, put it in my pocket, and sipped my coffee. "Thank you."

"You want to tell me why you were doing surveillance on Deacon Emmanuel Carter and the sister of the man who kicked this war off?"

"Not really," I said.

"Bullshit, Alex!"

I raised an eyebrow. "Who?"

"Wilson or Troy or whatever you're calling yourself these days," he said as he leaned in. "You know people thought they saw you at the funeral."

"Really?"

"Becky from the crime lab posted about it on social media," Hyatt replied. "Most people just wrote it off as fog of war and your spirit intervening because it could've been much worse."

"Well, she's not wrong. It's just that my spirit was still attached to my body at the time. How is Becky, by the way?"

"Seriously? She's fine. Why are you acting like this? Last time we talked, you were begging me to keep your identity safe and now you're blowing it off like it's no big deal?"

I thought about what he was saying as I perused the file. It had been a long few days, and I realized I wasn't thinking clearly.

"You're right."

Hyatt made an exaggerated movement back and grabbed his chest. "I'm *what*?"

"You're right. I'm sorry. It's been a fucked up couple of days here."

"I'm right? *You're sorry*? Yeah, you are definitely not Alex Shepherd."

"He's been gone a long time, man. But seriously, I should've told you."

"Told me what?"

"I think that church is involved in the attacks on law enforcement."

Hyatt frowned. "It's unlikely, man. That church has done a lot of big stuff for the community since you've been gone. What makes you say that?"

I looked around the small coffee shop to make sure no one was listening to our conversation and then said, "You know the car they pulled out of the canal recently with the dead guy?"

"I vaguely remember hearing something about it on the news, but what does that have to do with anything?"

"That car and driver were involved in the attempted attack on the NOPD officers at the Super Dome."

"And you know this…how?"

"Because I watched that attacker get out of his car."

Hyatt's eyes widened. "Jesus, Al..err..Troy…that was *you*?"

I nodded. "And after spending a night in jail because of it, I found the car when I went to get my truck out of impound."

I reached into my pocket and pulled out the card I had taken from the glovebox. I slid it across the table to Hyatt who picked it up and studied it.

"I decided to look into it and that's when I took the pictures I sent you. And right after those pictures, NOPD hemmed me up and I had another face-to-face meeting with Detective Jackson. Ever heard of him?"

"No. Should I?"

I shook my head. "Probably not, but he interrogated me after the Super Dome incident and then his NOPD boys had me meet him after they stopped me by the church. He strongly discouraged me from looking into the church any further."

"Jesus, Troy. When you said you wanted to meet me for coffee across the lake, I thought you maybe had a real lead. You don't think corrupt cops are involved in attacking their own people, do you?"

"No, that's not what I'm saying. But they're protecting the church."

"I could have told you that, even without hearing the story. You know how it goes, man. Hell, we still have churches like that here. When there's big money involved and politicians, they're going to be protected. That doesn't mean they're doing anything illegal."

"They had a lot of security in addition to NOPD."

"And? If I remember correctly, it ain't the safest neighborhood in New Orleans."

I tapped the folder in front of me. "So, it's just a coincidence that the sister of Terry Haynes is there?"

Hyatt shrugged. "Maybe. Maybe not. She wasn't involved in either attack."

"My gut tells me there's more to it."

"Look, man," Hyatt said as he leaned in. "I am glad you're still alive. I really am. I never thought I would see you sitting across from me like this and I'm thankful for it, but you have got to let this go before it really does kill you. We're making some good progress on Cindy's killers and the gangs behind the ambush. It's going to take time, but we're going to make every one of those fuckers pay."

"I can't just do nothing," I said, clenching my fist as I thought about Cindy and her family.

"Unless you want to tell the world that Alex Shepherd isn't dead, you're going to have to let us handle it. Sniffing around crime scenes and running over assholes is a great way to tell the world you're back, but it doesn't sound like that's what you want. So, my advice to you is to go back home – *to Texas.* I can keep you updated with our progress from here."

I opened the file up again, staring at the mugshot of Haynes.

"Go home, Troy. I mean it," Hyatt said as he slapped a twenty on the table and stood. "This isn't your fight anymore."

CHAPTER SIXTEEN

As I drove back to the bed and breakfast. I couldn't stop thinking about what Hyatt had said. *It's not your fight.*

In some ways, he was absolutely right. I was dangerously close to a repeat of last year when a YouTube video had caused Russian mobsters to find me, putting everyone I loved in danger. Despite Jenny being safely at home, it was not something I wanted to repeat.

I was living a new life and should have moved on. Alex Shepherd had long been dead, and my new identity as Troy Wilson had no real ties to the situation, other than being angry that fellow cops were being targeted by assholes. I was only there to pay respects to a fallen officer and nothing more.

On the other hand, I couldn't just forget about the loss of my friends. Cindy and Jacobs had been there for me during the worst time of my life. They had both been important parts of my former life. No matter how much I tried to tell myself that Alex Shepherd was dead, it didn't make things any better. I was sad, but more than anything, I was angry.

Part of me felt responsible for both their deaths. I had abandoned my team to quench my thirst for vengeance in the Middle East. I wondered if Cindy would still be alive if I had been there. Would I have let her go to the call without backup? Would I have been the one ambushed instead?

I knew that there was really no way to know for sure. We went to calls solo all the time when other units were tied up on calls. It wasn't uncommon to arrive before backup was there, and as the shift's corporal, I may have been tied up with other administrative actions and not even been in the area. I knew better than to blame myself for what happened, but it still didn't stop me.

There was heavy traffic as I reached Uptown in New Orleans. I turned on the radio, but the news report just made me angrier - protestors had turned violent in front of Louisiana State Police headquarters. Two troopers had been injured when someone threw a Molotov cocktail at a patrol car. Tensions in the city were as high as the heat index, and officials were worried about widespread rioting if charges were not filed against Trooper Simmons for killing Terry Haynes.

Leaving the city before things got worse was probably the right call, but something about that church was still gnawing at me. Why had NOPD been so quick to accept the idea that LeShawn Revis had committed suicide after dropping off the attacker at the Superdome? How was he related to the church?

As I sat in stop and go traffic, I decided to phone a friend. He was someone I had met after my time in the Middle East and hadn't known for very long, but I trusted him with my life. We had worked together in Odin and I knew I could trust him. And although we hadn't talked since they had helped me take down the Russian mobsters that had kidnapped Jenny, I was certain we could pick up right where we left off. That's just what war buddies did.

"Call Cowboy," I said, using the hands-free feature of my phone. His nickname was about as ironic as you could get, considering that Reginald "Cowboy" Carter was a former British Special Air Service Sniper.

"Calling Cowboy," my phone's virtual assistant replied as the screen showed that it was dialing his number. I wondered what he would say when he picked up. I could only imagine what kind of wild stories he could tell since we last spoke.

A robotic voice answered without so much as a ring. "This number has been disconnected or is no longer in service,"

"Huh." I tried one more time.

Once again, the automated voice informed me that the number no longer worked. Curious, but not completely surprising. It had been just shy of a year and the clandestine nature of Odin meant they may have had to go dark or change identities as I had done.

I called the emergency number I had listed for the new head of Odin, Freddie "Kruger" Mack. He was a former Army SFOD-D "Delta" operator who had inherited billionaire Jeff Lyons's fortune after Lyons was assassinated by a sniper. He had been the leader of Odin before that, and I had saved his girlfriend's life. I figured he'd at least humor me and talk me out of doing something stupid in my current situation or tell me how to find Cowboy.

"Call Mom," I said, using the contact name I had stored the Odin emergency number as just in case prying eyes accessed my phone. Of course, my mother had been dead for nearly fifteen years so there was no chance of me calling the wrong mother.

Once again, a robotic voice and loud tones announced that the number I had dialed was no longer in service. While Cowboy's number being disconnected might not have been cause for alarm, *this was bad.* The number I had stored under "Mom" was a 100%, call anytime and we will answer, phone number. If it had been disconnected, that was *very* bad.

As a last ditch effort, I decided to try the only other number I knew. I dialed the number, wincing until the phone actually started ringing this time.

"Special Agent Tanner," she answered on the second ring. Thank God.

"Maddie, it's Troy Wilson."

There was a pregnant pause and then she said, "Troy! Hold on a second, let me step away from my desk."

I waited as I heard papers shuffling and people in the background.

"How are you? Is everything okay?" she asked.

"It's complicated," I said, "but that's not why I'm calling. Do you have a good number for Cowboy or Kruger? I tried both numbers I have and they're disconnected."

"Oh, Troy," she said as the tone suddenly changed in her voice. "I'm so sorry. You didn't know?"

"Know what?"

She hesitated and then said, "Troy, Cowboy was killed in an operation earlier this year."

My heart sank. "No! C'mon! No!"

"I'm so sorry. I know he was your friend."

"Why didn't anyone call me? What about Kruger?"

"We think Kruger was killed by Natasha," Maddie replied softly.

"What?" I yelped. "No fucking way!"

"I'm sorry, Troy, I can't really talk about it on an open line because it's all classified, but she wasn't the person we thought she was."

"How did he die? What about the rest of the team?"

"They've moved on. Tuna was the sole heir and is still sorting out the estate, but he said they won't be carrying on the...special line of work."

"You didn't answer how he died."

"We really aren't sure."

"And you're sure he's really dead?"

"His remains were positively identified, Troy," Maddie replied. "Where are you? Why are you looking for them?"

"It doesn't matter," I said, still in shock that the two seemingly most invincible men I had ever known were dead. "Thanks for letting me know."

"I'm so sorry, Troy. Is there anything I can help you with?"

"I don't know," I said.

"Well, listen, I'm heading into a meeting, but if you think of anything or need anything at all, you've got my number. I'm sorry you had to find out this way, Troy. I really am."

"It's okay," I said.

"Seriously, call me if you need anything at all. I'll talk to you later."

"Okay," I said as I ended the call.

I sat in stunned silence before a car honked behind me. I had just lost four good friends in less than a week. It was almost too much to process.

"Fuck it," I said to myself as I changed lanes and made a u-turn back toward the church.

"Hold on, sweet girl," I said to Kruger in the back seat. "We're not going home just yet."

CHAPTER SEVENTEEN

The news of Cowboy and Kruger was hard to swallow. It seemed like the most important people from my past were dropping like flies. Jacobson and Kruger had been seemingly invincible to me and yet they were both dead. I wondered who might be next or if my number would soon be called.

The address Hyatt had given me for Cynthia Haynes was a few blocks from the church. It took us almost an hour with five o'clock traffic to make our way there. In front of the church were four men in suits standing watch next to two SUVs. We drove by, careful not to slow too much to draw their attention.

I pulled into an empty spot across the street to watch. Deacon Carter emerged with his security detail and one of the men in suits opened the rear passenger door of the SUV. A man appearing to be in his late 30s or early 40s with sandy blonde hair emerged. He was wearing a three-piece suit and sunglasses and carrying a black attaché.

Carter greeted him with a hug and then the man handed him the attaché and they both went inside. Carter's security team followed while two of the unknown man's team stayed outside with the SUVs.

I tried to write down the license plates, but only managed a partial of the rear SUV before I looked up and saw an NOPD cruiser approaching in the distance. I decided that a third interaction with Detective Jackson was unwise and pulled back onto the street before making an immediate right to avoid catching their attention.

I took the long way to the address for Cynthia Haynes to make sure no one was following me and there weren't any more surprises. The streets were extremely narrow and poorly maintained, making it tough to find a place to park and establish surveillance.

I passed by the house at a crawl as I confirmed the address. An SUV very similar to the ones in front of the church was parked out front, but this time there were no guards standing watch outside. The engine appeared to be off, and the vehicle was unoccupied.

I continued past the house and found a place to park on the side of the street a few blocks down. I grabbed Kruger's leash and hooked it to her collar as she jumped over the center console and exited the driver's side with me. "Let's go for a walk, girl."

We crossed the street and walked toward the house, stopping to let Kruger sniff around a bit and do her business. I knew being cooped up in the truck so much the last two days had taken its toll on her. She was used to being much more active but was still handling it very well.

I kept an eye on the house as Kruger finished and I gave her her Kong. "Good girl."

We continued down the sidewalk toward the house, walking slowly as I glanced over at the house across the street every so often. As we got closer, a man in a suit very similar to the security detail from the church emerged from the house, followed by Haynes and another similarly dressed man.

We stopped by a tree, and I took the Kong from Kruger as I watched the first man walk to the SUV and open the passenger door. He motioned for her to get in as she stopped ten or so feet short. The man behind her nudged her to keep going, but she refused, shaking her head as she said something to the man.

The man who had opened the door stepped toward her. He put his finger in her face, appearing to threaten her as the man behind her grabbed her by the arms. She tried to resist but the man holding her was easily a foot taller and outweighed her by at least a hundred pounds. He had no trouble holding her in place.

With their attention on the woman, Kruger and I crossed the street. We continued toward the house as I watched the man who was holding Haynes attempt to force her into the back of the SUV. She struggled to break free of his grip.

"Let me go, asshole!" I heard her yell as we got closer.

The man holding the door open turned and mean-mugged me as we approached. It was intended to be a clear warning that whatever they were up to was none of my concern. But given the recent news and the brewing anger I had as a result of the loss of my friends, I took it as more of an invitation and left the sidewalk heading straight for them.

My direct approach caused the man to put his plans for Haynes on standby as he squared off with me and my fifty-pound fur missile.

"Can I help you?" he asked, pulling his suit coat to the side, revealing a nickel-plated handgun of some sort in a shoulder rig. It was about as clichéd as I could've imagined for a hired thug like him.

"Everything okay here, ma'am?" I asked as I continued toward them. I stopped a few feet from the man, which was another ten or so feet from Haynes and the man holding her. Her face was wet with tears and her face bruised. She looked at me and mouthed, "Help me."

"You need to go on about your business," the man near me warned as he made an exaggerated motion to unsnap the holster. "Wouldn't want anything to happen to you or your dog."

"Look, buddy, I've had a long day. We can go back and forth all day about what you will do to me if I don't and what my fifty-pound velociraptor with titanium incisors will do to you if you try. But how about, instead, you snap your holster, let the girl go, and get back in your vehicle?"

Angered by my resistance, the man drew his weapon.

"*Fass!*" I yelled, giving Kruger the command to attack as I engaged the man.

I dropped the leash as I stepped to the left and pushed the man's right wrist away from me with my left hand, and placed my right hand on the slide. Kruger bolted toward the man's left leg as I relieved the man of his weapon by using the leverage to twist it toward him. As an added bonus, his finger was caught in the trigger guard and broke with a satisfying *crack* as I ripped the gun away.

Kruger went to work on his leg, causing him to scream in agony as he fell to the ground. The man holding Haynes pushed her away and attempted to draw his weapon, but before he could, I had the first man's weapon pointed at him.

"Don't," I warned.

"Get the dog off me!" the man on the ground screamed.

I walked over to the second man and relieved him of his weapon. I tucked it into my waistband before returning to the man on the ground.

"The more you resist, the harder she'll bite," I said as I squatted down next to him, keeping my newly acquired gun trained on the other man.

"Fuck you!"

"That's not nice," I said, grabbing his broken finger and twisting it. With Kruger still gnawing on his leg, I wasn't sure it would have any effect, but it appeared to add to his agony.

"Stop! Please!"

"Who are you working for?"

"Mike Houston!"

"Let's all go back inside and have a little chat, shall we?" I gave Kruger the command to release, and rewarded her with the Kong.

CHAPTER EIGHTEEN

I found several pairs of Flexcuffs in the SUV and used them to bind my new friends once inside the house. Cynthia Haynes was nice enough to provide duct tape to keep them quiet, so I could figure out what to do next.

I fed Kruger and sat with Cynthia at the small table in her kitchen. She had brewed coffee for the goons tied up in her living room and offered me a cup. I accepted as she sat down and brushed a strand of hair away from her face. Her hands were shaking, and I could see she had tried to cover up a bruise on her face with makeup.

"I'm sorry they're bleeding on your floor," I said, nodding to the man Kruger had gnawed on. Both men were hogtied in the living room.

"They'll just send more, you know," Cynthia said. "That man is very powerful."

"Well, let's talk about that. Who are they and what do they want with you?"

"I don't even know who you are. You some kinda cop or something? That ain't no normal dog."

I looked at Kruger as she just finished licking her bowl clean. "No, she's not. I'm not with NOPD. I'm just trying to get some answers."

"For what? Is that why you were here?"

"Yes," I said before sipping the coffee. "I came to talk to you."

"I don't know nothin'!"

"Relax," I said, noticing her body language suddenly turn very defensive. "I'm not here to hurt you. In fact, I think you may need my help. Why don't you tell me what those two wanted from you?"

Cynthia looked away and folded her arms. She rubbed her neck as she avoided eye contact.

"Would you rather I let them go and let them take you wherever they were going to take you?"

"No!"

"I promise you I'm here to help. But I can't help you if you don't tell me what's going on."

"They wanted to take me to go see that man...Mr. Houston."

"Mike Houston? Who is he?

Cynthia sighed. "You promise you won't let those men take me?"

"You have my word," I said before nodding to Kruger. "And hers too."

"When my brother died," Cynthia began, pausing to close her eyes. "I still can't believe they killed him."

I nodded, not wanting to get into an argument about poor life choices leading to her brother's death.

"Go on."

"When that state trooper killed Terry, Deacon Carter told me he could get my family some money. All I had to do was say what they told me to the reporters and talk at the rallies. I was so mad that they killed him just for being black. I didn't think nothing of it," she said as she started to cry.

"It's okay," I said as I reached across the table to stroke her hand.

"I did what they asked. I did everything. I got the money and I kept my mouth shut. But then I overheard them talking about LeShawn yesterday. They killed him!"

"Wait," I said, as I leaned back to process what she had just said. "LeShawn Revis?"

Cynthia nodded. "I knew him from the church. He was a good man. He didn't deserve that."

"How do you know they killed him?"

"I heard Deacon Carter talking to one of his body guards about how they dealt with him and made it look good. I didn't think nothing of it until they said he killed himself. That man did not kill himself. He loved his wife and baby. He had gone straight, you know? He didn't kill himself."

"So, what did you do?"

"I confronted him. I told Deacon Carter that there was no way he killed himself, and I didn't know what they was doing but I didn't want no part of it anymore. I told him I ain't doing no more interviews or talking in public."

"So he yelled at you?" I remembered the scene at the playground.

"Not at first. At first he just said 'we'll see' and then walked away. But then I was out watching the kids and he got real mad and came out and told me I needed to act right or I'd have to give the money back. He said they needed me to do some more stuff."

"That was earlier today?"

"Yeah, how'd you know?"

"Just a guess."

"So when I went home, these two showed up at my door and said I need to go talk to Mr. Houston himself. They said he wanted to talk to me, and he would give me more money if I went with them. When I said told them I wasn't gonna, they said I didn't have a choice. Then you showed up."

"Do you know who this Houston guy is?"

"Some rich big wig. That's all I know."

I pushed my chair back from the table and stood. "I'll find out."

"Wait," she said. "You're still gonna help me, right?"

"I'm going to get you somewhere safe, but first I'm going to have a chat with our friends in your living room."

I walked into the kitchen and started opening drawers, looking for something useful to help me coerce our guests into talking. In the fourth drawer, I found a corkscrew and decided it would be good enough if they decided to resist.

As I walked into the living room, the guard with the fresh bite marks on his leg groaned. I ignored him as I walked to the other guard and squatted down, tossing the corkscrew on the ground in front of his face.

As the guard nervously eyed the object in front of him, I ripped the tape from his mouth and balled it up. I toyed with it for a second and then tossed it to the side before I reached down and picked up the corkscrew.

"Who are you?" the guard asked nervously.

"It doesn't matter," I replied. "I'm not the one hogtied on the floor."

With a sudden gain of confidence, the guard laughed. "They'll kill you, you know. You're a dead man."

I squatted down and looked the man in the eye.

"I've been dead for a long time."

"Real funny, but you have no idea what you're getting into."

"Let's start with names. You and your bleeding friend. And which one of you is in charge here. You?"

"I just work here."

"Do you, though?" I asked, toying with the corkscrew in my hand.

"What? So you're going to torture us? You think we're scared of you?"

"Good point," I said before whistling.

The sound of her claws on the hard floors preceded Kruger's entrance as she trotted in. The other guard squirmed and grunted through the duct tape covering his mouth.

"Winner, winner," I said as I stood and walked over to the other guard.

I squatted down and ripped the tape from his mouth, balling it up and tossing it aside as Kruger walked up to me. I scratched behind her ears as I watched the guard look up in terror.

"You heard the questions," I said.

"We work security for Mr. Houston!"

"And what did you want with Ms. Haynes?"

"He told us to come get her."

"And take her where?"

"He said to call him when we were on the way and he'd tell us."

"Does he have an office or house in the city?"

"Yeah, but he wouldn't have us take her there."

"Why not?"

The other guard interjected. "Shut up, dumbass!"

I stood and grabbed the duct tape. "That's enough out of you."

I duct taped the other guard's mouth and then returned to the other one.

"He's right. I ain't talking!" the guard said defiantly as I squatted down next to him.

"Looks like we struck a nerve," I said as I reached behind the guard's back and grabbed his broken finger. "Why not?"

"Because Mr. Houston isn't coming back to the city until it's over," he replied as he winced in pain.

"Until what's over?"

"The attack!"

"What attack?" I asked, applying pressure to his finger.

"I don't know! I swear! I just know it's going to be big. Real big. They told us to get everyone we love out the city."

"When? When is the attack?"

"I don't know! Two or three days! They didn't tell us specifics, I swear!"

"Where?"

"Everywhere. It's the whole city. That's all I know. They didn't tell us."

"Shit," I hissed as I picked up the duct tape roll and taped his mouth.

I walked back into the kitchen and found Haynes still crying at the table. "Pack a bag. We're leaving."

"Where are we going?"

"I'm going to get you to safety," I said. "Go!"

She reluctantly complied and disappeared toward the bedroom. When she was gone, I pulled my cell phone out of my pocket and dialed Tanner.

"Special Agent Tanner," she answered.

"Hey, it's Troy. I think you might want to get down here."

CHAPTER NINETEEN

"Where are you taking me?" Cynthia asked nervously from the front passenger seat of my truck.

"Somewhere safe," I said. I had left the two guards tied up in Cynthia's house and called 911 before we left. After explaining the situation to Tanner, she had agreed to put a team together and fly down to New Orleans as soon as she could arrange transport through the Bureau.

"I'm scared," Cynthia murmured.

"You're going to be okay," I said. "You're just going to have to trust me."

"I don't even know you."

"I saved you from those two assholes, didn't I?"

"Yeah, but that don't mean nothin' around here. You could be just as bad as them?"

"And yet here you sit - in a truck with a stranger that you don't trust."

"You don't know me."

"You're right. I'm just trying to get you somewhere safe so you can tell the right people your story."

"What people? What story?"

"I'm just going to introduce you to some friends of mine that can keep you safe, and you can tell them what you told me."

"Cops? I ain't no snitch!"

"Do you want to go back to those men?"

"Well, no..."

"Do you think it's right what they're doing in your brother's name?"

"Some of them cops deserved it."

It was hard to bite my tongue. I had lost friends that had been like family to me because of how they had used her brother. But I knew that picking at that scab wouldn't solve anything. I needed her to be willing to tell Agent Tanner her story, so we could put an end to the attacks against law enforcement and the pending act of terrorism.

"Innocent people are going to die if we don't stop this right here and right now. And if I bring you back, they will kill you. Is that what you want?"

"Well, no..."

"So, trust me and-"

Arguing with Cynthia had caused me to drop my guard long enough to miss the SUV barreling toward us. I looked up just as its push bar impacted the rear bumper of my truck, causing me to lose control as the truck took a hard right into a parked car.

The airbags deployed as we crashed. I heard Kruger yelp in the back seat as time seemed to stand still. The airbag hit me in the face, knocking the wind out of me as we bounced off the car and back into traffic.

We rolled to a stop, and I looked over at Cynthia. She was unconscious, and blood covered her face. As I turned to check on Kruger, I saw two men in suits approaching with guns drawn.

I managed to get my seatbelt off as I pushed the deflated airbag away from my face. Pain shot through my right arm as I tried to draw my Glock from the holster in my waistband. My vision was blurred, and I felt like I was in a haze as I tried to open the door while searching for the two men. I had lost them as I had struggled with the seatbelt.

Gunshots rang out as I finally got the door open. A round went through my right leg and another through my shoulder, causing me to drop my gun as I fell backward out of the truck and onto the street.

My adrenaline surged as I tried to fight through the pain and get back up. I frantically searched for my gun only to realize it had fallen under the truck.

As I bent over to get it, I heard two more gunshots and then turned to see one of the men in suits. He kicked me squarely in the chest, knocking me back to the hot asphalt.

My head hit the side of the bent driver side wheel as I landed. The world started to dim as I drifted out of consciousness.

"He's down. You want me to finish him?" I heard a voice say before everything went black.

CHAPTER TWENTY

The first thing I noticed when I came to was the rhythmic beeping of the heart rate monitor. It was an all-too-familiar sound that had been seared into my brain what seemed like a lifetime ago when I was recovering from a coma after the school bus attack.

As my eyes adjusted to the dark room, I realized I was once again in a hospital bed. For a moment, I wasn't sure if I was back in that same hospital bed, I had spent so many weeks recovering in after my family had been taken from me. It all felt so familiar.

My shoulder and leg were both throbbing as I tried to move. As I tried to roll to my side, I realized my left wrist was handcuffed to the bedrail. I pulled against it as it dawned on me that I was, in fact, someone's prisoner.

"You're awake!" I heard in the darkness.

"Jen?" I asked as I tried to process the voice.

Seconds later, the light came on. Jenny rushed to my bedside as a uniformed NOPD officer stood by the light switch. I was suddenly very confused as I tried to process it all. In that moment, the only thing I could remember was dropping Jenny off at the airport. Everything else was a blur.

"What? Where am I?" I asked as she reached my side and kissed me.

"Ma'am," the male NOPD officer warned as he took a step toward us.

"Sorry," she said as she took a step back. "I'm not supposed to touch you."

"What? What's going on?" I asked, pulling on the handcuff chain. "What is this?"

"You're in NOPD custody, sir," the officer replied.

"What the hell for?" I asked. I was still trying to process the events of the last few days when suddenly I remembered seeing Kruger bleeding and in the back of my truck. "Where's Kruger?"

"Relax, sweetie, she's fine," Jenny said, trying to be as soothing as she could. "Sergeant Maclin sent Deputy Michaels to go get her. NOPD found her and turned her over. She was scratched up, but the vet said she's fine."

"What about the girl…ahhh…I can't think of her name…." My mind was drawing a blank. I couldn't seem to remember anything or shake the fog. Some of it was starting to come back to me. I remembered an accident and the girl, but everything seemed so fragmented.

Jenny frowned. "You really don't remember anything?"

"Just tell me what the fuck is going on!" I was frustrated and angry that I couldn't remember anything. I knew I shouldn't have snapped at her, but I just wanted answers.

"I'm sorry," I said as Jenny jumped with my outburst. "It's not your fault. I just don't know what happened."

"I sent a text to Detective Jackson," the uniformed officer said. "They're on their way."

"Thank you," Jenny said to the officer.

"I don't remember anything," I said, trying to calm myself down. "Everything is in fragments since I dropped you off at the airport. I remember some kind of car wreck and Kruger was bleeding and there was a woman…Candace…Cindy…Cynthia maybe? Yeah, that's it!"

"Troy, she's dead," Jenny said, ignoring the officer's previous warning not to grab my hand. "That's why the cops are here. They think you killed her."

"What? No way!"

"I don't believe it either, Troy, you know that."

"How long have I been here?"

"Two days," Jenny replied. "They called me yesterday afternoon, and I rode here last night with Deputy Michaels. He dropped me off and started the drive back. You had been in and out of surgery all day. They had to remove bullet fragments from your shoulder and leg."

"Wait, I was shot. What about the men that shot me? How am I a suspect?"

"We'd better not say anymore until your attorney gets here, Troy."

"*My attorney?* I don't understand!"

There was a knock at the door and the NOPD officer opened it. Detective Jackson walked in followed by Special Agent Tanner and another man in a dark suit that I didn't recognize. Jenny stepped back as the trio surrounded my bed.

"Mr. Wilson, good to see you up and about again. I'm here to inform you that you've been charged with two counts of battery, kidnapping, and the murder of Cynthia Haynes," he said before pulling out card and reciting my rights per Miranda.

"Do you understand your rights, Mr. Wilson?" Detective Jackson asked as he put the card away.

"I do," I said slowly.

"And do you wish to answer my questions at this time?"

"I just want someone to tell me what the hell is going on," I said. "I don't remember anything."

"So, you're willing to speak to us at this time?"

I ignored him and looked at Agent Tanner. "I'm probably hopped up on morphine or something, but none of this makes sense. What are you doing here?"

"You don't remember calling me?" Tanner asked.

"I don't remember anything."

"Maybe this will refresh your memory," Jackson said as he turned his phone around to show me pictures from the crime scene.

I grunted as I tried to sit up. Pain shot through my shoulder as I tried to get a closer look at the screen.

"Take your time," Jackson said.

It was a close-up picture of Cynthia Haynes with a gunshot wound to the head. The picture was extremely close, so it was hard to tell where she was or what position her body was in.

Jackson swiped to the next picture on the phone. It was less zoomed in. Cynthia appeared to be lying on carpet next to an end table. As I stared at the picture, images of being in her house came rushing back.

"That's her house, isn't it?"

Jackson nodded and then swiped to the next picture. It was clearly in her living room. There was an evidence marker a foot or so away from her hand next to what appeared to be a revolver of some sort.

"Okay, that's enough," I said as I laid back down in the bed.

"So, you recognize her house?" Jackson asked as he put his phone back in his pocket.

I looked up at Tanner who discretely shook her head for me not to answer.

"Someone needs to tell me what the hell is going on here," I said, looking back at Jackson.

"Can we have a moment alone with the suspect?" Tanner asked Jackson.

"This is my investigation," Jackson protested. "You can ask him anything you want with me here."

Tanner brushed her brown hair from her forehead as she turned to square off with the much bigger detective. "I was being polite, detective. We believe your suspect may have information regarding a federal terrorism investigation. As you can imagine, this information is highly sensitive."

"I understand, but-"

"But nothing, Detective. Please give us the room. I will let you know when you may return."

"Ten minutes, and that's it," Jackson replied.

"We'll let you know when you can come back in," Tanner said before turning to the uniformed officer. "That goes for you too, officer."

Jackson reluctantly complied and motioned for the officer to follow him.

"Ten minutes," he said as he opened the door. "And we will be right outside."

Tanner waited for the detective and officer to exit and then let out a sigh. "Holy shit, Troy, what the hell have you gotten yourself into this time?"

"Everything is a blur," I said.

"Well, you'd better figure it out quick because NOPD is looking to make an example of you for killing the sister of Terry Haynes. I would not be surprised if they really do bring in the FBI to prosecute it as a hate crime."

"My office," the male FBI agent said.

"Troy, this is Special Agent Davis Wells with the New Orleans Field Office," Tanner said. "His office would be the one investigating if it does come to that, so watch what you say. Your lawyer should be here any minute if you'd rather wait."

"Look, I just want to know what happened. I'm remembering bits and pieces, but nothing seems to make sense."

"Well, according to reports, you visited Cynthia Haynes at her home demanding answers after being warned by NOPD to stay away from the area. Apparently, they caught you doing surveillance on some church?"

"I guess," I said, still trying to remember.

"Well, surveillance cameras from that church had you there shortly before going to the victim's house. Witnesses saw you and your dog fighting with her security detail before you forced them all into the house."

"That sounds like bullshit," I said. Images of Kruger taking down one of the bodyguards were suddenly coming back to me. I remembered seeing them trying to kidnap Cynthia and bringing them into the house, but I knew I didn't kill Cynthia.

"They found Kruger's hair in the house, Troy, as well as your fingerprints on the door and in the kitchen. The security detail said you knocked them both out and when they came to, you were gone and Cynthia was dead next to her revolver," Tanner said. "That's pretty damning evidence."

"I know I didn't kill that girl," I said.

"NOPD thinks she may have pulled a gun she had hidden in the house and shot you. Ballistics still have to be run. You may be able to argue self-defense, but that's something your lawyer will have to argue," Tanner said.

"So, how did I get here?"

"You crashed your truck a few blocks from the victim's house. You and Kruger managed to escape before your truck burst into flames. I think they said you had a concussion which is why you probably can't remember much," Tanner said.

There was a knock at the door. Tanner nodded for Agent Wells to answer.

"Where did they find me?"

"On the ground next to the truck."

"And Kruger?"

"It's the suspect's lawyer," Wells said as he held the door partially open.

"Let her in, "Tanner said and then turned back to me. "NOPD found her guarding you."

"None of this makes sense."

A tall, attractive blonde woman entered the room carrying an attaché. She placed it on one of the chairs as Tanner turned to greet her. I was expecting them to shake hands, but instead, they hugged.

"You remember Cal Martin's wife, Michelle?" Tanner asked.

"Cal Martin…" I said, not really sure why I knew that name.

"You might have known him as Spectre," Michelle said.

"Oh, right! I remember you now. Sorry, I'm having trouble remembering anything right now."

"It's okay," Michelle said as she walked around to my bedside. "Maddie called me as soon as she heard you were under arrest. I'll be representing you if that's okay with you. Friends and family, discount, of course."

"Thank you," I said. "I didn't do anything, though."

"I know, but-"

Before she could finish, Detective Jackson and the uniformed officer came storming in. "You all need to leave right now!"

"Not until I've had time to speak to my client," Michelle replied angrily.

"Ma'am, the rioters are headed this way; we need to get all of you to safety."

"Rioters?" I asked. I remembered something about an attack but couldn't quite remember what it was.

"Yeah," Jackson said. "What did you expect would happen after murdering the sister of a man that has caused so much unrest lately?"

"I didn't kill her, and you know it."

"What happened?" Tanner asked.

"Protests started a few blocks from here in front of the precinct and turned into riots about an hour ago. Our best guess is that the protesters found out Mr. Wilson is here and are coming to demand justice. We're locking this place down and moving out all non-essential personnel just in case."

"What about my client?" Michelle asked.

"Doctors are making rounds right now to assess which patients can be transported and which will have to stay. If he can be transported, we'll move him to the Orleans Parish Correctional Facility. If not, he'll have to stay here, but from what I'm hearing, they're worried the riots are moving this way. We have to get you out of here. Come on."

CHAPTER TWENTY-ONE

I don't know how long I had been asleep when the Orleans Parish Sheriff Deputies entered the room and flipped the lights on. I had drifted off shortly after Agent Tanner left with Jenny and Decker, promising to keep them safe until we could be reunited and come up with a plan to fight the charges against me. Whatever painkillers or sedatives they had me on were kicking my ass and all I wanted to do was sleep.

"Rise and shine. Your ride is here," Detective Jackson said as he walked in behind the two deputies.

One of the deputies went to work releasing my restraints as the other stood at the bedside holding a belly chain and leg shackles. I groaned as the pain hit me when the deputy sat me up in the bed.

"Get dressed," Jackson said, tossing a bright orange prison jumpsuit and black bulletproof vest on the bed next to me.

"A vest? Seriously?"

"You're going to live long enough to answer for what you've done to this city," Jackson said.

I slowly stood and put on the jumpsuit. The deputy had to help me get my arm in as the pain was nearly unbearable. He put the vest on me and then tightly clasped the Velcro straps. I grunted as more pain shot through my arm and chest.

The deputy helped me put on a pair of wool socks and Crocs and then turned me toward the other deputy still holding the belly chain and shackles. He held me in place while the other slid the chain around my waist and locked it before cuffing both hands, pinning my arms to my sides. He then squatted down and attached the shackles, completing the ensemble.

"C'mon, man. Is all of this really necessary?" I asked, looking at Jackson as he seemed to enjoy watching me suffer.

An orderly arrived with a wheelchair and helped me sit. I could walk, but I was relieved that I wouldn't have to walk very much with my injuries.

"Just following protocol," Jackson said without even trying to hide the smirk on his face.

"Really? Is that why you're coming with me? Protocol?"

"Actually, yes," Jackson said. "I volunteered to go along as extra security."

"You still think I'm guilty," I said, shaking my head as the other deputy walked around the bed to open the door.

"That would be the reason you're going to jail, yes."

"It's bullshit and you know it."

"Then tell me what happened," Jackson said.

No matter how hard I tried, I couldn't quite piece it all together. I was still in a haze. I remembered bits and pieces – men in suits, a car crash, hearing gunshots – but it wasn't enough to build a clear picture of how I had ended up in this situation.

"I don't remember," I mumbled.

"Yeah, right. That's what I thought," Jackson said with a fake laugh. "Let's go."

The deputy behind me grabbed my arm and led me out. The chains jingled as I was wheeled out of the door and into the hallway where two NOPD officers carrying rifles and wearing plate carriers were waiting to escort us.

"All of this for me?" I asked.

"Wait until you see the shit storm you started outside," Jackson replied as he walked next to me.

Nurses and doctors at the nurses' station turned to watch as we went by them toward the elevator. I could almost feel their disdain as they glared at me as I passed by them. How dare I bring this unrest upon their hospital! After all the city had been through in the last week, I was only fueling the fires in their mind. There was no doubt they all thought I was guilty as charged.

The memory fragments of the last twenty-four hours came and went. I would see, hear, or even smell something and suddenly I'd get a brief flashback, but there wasn't enough to put it all together.

We piled into the elevator and headed down to the Emergency Room level. They escorted me through the waiting area and out into an open area next to a parking garage. There was a covered walkway with a big red sign that said EMERGENCY DROP-OFF. Parked next to it were the vehicles of what I assumed to be our convoy – two NOPD SUVs, an Orleans Parish Sheriff prisoner transport van, and a black unmarked Tahoe which I assumed Jackson would be driving. They all appeared to have engines running and emergency lights activated.

Stepping into the muggy night air, I heard the protesters raging in the distance. The University Medical Center Emergency Room was on an upper level and had a ramp to the street level. I could see NOPD units blocking the roads at the end of the ramp for our departure, but I couldn't see any protesters near them. I wondered just how bad it was going to get before it was all over.

The deputies helped me out of the wheelchair and into the back of the prisoner transport van as Jackson watched.

"I'll be right in front of you," Jackson said as they seat belted me in and secured my chains. "Don't get any ideas."

"Doesn't look like I have much of a choice," I said.

The deputy shut the door and then got in the front seat of the van. We were separated by a plexiglass divider, but I could hear them talking about our route to the prison. Although it was only a few blocks away, it sounded like the riots were going to force us into taking the long way around.

I leaned my head against the metal bars on the window as the convoy started to move. I started to drift off as I thought about Jenny and my K-9 partner. I missed them and just wanted to be home. This whole ordeal had become another bad nightmare – one that I had brought upon myself by foolishly chasing my rage. *Again.*

I felt the van turn and accelerate. I knew I should stay awake, but I was so exhausted. I just wanted to sleep. I would need my strength in jail if they put me in the general population and the inmates discovered I was a cop. Even more so when they realized I was accused of killing Haynes.

The siren of the lead police Tahoe jolted me awake. It was followed by the air horn blasting three times before I heard the deputy in the passenger seat yell, "Stop!"

My head nearly hit the plexiglass as he slammed on the brakes and we slowed to a stop. I looked up and saw what appeared to be a burning car in the middle of the road. It looked like a war scene out of Syria or Iraq.

The reverse lights on the Tahoe came on, and I heard him say something over the radio that I couldn't quite make out. I assumed it was something along the lines of *"Back the fuck up!"*

based on the reaction of my driver and his subsequent fumbling around with the gear shift to put the van in reverse.

I tried looking around to get my bearings, but I had no idea where we were. It was too dark and, despite the action going on around me, I still couldn't seem to shake the haze and think clearly.

The engine roared as the driver missed reverse and went into neutral instead. He found reverse just as the lead Tahoe slammed on its brakes, stopping within inches of our front bumper.

As the driver gunned it, I heard the unmistakable cadence of automatic gunfire. I ducked down on the plastic bench seat as much as I could within the limits of my restraints as the rounds shattered glass around me.

"Fuck!" one of the deputies yelled. "Keep driving!"

I managed to hit the release and unbuckled my seatbelt. The inertial reel had locked as the driver had hit reverse. It gave me more room to maneuver despite my shackles being connected to the floor. I was able to slide down and get low on my side beneath the windows as more glass shattered around me.

"Alan! You're hit!" I heard.

The van suddenly swerved and I slid toward the door, held in place only by my chains. The pain in my shoulder and legs was excruciating. I heard tires squealing immediately before we ran over something and I was launched into the air.

For a moment, I was airborne and time seemed to slow down. I saw the driver slumped over and bullet holes through the windshield. His foot was still on the accelerator as I landed back on the floor of the van.

We crashed into something. I didn't know if it was a parked car or other solid object, but the force of impact slammed me into the divider. I tried to move, but in the crash my shackles and become tangled even more, locking me to the floor.

I heard what sounded like return fire in the distance. It sounded like some of the battles I had encountered in Iraq and

Syria. I hadn't heard anything like it in a while, but the sound was unmistakable. I only hoped the good guys weren't outgunned and outnumbered this time.

I tried to unbind my restraints to at least allow me to get out of the awkward position I was in, but they wouldn't budge. Despite the gunfire outside, I couldn't hear anything from the front seats. I assumed they were either both dead or incapacitated.

The gunfire suddenly stopped as I tried unsuccessfully to free myself. I heard the door open, but I wasn't in position to see who it was. All I could do was wince and hope whoever it was either planned to put a bullet in my head and end it quickly or was a good guy.

I felt someone grab me by the shoulders and push me up only to realize I was stuck in place.

"What the fuck did you do in here? Were you trying to escape?"

I immediately recognized Jackson's voice as he fumbled with his keys to release the lock from the mounting bracket. He then went to work untwisting my chains until finally he gave up and unlatched the cuffs and leg restraints.

"If you try to run, I'll shoot you," he warned as I sat up. "Now come on, we have to get out of here. We've been ambushed and backup can't get to us here. We gotta move!"

CHAPTER TWENTY-TWO

Walking proved to be difficult but manageable. Running, however, was pure agony. But it was my only option as I pushed through the pain to keep up with Jackson as we moved from the prisoner transport van toward his Tahoe.

The scene outside the van was just as bad as I had imagined it. The lead Tahoe had been shot up and was on fire in the middle of the street. Luckily, the driver's side door was open and at least initially it appeared that the NOPD officer had gotten out.

Both front doors of the prisoner transport van had been opened. There was a blood trail from the passenger side. It led to the rear NOPD Tahoe where I saw one of the uniformed officers using the engine block as cover next to one of the deputies leaning against the left rear tire and clutching his shoulder. I couldn't see the other deputy or NOPD officers, but I hoped they had at least made it to cover.

I heard a few rounds zip by and impact a tree in the neutral ground as I followed Jackson. He had his patrol rifle up and pointed toward the burning Tahoe, but he did not return fire. I didn't blame him. The power on the street had gone out and it was far too dark to tell who was friend or foe.

As we reached the Tahoe, Jackson opened the left rear passenger door. "Get in!"

I climbed in the back as I tried to catch my breath. I was slightly surprised to see that Jackson's unit had a cage. Most detectives I had known drove unmarked Ford Fusions that were no different than their civilian counterparts, other than aftermarket lights and siren. Jackson slammed the door and hurried to the driver's seat.

"What about the others?" I asked.

"They won't all fit in the other Tahoe so they're going to hunker down and wait for SWAT to arrive with medics. Should be five to ten out."

"If we put some in here, they'll fit," I said.

Jackson slammed the column shift lever into drive and looked over his right shoulder as he started to make a u-turn away from the burning vehicle in front of us.

"You're the reason they're shooting at us," Jackson said. "If I get you out of here, it'll draw them away."

"What? How do they know it's me?"

"Someone tipped them off. They were yelling for your head before I pulled you out of the van."

"This is a stupid idea," I said as I looked back to see one of the NOPD officers tending to the wounded while the other returned fire over the hood of his unit. "You don't stay and fight in an ambush. You get the hell out of there."

I struggled to keep my balance as Jackson floored it and swerved around the prison van as he hopped the curb onto the neutral ground. The Tahoe bounced violently as we crossed the streetcar tracks toward the opposite lane of traffic.

As we made it back onto the roadway, rounds peppered the Tahoe. I ducked down as glass shattered around me. We swerved violently, throwing me to the other side of the seat before I was able to grab onto the door for support.

We sideswiped a parked car and rolled to a stop. I managed to pick myself back up to see Jackson slumped over the steering wheel.

"Oh shit!" I yelled as I tried to open the door. I immediately remembered that I was in the back of a police vehicle and that the doors wouldn't open. Both windows in the back were splintered from rounds going through them but still intact.

I pushed through the pain and positioned myself to kick out the window. I was lucky the side windows didn't have bars like some units. Despite the bullet hole having done some of the work for me, my first attempt failed. My leg just didn't have enough strength at the angle I'd managed.

I repositioned myself to get a better angle on the window with my left leg and braced against the hard plastic seat. It was smooth and hard not to slide, but I managed to latch onto the seat belt receiver to hold me in place. I kicked as hard as I could until the window completely shattered around my flimsy Croc shoes.

With the window no longer in my way, my next task was to get out through the window. I knew the door would be locked, but I tried it from the outside anyway just to be sure. As I unsuccessfully pulled on the door handle a few times, I heard a few rounds ricochet off the nearby asphalt. I didn't have much time, and if Jackson was still alive, he had even less.

I took a deep breath as I climbed through the window. The pain was overwhelming as I pulled myself through and fell onto my shoulder onto the asphalt. It wasn't graceful, but I was out and still able to fight.

Surveying my surroundings, I slowly picked myself up to a crouching position next to the driver door. With the streetlights out, it was so dark, but my eyes had adjusted enough that I could see a group of rioters approaching about a hundred yards away. Based on the sounds of gunfire, I assumed that's where the rounds had been coming from also.

I pulled myself up to check on Jackson. He was no longer slumped over and was now leaning back against the headrest clutching the right side of his neck.

"Open the door!" I yelled.

Jackson barely moved in response to my command.

"Open the door!" I repeated. "We have to get you out of here!"

Jackson weakly tried to raise his left arm to reach the door's unlock button. He fumbled around until he gave up and leaned back in his seat. He was in bad shape and needed to get to a hospital immediately.

I looked back at the crowd. They were closing the distance rapidly and would be on us in a minute or less. I didn't want to stick around to find out what they would do once they reached us.

I leaned back and forced my elbow through the window as hard as I could, shattering it. I ignored the pain as I reached in and manually unlocked the door.

"Don't try anything, Wilson," Jackson warned weakly.

"I'm trying to save your ass," I said as I opened the door.

I reached across him and put the Tahoe in park before assessing his wounds. He was shot in the neck and chest as far as I could tell. The dome light in the vehicle was barely enough to illuminate him, but enough to illuminate us to the bad guys resulting in more rounds impacting nearby.

Jackson's seatbelt wasn't buckled, making it only slightly easier for me to move him. He was a large man who hadn't skipped a meal in a while.

"Keep applying pressure as best you can," I said. "I need to move you to the backseat."

"I'll wait for the ambulance," Jackson mumbled.

"If we do that, you'll die."

"You're not going to escape," he said.

"Don't be an idiot," I said as I pulled him out of the driver's seat. "Hold pressure."

Jackson was pretty much dead weight as I struggled to get him out. I barely had the strength to move him, but a combination of adrenaline and a sense of urgency knowing that the crowd was steadily approaching kept me going.

I got him out of the SUV. He was able to stand up, which was a good sign. Getting him into the backseat was easier than getting him out of the driver's seat.

Once he was lying on the bench seat in the back, I closed the door and jumped in the driver's seat. The crowd was now less than twenty-five yards away, and the rounds coming our way were getting closer.

I put the Tahoe in reverse and punched the accelerator. Once we were back in the roadway, I slammed it into DRIVE and floored it.

"Where's the hospital from here?" I asked as I tried to read the nearest crossing street sign.

Jackson said something inaudible as I accelerated away from the mob behind us. When we had some distance, I used the spotlight in front of the A-pillar to illuminate a street sign.

We were on Canal Street. I saw a convoy of police vehicles on the opposite lane of traffic and figured we must be heading east back toward University Medical Center. It had been a while since I had spent any time in the city, but I was pretty sure all I needed to do was stay on Canal, and I'd get us there.

"Hang on back there," I said as I hit the siren and pushed through eighty miles per hour on the narrow two-lane street.

I saw signs for University Medical and the interstate a few blocks away. I started to breathe a sigh of relief until I started seeing more crowds. The rioters we had just escaped weren't the same rioters that had closed in on the hospital.

I looked in the rearview mirror and could no longer see Jackson. He was below my sightline and not moving. If he didn't get medical attention soon, he'd be dead.

A block away from the hospital, a crowd was standing in the roadway, blocking traffic. I hit the horn and yelped the siren to no avail as we approached. I slowed, trying not to run over anyone, but the crowd surrounded us and began throwing things and trying to reach into the vehicle.

It was us or them. I chose us.

I pushed through the crowd, knocking people over with the push bar as they refused to get out of the way. We ran over something – I wasn't sure if it was a leg or a whole person, but at that point, I didn't care anymore. They had chosen poorly and left me no other options.

We made it through the crowd and onto the emergency room ramp we had just descended not long prior. I pulled up to the entrance and hit the horn once more, hoping someone would come out to meet me.

As I got out of the vehicle, two NOPD officers that had been walking out saw my orange jumpsuit and drew down on me.

"On your knees!" one of them yelled. "Do it now!"

"Detective Jackson is in the back!" I said as I put my hands on my head and complied. "You need to get him in there or he will die."

Two people in scrubs came out to see what was going on as the officers covered me.

"Gunshot wound to the neck!" I yelled, hoping they would hear me. "He's in the back seat!"

One officer covered as the other pushed my face down into the concrete. He cuffed me and the other officer cleared the vehicle.

"He's right. We've got a man down back here," I heard him say as the officer patted me down for weapons. "We need a stretcher over here!"

CHAPTER TWENTY-THREE

I felt like I had gone a long way to end up right back where I had started. It was after midnight, and after being detained by NOPD once more, I found myself once again chained to a hospital bed in an exam room waiting for the doctors to clear me for transport.

Despite my efforts to rescue Jackson, no one from either the medical or police side was really friendly to me. I didn't know what his status was, other than overhearing them talk about taking him to the operating room for emergency surgery.

The uniformed NOPD officer tasked with guarding me was sitting in a chair next to my bed playing a game on his phone. I had tried to engage him in conversation a few times to no avail. As far as he was concerned, he told me, I was the reason his city was turning into a war zone and the hospital was at risk.

The silence was broken by a knock on the door. The officer put his phone in his BDU pocket and walked to the door. He opened it, ushering in an attractive brunette nurse who wheeled in a blood pressure machine.

"How are you feeling?" she asked. It almost startled me that someone was finally talking to me after the way everyone had been treating me.

"Like shit, but I'm still alive," I said.

The nurse pulled out a full syringe with a capped needle from her scrub shirt pocket and placed in on the rolling table next to my bed. "This should help with pain."

"I don't think that's a good idea," I said.

"Why not?"

"After everything that's happened tonight, I think it would be best to stay alert."

"Everything you did, you mean," the officer mumbled under his breath.

"What?" I asked.

"A good man is in surgery because of you," the officer said, breaking his previous refusal to talk to me.

"You're right," I said. "I could've left him to die and taken his unit. Is that what you mean? If so, you're welcome."

"No, asshole, I mean the riots and the reason this hospital is under lockdown is *your* fault."

"Officer, please," the nurse said, intervening as she could see me starting to get visibly upset. "He doesn't need to be agitated."

"Whatever," the officer replied, throwing up his hands as he went back to his chair.

"Let's get your vitals," the nurse said as she turned on the blood pressure machine and wrapped the cuff around my arm.

She secured the cuff and then hit the button. The cuff inflated and then slowly deflated as it pulsed, checking my blood pressure.

"150/85 and your pulse is 93," she said. "Do you have a history of hypertension?"

"Only when I've been shot at."

"The pain meds will help you relax," the nurse said as she took the cuff off my arm.

"No, thanks," I said. "I'll manage."

"Suit yourself," she said with a shrug as she put the syringes back in her pocket. "Doctor Siddarth will be with you in a few minutes."

"Thank you."

The nurse wheeled the blood pressure machine out and closed the door behind her. I looked over at the officer who had gone back to playing games on his phone. I started to say something, but I realized it would be pointless. He had already made up his mind about me and there was no point in agitating him further.

I closed my eyes, hoping to get some rest and maybe the pain would subside. As I drifted to sleep, I saw Cynthia Haynes and two men in suits. I saw Kruger taking one of them down in a driveway somewhere in New Orleans. I wasn't sure if I was dreaming or remembering. I felt half -awake as if I was reliving it.

And then we were in my truck, but only for a split second before crashing. A man in a suit – different from the ones in the driveway – walked up and shot Cynthia. I tried to get out of the truck. The last thing I saw was a fancy leather shoe in my face.

A knock on the door jolted me back to reality. The officer put down his phone and opened the door. As I shook off the brief slumber, I was surprised to see Special Agent Tanner standing next to my bed.

"Can't stay out of trouble, can you?"

"How's Jenny?"

"Safe," Tanner said. "Michelle took her to her house outside of Baton Rouge."

"She needs to go back to Texas. She can't visit me in jail."

"Well, good news on that," Tanner said, pulling a folded paper out of her pocket. "You're going into federal custody."

"Wait, what?" the officer sitting next to the bed asked, suddenly perking up. "I haven't heard anything about this."

"And now you have," Tanner said, handing him the paper. "Mr. Wilson will be in federal custody going forward."

"I'll have to confirm this with my sergeant," the officer said, studying the paper. "I haven't heard anything about this."

"That's fine," Tanner replied. "As soon as he's cleared by the doctor, he's coming with me. So, you might want to hurry."

The officer unlocked his phone and started scrolling through his contacts, frantically searching for his sergeant's number as he stepped out of the room to make the call. "I'll be right outside."

"How'd you pull that off?" I asked as I tried to sit up in the bed.

"I didn't," Tanner said with a knowing grin. "Your attorney did. She pulled some strings to get you into federal protective custody due to the threats to your life and possible ties to the terrorism case."

"I didn't kill the girl," I said. "There were men in suits. We wrecked. It's still fuzzy, but you know I didn't do this right?"

"I know, Troy," Tanner said. "And NOPD located your truck about an hour ago, so hopefully that will help once forensics gets done with it."

"I don't know," I said, thinking back to my interactions with NOPD so far. "They're not big fans of me right now."

"They'll do their jobs, Troy. This city is a war zone. Everyone is stressed out right now."

The door opened, this time without a knock, as the officer returned with the same nurse as before and the doctor in tow. They turned on the main light in the room as the doctor flipped through my chart.

"I'm Dr. Siddarth," he said as he set the chart on the nearby counter. "How are you feeling?"

"I'll be fine."

"Any shortness of breath? Coughing?"

"No."

He took his stethoscope from around his neck and put it in his ears. He nodded to the nurse to help him as he had me sit up so he could listen to my heart and lungs.

"Your chart says you're refusing pain meds," Dr. Siddarth said as they helped me lie back down.

"Need to stay sharp."

"He's going to be taken into federal protective custody," Tanner interjected. "Is he okay to travel?"

"I would prefer to have him here for observation for at least forty-eight hours given his condition, but considering what is going on outside, I'd say that's unlikely. I will discharge him under the condition that he is discharged with appropriate pain medications and antibiotics. I don't know why this was allowed the first time, but I won't have it."

"We'll do whatever you want, Doctor," Tanner said.

The doctor looked at me, waiting for a reply. "Your body must rest and heal. You cannot just suck it up."

"I'm not arguing, doc, but the reason I'm sitting here right now is because the people outside just tried to kill me."

I turned and glared at the NOPD officer. "And I wouldn't have been able to get Detective Jackson to the emergency room had I been all drugged up."

"Don't worry, you're not driving this time," Tanner said. "We've got a helicopter waiting to take you out of here."

"Fancy," I said. "But since we're on the subject and the young officer won't talk to me, how is Detective Jackson doing anyway?"

"Last I heard, he's in surgery," Tanner said before turning to the doctor again. "So, he's good to go? We've got a helicopter to catch."

"Yes, he may leave," the doctor replied before picking up my chart and walking out.

CHAPTER TWENTY-FOUR

I spent a lot of time in helicopters when I worked with Odin, but for some reason I was a little nervous about my upcoming helicopter ride. Maybe it was because I had no idea where we were going. Or maybe it was because I overheard cops talking about the possibility of the hospital being shut down because of the rioters. No matter what the reason, I found myself just wanting to stay chained to the hospital bed and get some much-needed sleep.

Tanner escorted me out to the helipad alone where we met Special Agent Wells. The NOPD officer had been reluctant to let her take me solo, but after several calls to his leadership, he finally relented. As we left the exam room, I could feel the hate the man had for me through his angry glare.

We were only waiting a few minutes next to the helipad when I heard the helicopter approaching in the distance. It came in low and fast, turning its spotlight on at the last minute as it slowed to a hover and lowered its landing gear.

"What kind of helicopter is that?" I asked.

"Louisiana State Police Bell 430," Wells replied.

"Looks like Airwolf," I said. I don't think anyone heard me as the noise became deafening.

The helicopter gently touched down on the helipad and a Trooper emerged from the back. Tanner and I stood back as Wells ran up to meet him. They appeared to confirm that we were the right people and then Wells motioned for us to approach.

Tanner escorted me to the helicopter. I wasn't shackled as before, but my hands were cuffed behind my back, and I was wearing the same Level IIIA soft body armor vest as before. I hoped that wherever we were going involved being treated like a human again and ditching the bright orange jumpsuit.

We boarded the helicopter and strapped in. My hands being cuffed behind my back was hell on my shoulder, but I understood their protocols and did my best to suck it up and push through the discomfort. Since it was a Louisiana State Police helicopter, I knew we were at least going to stay within the state, so the flight wouldn't be too long.

I looked out the window as we took off and turned away from the city. It looked like a war zone. The power was out for most of the area surrounding the city and there were fires everywhere. Spotlights and the blue police lights illuminated huge crowds of people surrounding the hospital and in the streets. It was bad the first time, but it had gotten even worse since returning to the hospital.

"All those people," I said over the intercom.

"We're going to get to the bottom of this, Troy," Tanner said. "Don't worry."

"And they're all down there for me?" I asked.

"You're just an excuse for them, Troy," Tanner replied. "They're down there because they're unhappy."

"That looks a little more than just *unhappy*."

"Well, when you can remember what happened, maybe we can put an end to it."

"I didn't kill the girl," I said. "I went to go talk to Cynthia after seeing her at the church and found two men in suits trying to take her away."

"So, you remember, now?"

"Kruger and I had a little chat with them. They were planning something big in the city. That's why I called you."

"I still can't get over you naming the dog Kruger, but go on."

"I don't remember what happened in between, but somehow I was with her in my truck. We wrecked and they shot her and got me too."

"Was it the same men?"

"I don't remember seeing their faces, but I don't think so. I think these men worked for the same people though. They wanted her gone."

"We sent a forensic team to assist NOPD with the crime scenes related to your case. Hopefully, they can clear your case so we can get you back home and you and Jenny can move on with your lives."

Her last sentence caught me off guard. *Move on with our lives.* I had been so fixated on getting justice for Cindy that I had not given any consideration to getting back to any sense of normalcy.

"What do you mean?"

Tanner's brow furrowed. "What do I mean? About the forensic team or moving on with your life?"

"This isn't over," I said.

"No, of course it isn't. But for *you*, it is. *If*, and that's a big *if* right now given the evidence against you…but if we can get the charges dropped, you and Jenny will be on the first plane, bus, train, or rental car you can get back to your home in Texas. You've done quite enough here."

"The people responsible for this…*war* are still out there."

"Do you trust me, Troy?"

"What?"

"We've worked together in the past, right? Like the last time you decided to play hero and ended up getting sucked back into the life you tried to leave behind. Do you still trust me?"

"Well…yes. I wouldn't have called you otherwise."

"Then trust me when I tell you, I've got this."

"It's not that easy."

"Maybe. Maybe not. But you need to let me do my job. And it's all official and above board now. No secrecy. I'm going to do a thorough investigation and bring the people responsible to justice."

"Can you at least tell me where you're taking me?"

"Baton Rouge. There's a field office there and a safe house. You're going to be under federal protective custody at a U.S. Marshal's safe house near Baton Rouge. The prosecutor has basically given us three days to either work out a plea deal in exchange for your cooperation on our terrorism investigation or return you to NOPD's custody."

"Or prove my innocence," I added.

"Well, yeah, but no one in that department or prosecutor's office believes that to be a possibility. You haven't made a lot of fans since you've been down here, Troy."

"I never do."

CHAPTER TWENTY-FIVE

Two days in the safe house seemed like an eternity. I had slept for most of my time in custody. The pain meds the doctor had ordered to go with me were highly effective. I hated how cloudy they made my head feel, but I needed the rest and they were very good at accomplishing that goal.

And somehow through it all, Jenny had been there for me. Despite only being allowed an hour in the morning and an hour in the afternoon during the two days I was in the safe house, Jenny stuck around and spent every moment she could with me.

"I really like the Martin family," she said as we watched TV in the small living room.

The U.S. Marshals housed me in a small three -bedroom home just outside of Baton Rouge. Two agents stayed with me while two others took turns maintaining surveillance somewhere outside the house. All of my visits with Jenny had been under their watchful eye while we were given an hour to sit in separate chairs without any contact allowed.

"They were all really nice. The old man they call Bear is really funny," she said.

"Did you meet Spectre?"

Jenny tilted her head slightly. "Oh, is that Michelle's husband, Cal?"

"Yeah, I've worked with him in the past."

"He was really nice. Super funny. I think he said he's writing another book."

"Did they mention anything about Kruger?"

"Your dog?"

"No, there was a guy who ran the group I used to work for. His nickname was Kruger. Tanner told me he died not too long ago."

Jenny shrugged. "We didn't talk about anyone from your past. I just mostly played with Cal Jr. and laughed at Bear. They're a fun bunch to hang around with."

"I think you should probably start thinking about going home," I said. "They're only going to keep me here another day and then back to lockup. You don't need to wait around for me."

"You know I'm not going to do that, Troy."

"You won't have a choice," I said. "They're not going to let you visit me this much when NOPD takes me back. Besides, Bear and Kruger need you back home."

Jenny let out an exhausted sigh. "You're so hardheaded."

"Me? Never," I said with a boyish grin. "But I'm serious here. There's no reason for you to stick around when I'm in jail and you can't visit me."

"Or you can both go home together."

Jenny and I both turned around to see Special Agent Tanner standing next to the Marshal watching us. She was holding a folder that I assumed meant my luck had finally changed.

"No way!" Jenny said as she leapt from the couch to meet Tanner. "They finally figured it out?"

"Official results came in this morning," Tanner said, holding up the folder. "Working with our field team, NOPD Crime Lab has conclusively proven that you were not the one that killed Haynes. Michelle is in New Orleans now working with the District Attorney's Office to drop all charges."

"That's awesome!" Jenny replied with a clap. "Finally!"

Tanner studied my reaction for a second and then said, "I thought you might be *a little* more excited."

I hesitated for a minute as I considered her statement. I didn't really know why the news wasn't exciting for me. Most of my memory had returned in the last twenty-four hours, and I had given Tanner all I knew about Haynes and the men who more than likely killed her.

I respected Tanner and knew she was the most qualified person to bring those people to justice, but even knowing that, I couldn't stop thinking about Cindy and her family. Her kid was an orphan as a result of whatever was going on behind the scenes, and no matter how much I trusted Tanner, I still felt like I was letting Cindy's family down by not doing more.

"Yeah, it's great," I finally managed.

Jenny walked back over to me and squatted down next to my chair as she put her arms around me. "What's wrong?"

"How is your investigation going?" I asked Tanner.

"We're bringing Deacon Carter in for questioning and pulling prints from the Haynes house. Once we know who the men worked for, we'll-"

"Houston," I said as the name suddenly popped in my head.

"The city?"

"Mark...Mitch...Something with an M...Mike maybe"

Tanner pulled out a notepad and wrote the name down. "Is that who they worked for?"

"I think so," I said. "That's the name I remember."

"Okay," Tanner replied. "I'll run that name and see what comes up. In the meantime, we're going to take you back to New Orleans for out-processing so you can get home. With your truck totaled, I've arranged for an FBI jet to take you back to San Antonio."

"Finally," Jenny said. "Is it still bad in New Orleans?"

Tanner shook her head. "No, the rioting has stopped. There are still a few protests in the city, but they're peaceful."

"Can I go with you or do I have to get my own ride home?"

"Troy is still technically in U.S. Marshal custody, so he'll ride with them, but you can come with me. It shouldn't take long to get the paperwork done and get him released."

"Thank God!" Jenny said. "We can finally put this mess behind us."

"Yeah," I said. "I guess it's over."

CHAPTER TWENTY-SIX

Heavy traffic turned what should've been an hour and a half drive into a nearly three-hour ordeal. Despite the riots being quelled for the time being, the city was still under lockdown. And with so few routes into the city, afternoon traffic and a couple of wrecks led to total gridlock.

The ride in the U.S. Marshals transport gave me plenty of time to think. Despite everything that had happened to me since returning to New Orleans and being lucky enough to have my freedom once more, I couldn't shake the nagging feeling that I still had unfinished business.

To some extent, I was right. The people responsible for the deaths of my friends and Cynthia Haynes were still on the loose. I couldn't quite figure out how or why, but it was clear to me that something bigger was going on behind the scenes. Someone wanted to takedown law enforcement and cause unrest in the region.

On the other hand, I trusted Special Agent Tanner. She was young but extremely smart and a highly competent agent. If she believed she could bring the people responsible to justice and do it the right way, I believed in her. She had proven herself to me when I worked with Odin.

And then there was Jenny. She had refused to leave my side throughout it all. And as I turned back to see her sitting shotgun in the SUV with Tanner, I realized that her patience was far more than I deserved. She was a good woman – too good for me. If I had any hope of a normal life ever again, I needed to take the next step in our relationship before she got tired of waiting and moved on.

I started to doze off as I pictured how I might pop the question. My wounds were doing much better since leaving the hospital. I had stopped taking painkillers, but I still felt tired most of the time. I felt like I hadn't really gotten a good night's sleep since leaving Texas.

I woke up briefly as I felt the pace start to pick up. I didn't even open my eyes as my head rested against the cold steel bars of the van. I dreamed about Jenny and Kruger and the family we were going to have together. It felt so peaceful and serene – a stark contrast from the darkness I had felt over the last couple of years.

"Wake up, Wilson," I heard a gruff male voice say. I felt something touch my shoulder and jolted awake.

It took me a second to process that it was the burly U.S. Marshal squatting next to me in the van.

"Easy, fella, we're here," he said. "Time for you to outprocess and go home."

I shook off the grogginess and slid across the seat as the Marshal helped me out. The thick, moist air hit me as I stepped out into the parking lot. It looked like a rain shower had just rolled through, creating steam on the hot asphalt.

Tanner and Jenny parked behind us. I started to turn around to greet them, but the U.S. Marshal motioned for me to keep walking.

"You'll have plenty of time to say "hi" once we get you out-processed. Let's get it done."

"Hot date tonight?" I asked.

The Marshal smiled. "Just trying to avoid an angry wife."

"I hear ya," I said with a chuckle. Despite everything that had happened, the little bit of humor was good. It was a subtle acknowledgment that things were hopefully going to get a little better and, at least for now, I was no longer public enemy number one.

I looked back and winked at Jenny as we walked into the intake area of the jail. The corrections deputies went through the process of searching me for contraband and weapons and then escorted me to a holding area, leaving behind my U.S. Marshal escorts and Tanner and Jenny.

It took nearly an hour for them to go through the process and then return the items I had when I entered custody. The box included little more than my bloodied and torn clothes from the shootout and my wallet and a plastic bag with all of the contents of my wallet.

"You'll have to go to NOPD to get anything they inventoried from your vehicle," the deputy said as he had me sign for my items.

"Thanks."

I took my items and walked out. Jenny and Agent Tanner were in a small waiting area as I exited the secure side of the facility. As soon as she saw me, Jenny immediately jumped from her chair and hugged me, giving me a big kiss.

"I'm so glad you're finally free and this is finally over."

"I've booked a flight for you back to San Antonio," Tanner said, waiting until Jenny and I were finished reuniting.

"It might be easier to just get a rental car and drive home," I said. "I also need to swing by NOPD and get my duty weapons and figure out what to do with my truck."

"I think we can do that for you," Tanner said as she pulled her cell phone out of her pocket.

"You're busy," I said. "I can figure it out."

Tanner shook her head as she typed away on her phone. "Taken care of. I'll bring you to NOPD to get your stuff and then drop you off at the rental car place."

"Wow. Why are you being so nice?"

Jenny gently slapped my shoulder. "Troy! *You* should try being nice. She's trying to help you."

"It's fine," Tanner said. "You've been through a lot, and I just want to make sure you get home safely. Before you get yourself into any more trouble here."

"I'll be fine."

"Of course you will," Tanner said with a smirk. "Let's get going."

I insisted on Jenny taking shotgun as we piled into Tanner's government SUV. It was both chivalrous and slightly selfish since I knew some people in the public either hadn't gotten the memo that I was innocent or didn't believe it. The less drama in my final hours in the city, the better.

We arrived at the NOPD precinct just as the next shift was finishing up their roll call. They appeared to be gearing up for more riots. They were all wearing plate carriers and some even had on riot gear.

"What's going on?" I asked Tanner.

"There was a riot today in Atlanta and a protestor was killed by a rubber bullet. They're thinking it's going to get worse everywhere. That's why I am trying to get you out of here before the next round starts tonight," Tanner said in a hushed tone.

"Wow." It was all I could muster. The world seemed to be burning down around us. I just couldn't understand all the hatred that had driven people to turn on each other.

A few officers eyed me suspiciously as we walked to the evidence and recovered property locker. I showed my ID and signed the inventory sheet before the clerk returned with a box of the items they had inventoried in my truck.

I went through and checked off the items on the inventory sheet as the clerk disappeared into the back once more to retrieve my firearms.

As we waited for her to return, I tried to power on my cell phone. To my surprise, it did, but the battery showed critically low as it finished booting up. Within a few seconds, it started a continuous cycle of buzzing as text messages and voicemails were downloaded from the network.

"You'll have to sign for these separately," the clerk said as she returned with my rifle, handgun, and two plastic bags full of empty magazines. "We don't return ammunition."

The phone continued to vibrate with new messages but I set it aside and inspected my weapons. They were in good condition and appeared to be in working order, minus the ammo NOPD had confiscated from me. I placed them in the box and picked up my phone as I turned to Tanner and Jenny.

"Let's go," I said.

"Who are all those messages from?" Jenny asked, eyeing the phone in my hand.

"Probably my sergeant wanting to chew my ass for…everything."

"Don't you think you should check it?"

"It can wait."

"Troy! What if it's something about Kruger?"

"Fine," I said as I held out the box for her to hold.

She took the box from me. It was nearly as big as she was, and she stumbled back as she tried to wrap her arms around it.

I unlocked my phone and started swiping through the messages. Some of the messages were people wishing me well. Some were just asking what the heck was going on. But my heart sank as I saw the most recent one from Hyatt.

Why aren't you answering? They told me to get a lawyer. IA is calling me in.

"What the…" I said as I opened the message and tried to scroll back through the history. He had sent me at least twenty messages on the night Haynes was murdered.

"What's going on?" Jenny asked, still struggling to hold up the box.

My face felt flush as I read through the messages, starting from the most recent unread one. "How?" I mumbled.

"What is it?" Tanner asked, now also gaining interest as we stood in the lobby of the precinct.

My phone warned of impending shutdown as it reached 1%. I tried to read them as quickly as possible, but missed the last few before the phone finally shut down.

"Fuck!" I yelled, causing a few of the officers to turn and look at me.

"What is it?" Jenny asked.

I took the box and headed toward the door.

"Not here. Let's go."

CHAPTER TWENTY-SEVEN

"Troy, what's wrong? What was on your phone?" Jenny asked, needling my arm as we walked out of the police station.

"I'll tell you in the car," I said as we passed a group of officers in riot gear heading back into the station. They all looked tired, battle-worn from dealing with the events of the last few days. Although things seemed to have calmed down, there were still pockets of protests throughout the city that these men and women had to deal with to protect people and businesses in the city.

Tanner also gave me a look of concern as she eyed the phone still in my hand. I was carrying the box containing my weapons and inventoried items, but I hadn't released the grip on my phone since reading the texts. It was now little more than a paperweight until I could get to a charger, but the texts I had received from Hyatt had my mind racing. *How the hell had it come to this?*

We made it to Tanner's SUV, but this time I accepted Jenny's offer to ride shotgun after placing my effects in the cargo area. I was still holding the dead cell phone in my hand as Tanner started the vehicle and the two women waited for me to explain.

"*Well?*" Jenny asked, out of her seat and leaning on the center console. "Out with it!"

I dropped the dead phone in the cupholder and turned toward them nervously, making sure no one could overhear us before I began.

"In my…previous life…Jason Hyatt was one of the deputies on my shift."

I paused, looking for acknowledgment from both of them that I was talking about my life as Corporal Alex Shepherd with the St. Tammany Parish Sheriff's Office – a life I had given up after going to Syria to fight ISIS and joining Odin. Tanner nodded.

"Go on," Jenny said impatiently.

"Well, he's a detective now. After I brought you back to the airport, he happened to be working the crime scene and recognized me. We had coffee and caught up and he promised to keep my identity a secret. When I was looking into the church, I had him run some information for me, which led me to Cynthia Haynes."

Tanner's eyes widened. "Oh no," she mumbled as she realized where this story was heading.

"Wait, the woman everyone thought you murdered?" Jenny asked.

I nodded. "Hyatt ran a few people for me, and I got her address. Apparently, someone found out because while I was in the hospital, Hyatt sent me a dozen texts and left a few voicemails. I didn't get a chance to listen to the voicemails before my phone died, but apparently someone discovered him searching NCIC for me and giving me the information. He also said they had wire transfers from me to him, which is not true."

"Jesus, Troy," Tanner said, shaking her head.

"What? What does that mean?" Jenny asked.

"I'm surprised they never added that to your charges," Tanner said.

"Troy, what does that mean?"

"The last text I got from Hyatt was that they were pulling him into a meeting with internal affairs and he wanted to know what I had done. It was sent while I was in the hospital and there's been nothing since. It means someone was trying to implicate him in the murder of Haynes."

"But why?" Jenny asked.

"Guilt by association, I'm guessing," I said. "I had been convicted of killing Cynthia in the court of public opinion and tying it to another corrupt cop was the obvious icing on the cake."

"Well, you did break the law, Troy," Tanner said.

"I didn't pay him off. And it's more of a policy violation than anything. Someone knew I was getting too close and wanted to bury me with charges. And take Hyatt down with me."

"How? Were they following you?"

"I don't think so. I was careful."

"I'll look into it. The field office here may be able to help," Tanner said.

"This is my fault. I shouldn't have asked him to help. I can't just let him hang like that."

"What are you going to do, Troy?" Jenny asked.

I stared at my phone as Tanner and Jenny waited for my reply. The right answer was probably to go home and let Tanner do her job, But I couldn't leave Hyatt hanging like that. He had gotten caught in the middle of something that was obviously my fault.

"Troy, no…" Tanner said, seeing the apparent look in my eye. "Don't even say it. You and Jenny need to get in the rental car and go home."

"Let's go to the rental car place," I said to Tanner.

"So, we're going home?" Jenny asked with a raised eyebrow. "That's it?"

"That's first."

"Whatever you want to do, sweetie, I'll support you," Jenny said as she squeezed my hand. "But I'm staying with you."

"I hardly think that's a good-" Tanner was interrupted by her phone vibrating. She pulled it out of her pocket and read the message. "…idea."

"Let's go get the car and then we can figure it out after," I said, watching Tanner as she reacted to whatever the message was. "You okay?"

Tanner scrolled through the text and put the phone away before slamming the column-shifter to Drive. "I've got to get you to your car and head to the airport."

"What happened?" Jenny asked.

Tanner looked at me and shook her head. "Looks like they're going after me too."

"Going after you? For what? How?" I asked.

"My guess is the same reason your detective friend is in hot water."

"What did the text say? Can you tell us?" Jenny asked.

"There wasn't much to it," Tanner said. "It was my boss telling me to get on the first commercial flight back tonight because OPR wants to have a chat with me at 9 a.m. tomorrow about my involvement with you."

"What's OPR?" Jenny asked.

"Office of Professional Responsibility," Tanner said. "It's basically internal affairs. It means they think I did something wrong or have allegations against me."

"Shit!" I hissed. "Dammit, I'm sorry to drag you into this."

We passed a group of protesters squaring off with police in riot gear as we headed for the interstate. "You didn't do any of this," Tanner said.

"I know, but I called you down here. And now you're possibly in trouble."

"I'll be fine," she said.

"You've got a good attitude," Jenny said.

We stopped at a red light. Tanner turned and accelerated before the crowd could approach. They were chanting something that I couldn't make out.

"That doesn't seem off to you?" Tanner asked me, nodding toward the crowd as we passed them.

"Off?"

"Yeah. As in, not quite right."

"I'm gonna be honest here, *nothing* has seemed right in a long time," I said and then quickly turned to Jenny in the backseat. "Except you, sweetie."

"Nice save," she said with a smirk.

"I'm talking about everything going on down here – the ambush on your friends, the protesters, the money transfers with Hyatt. Something just doesn't sit well with me about it."

"People are pissed at cops," I said. "It's not the first time. And of course, the media stokes the fire."

"Yeah, I know," Tanner said. "But this is different. I was looking into your attack that happened when you were going from the hospital to the jail. The people that were killed or injured were all from out of state. In fact, a lot of people have been bussed in from other states. And not nearby states either – some as far as New York."

"Do you think it's related to the attack they were planning?"

"Hard not to. But it all sounds so familiar to what they were doing with Helios."

"But we destroyed it in Russia," I said.

"And the billionaires are all dead – I know," Tanner said. "I'm just saying, I don't believe this is all unrelated."

"Shit," I hissed as I considered the possibility that Helios might have fallen into the wrong hands again. "Fucking *Helios*."

"What's Helios?" Jenny asked.

CHAPTER TWENTY-EIGHT

Helios was the code name for a computer system that I barely understood created by billionaires who thought they were smarter than the rest of the world. My only involvement with it had been to aid in its destruction.

The billionaires were part of a group called Odin, an organization that had recruited me after saving me from ISIS in Syria. It was sold to me as a group that did good things around the world where most governments were unwilling or unable to act. The men I knew and worked with were mostly special operators from all over the world who were not only good at their jobs but seemed to be genuinely decent human beings.

We worked for a man named Jeff Lyons, a billionaire mostly known for his social media involving firearms and technology. Until it all fell apart, he was the only one I had interacted with. The other billionaires were mentioned in passing, but I didn't know much about them.

That was until Lyons announced his intent to run for President of the United States. An attempt was made on his life and everyone on our team. He faked his death only to end up getting killed by a sniper later. That was when I truly saw what too much money and arrogance could do to people.

Helios was capable of accessing any other computer system in the world, no matter how secure or encrypted. It had its own artificial intelligence and could fake video, audio, or documents with scary accuracy. And even though I didn't really understand how it worked, I knew that it was suspect in the right hands, but downright dangerous in the wrong hands.

Which is why, when it was stolen, I helped to destroy it. My role in that operation had been the reason Russian mobsters had come looking for me and kidnapped Jenny when I stopped an active shooter in Fredericksburg. My face blasted on social media had been enough for them to find me and attempt revenge. Luckily, Kruger and the rest of the team had still been around to back me up on that one.

"So, what happened to the billionaires?" Jenny asked as she listened to my explanation. Tanner seemed to be ignoring our conversation as she focused on maneuvering through the detours around the protesters to get us to the car rental place at the airport across town.

"Dead," I said. "In various ways, but they all ended up dead."

"And you're sure this Helios thing was destroyed?"

Tanner glanced at me in anticipation of my answer. I shrugged and said, "As far as I know."

"That's not very reassuring," Jenny said.

"I agree, but even if someone did get their hands on it, I am not sure why they would use it for something like this."

"You said that everyone who knew about Helios is dead?"

"Well, no," I said. "As far as I know, Tuna is still alive, right?"

"He was when I left to come here," Tanner said.

"Right, but I don't think he would have it or be using it. That thing takes up a huge amount of space. It's not small like a laptop. And the Russian mobsters who knew about it are all dead."

"So, that leaves Kruger," Tanner said.

"But isn't he dead too?" Jenny asked before touching my shoulder gently. "Sorry."

"Even if he were still alive, there's zero chance he'd be trying to start a war on police. He has spent time in law enforcement, plus, he's not a douchebag."

"I don't think he's alive," Tanner said softly. "I just meant he was the only other person who knew about it and could control it."

"What about the computer guy?" I asked as I tried to remember his nickname. "Coolio."

Coolio was the nickname for the computer hacker named Julio Meeks. He was an absolute genius when it came to computers and all things electronic and had helped Odin find me when I was captured by ISIS.

"Working for three-letter agencies doing black ops stuff," Tanner said.

"Maybe he can look into it," I said. "He'll be able to follow the money and figure out who framed me for paying off Hyatt."

"I'll see what I can do when I get back to D.C.," Tanner said as we hit the exit for the rental car terminal at the airport. "If I even have a job when I return."

"You didn't do anything wrong," Jenny said. "Right?"

"Neither did Hyatt," I said.

Tanner turned into the parking lot and put the SUV in park. "Look at me, Troy."

I looked her in the eyes, knowing she was about to warn me against staying and fighting for Hyatt.

She let out a long sigh and then said, "I know you're going to do whatever you want to do. And I can't make you get in that car and drive straight home. I can't make you not want to help your friend and to be honest; I'm not sure I can help you anymore either."

I nodded, not sure where she was going with that and bracing for the inevitable *but.*

"If I can get through whatever they're planning for me when I get back, I will do everything in my power to help you find answers. But if I can't, you'll effectively be on your own down here. I won't be able to bail you out. So, all I'm asking is that you be smart about whatever it is you're going to do and try not to take any more chances. You're not invincible, Troy."

"I know."

"This city is becoming a war zone. Before I left the office earlier, I heard rumblings of a sick-out from several agencies due to how the politicians are handling it and blaming them for everything going on. If that happens, it's only a matter of time before it descends even further into chaos. I know you've been through this stuff, but Jenny hasn't," she said, pausing to nod at Jenny.

"Hey! I can take care of myself!" Jenny protested.

"I know you can, but I still strongly recommend you both go home. And if you don't, I urge you to go into that terminal, rent a second car, and Jenny drives back to San Antonio tonight. You know I'm right, Troy."

"Absolutely not, Troy," Jenny said. "I'm not leaving you here."

"She's right, you know," I said to Jenny.

"I don't care. I will support whatever you decide whether it's going home or staying here to help your friend, but you're not doing this alone. I can take care of myself. Don't worry about me."

I let her words hang in the air as Tanner's eyes seemed to plead with me to reconsider.

"There you have it," I said finally. "I'll call you tomorrow to find out how your meeting went and let you know what I found out with Hyatt."

CHAPTER TWENTY-NINE

Despite Tanner's warning, we opted to only get one rental car and stick together. Jenny simply would not yield on the issue. I figured keeping her in my sight would be safer than risking the drive back home or someone trying to do something when she was back in San Antonio. And perhaps most importantly, I just missed being with her.

We picked up the car and headed across Lake Pontchartrain to Covington where we checked in to a hotel near the interstate. We had dinner at a nearby diner and then went straight back to the hotel.

After charging my phone, I listened to the half dozen voicemails from Hyatt. Like the text messages, they grew increasingly more desperate. They were all pretty much the same, however, with the latest indicating that he had been suspended and they were considering criminal charges.

The next morning, we checked out of the hotel and headed for Hyatt's house. I opted not to call or text him, in case his phone was being monitored – either by law enforcement or whoever was behind framing us.

Hyatt lived in a relatively new housing development just north of Covington. His house had been completed a few months before the attack that killed my family, and his housewarming party was one of the last events my wife and I had gone to together. As with everything else in the area, seeing it brought back a flood of memories of a life that I had buried years ago.

The house looked mostly as I remembered it as we pulled up short of his driveway and parked in our rented Jeep Grand Cherokee. The grass had grown out more and the landscaping was more complete, but otherwise everything looked the same. He still had his New Orleans Saints wreath on the front door.

"You're sure he's going to know it's you?" Jenny asked as we went over the plan one more time.

I looked over at Hyatt's driveway. His issued Fusion was there next to his pickup. I knew he parked his Jeep and his wife's minivan in the garage, so I couldn't be sure they were home. But if his wife and kids were there, we needed an excuse to get him outside to talk without his wife recognizing me.

"I'm sure," I reassured her. "Are you sure you're up for it?"

"I got this," Jenny replied before giving me a kiss and opening the door. Her shirt lifted slightly, revealing my backup Glock 43 I'd given her in its holster just behind her right hip. I hoped she wouldn't need it, but with everything going on, I wanted her to be able to defend herself. Back home, she was proficient and carried a Sig Sauer P365 which was similar in size and feel for her.

I watched her walk down the driveway and then take the sidewalk in front of the house to the front door. She stopped short of standing in the doorway just as I had taught her in the hotel room and knocked on the door. Moments later, Hyatt emerged in shorts, a t-shirt, and flip flops.

Jenny appeared to introduce herself and then Hyatt glanced toward me. He nodded as she went through the introduction we had rehearsed and then he stepped out onto the front porch, closing the door behind him.

They walked toward me and he shook his head as he saw me in the driver's seat. I was wearing sunglasses and a baseball cap to keep a low profile. Jenny opened the passenger door for him to get in as she took her seat in the back.

"Alex, you son of a bitch!" Hyatt said as he closed the door. He didn't appear to be happy to see me, but I couldn't tell if he was angry or just frustrated.

"Hey buddy," I said.

"First off, she is way too hot for you," Hyatt said before looking back at Jenny. "No offense."

"Oh, no, I agree," Jenny said with a grin. "None taken."

"Second, you're lucky my wife left me. Do you really think sending this smoke show to my door at 8 a.m. wouldn't raise suspicion?" Hyatt said before turning to Jenny again. "Once again, no offense."

Jenny smiled.

"You're lucky I remembered that crazy guy we used to always deal with sending his wife to the door to sell insurance… What did they call themselves?"

"Really Goodman Insurance," I replied.

Hyatt chuckled. "Yeah. *Lost Shepherd Insurance* was a little on-the-nose, don't you think?"

"Well, it's not like I could just go walking up to your door. Becky would have recognized me in a heartbeat. And more importantly, what do you mean, she left you?"

"She packed up the kids and went to her mom's last night. Couldn't handle being the wife of a detective that may or may not be going to jail and is probably going to lose his job. *Thanks to you.*"

"I haven't exactly had a vacation these last few days either," I said, pulling up my shirt to show my still-bandaged wounds.

"Jesus, man," Hyatt said as he winced. "Well, why don't y'all come inside. It's just me. She even took the dog."

I started to turn off the vehicle but Hyatt stopped me. "You can pull into the driveway. Neighbors will complain if you stay parked in the street like this for any length of time."

I parked as requested and then we followed Hyatt into his house. He offered us each a cup of coffee as we sat down at the high table in his kitchen.

"Please tell me you have a plan. I'm assuming you got my messages."

"I did. I didn't want to call you back in case someone is listening, so we decided to pay you a visit. I've been in the hospital and in custody for the last few days. Just got my stuff back yesterday."

"Well, while you were getting your freedom, I was being shown the door. They suspended me and told me to lawyer up for possible criminal charges for giving you that information. I'm supposed to turn in my unit and equipment later today."

"Then we'd better get to work proving your innocence, huh?"

Hyatt shook his head. "I told you I could get in some serious shit for this. I'm not innocent. Neither are you."

"You used the information for a law enforcement purpose. This is happening because you helped me, and I got too close. Not because you did anything wrong," I said.

I went on to explain everything that had happened since I left the diner with the information he had given me. Although it had been less than a week, it seemed like a lifetime ago. So much had happened since he warned me about sniffing around the church.

"But how did they know we met before all of that? Did you tell anyone?" Hyatt asked.

I shook my head as I considered telling Hyatt about Odin and Helios. To some extent, I felt like he deserved to know the full truth. But on the other hand, it would likely only muddy the waters and get him further involved in something that was far too dangerous for him and his family. Besides, the reality was that Odin no longer existed and Helios had already been destroyed. It was nothing more than a theory Tanner and I had come up with to try to explain what was going on.

"Then how did they know?"

"That's what we need to find out. I suspect someone traced my history and pulled the GPS locations from my phone. Maybe the security camera feeds from the diner. We need to find out who's behind the attacks on law enforcement and killing Cynthia Haynes."

"And the FBI Agent you were working with – Tanner – you said she's in trouble too?"

"She was recalled to Washington to meet with their version of IA, correct."

"So, if this is a big conspiracy, the feds are in on it too?"

"That's what we need to find out."

"C'mon man. This all seems a little far-fetched. This isn't some Hollywood movie. This is real life."

Jenny laughed, nearly choking on her coffee.

"What's so funny?" Hyatt asked.

"Sorry, I shouldn't laugh. But if you had seen some of the stuff I've seen with this guy in the last year, you wouldn't be so skeptical."

Hyatt raised an eyebrow. "Like what?"

Jenny stood from her chair and walked around the table to put her arm around me. "Take a look at Troy."

"He looks like shit, but go on."

"And what did he look like at his funeral?"

Hyatt's eyes widened. "Fair point."

"Look, I don't think any of this stuff is a coincidence. What happened to Cindy and Jacobson is part of something much bigger, and I intend to find out what and who's behind it."

Hyatt was staring off to space, still seeming to consider what Jenny had just made him realize.

After a brief pause, he nodded and then said, "I'm in. Where do we start?"

CHAPTER THIRTY

We followed Hyatt as he made the turn in his unmarked Ford Fusion at Vehicle Maintenance in Covington and then headed to the first lead he wanted to track down. It was a recently built mega church on Highway 190 in Covington across from the American Legion. We pulled into the empty American Legion parking lot to set up brief surveillance before making our next move.

"Holy shit," I said, viewing the giant church through Hyatt's binoculars. "When did they build this?"

"About a year ago. Huge influx of cash and all the permits and such were fast-tracked," Hyatt replied.

I panned past the fountain in front of the entrance and found a sheriff's deputy sitting in his patrol car underneath the covered drop off area by the front door.

"Is that a detail for the money drop?" I asked. One of the other mega churches in the area had a sheriff's office detail for 3-4 hours to guard the employees a few days per week as they took the money they received from services and transported it to the bank.

"Twenty-four-seven," Hyatt replied.

"No shit?"

"Yup."

"What does that mean?" Jenny asked from the backseat.

"They're spending a boat load of money on security. Unless the sheriff cut them a deal, the detail rate is $50 per hour. The deputy gets $40. So that's 2-3 deputies per day every day," I explained.

"Worse than that," Hyatt said. "They're paying $100 per hour to the deputy."

"Good Lord," I said.

"Indeed. It's the highest paying and most competitive detail to get."

"Have they had a lot of issues that require security?"

"Not that I know of. It's been that way since they started. Really easy gig."

"So, what are we doing here?"

"The name those men gave you – Mike Houston – it sounded familiar to me. Like, *really* familiar. I couldn't remember what it was for, but I remembered it coming up in the news here a while back. So, I asked Lenny when we were bullshitting while they inventoried my unit."

"Who's Lenny?" Jenny asked.

"Lenny Richmond. Used to be the sergeant over vehicle maintenance," I replied.

"Now, he's a lieutenant and runs the Maintenance and Acquisitions division. Basically, same job, more pay and rank."

"Good for him," I said. "I always liked Lenny."

"Anyway, he told me that Houston was in the news as one of the biggest backers of that church," Hyatt said, indicating the mega church across the street. "It was his team of lawyers that pushed everything through, and greased a few palms on the Parish Council."

"Was there resistance in the community?"

Hyatt shrugged. "I don't remember, honestly. It all happened pretty fast."

"Do you think he's in there?" Jenny asked.

"I have no idea, but short of going back across the lake and digging into the church where Haynes was working, this is our best lead. I think someone in there will know how to find Houston."

"And he's the one who killed Cynthia Haynes?" Jenny asked.

"His men were the ones who tried to abduct her when I went to her house. And I'm pretty sure they are the ones that killed her and tried to pin it on me too."

"So, what's the play here, boss?" Hyatt asked.

"You don't have a plan?"

"My plan was to bring you here and let you do your thing," Hyatt replied. "Teach a horse to fish and all that."

"You mean lead a horse to water?"

"I've heard it both ways."

"Seriously, boys?" Jenny asked. If she rolled her eyes any harder, I was afraid she might cause permanent damage.

"Sorry," I said as I put the Jeep Grand Cherokee in gear. "Let's go talk to them."

"And say what?" Hyatt asked nervously. "You planning on asking them if they killed Cynthia Haynes?"

"Well, that's one of many questions," I replied.

"Troy, are you serious?" Jenny asked. "What are you thinking?"

"Sitting here won't solve anything," I replied as I pulled up to the highway and waited for traffic to clear so I could cross over to the church's driveway. "We can poke around and ask some questions."

"Just like that?" Hyatt asked.

"Unless you have a better plan?"

"No, boss, I don't."

"Then let's see what they have to say."

CHAPTER THIRTY-ONE

The interior lobby of the church was just as lavish as the exterior. All of the fixtures appeared to be of the highest quality, with lots of gold on pretty much everything. It was just what you'd expect from a mega church raking in millions of dollars per month.

The only problem was that the area we were in simply couldn't support it. Sure, the Northshore was known for being a wealthy, across-the-lake suburb of New Orleans, but Covington was much more blue-collar and there was already another mega church a few miles away in Mandeville. Unless things had changed drastically since I had left the area, it just didn't make sense to me.

An older woman walked in from a side door that I assumed led to offices. She smiled and said, "Hello! Welcome! How may I help you?"

"I'm new to the area," I said. "We were thinking about joining a new church."

Jenny was standing right beside me with her arm in mine. She squeezed my arm tightly as she heard the lie. I knew I'd hear about it later – *lying in church of all things!* Given Jenny's upbringing, I was somewhat surprised she didn't step away from me for fear of lightning striking me down in the lobby.

"Well, my friends, you've come to the right place!" the woman replied enthusiastically. "My name is Jill Bowers, and I'm the office administrator here. What are your names?"

"I'm Kevin," I said, preparing for another squeeze or glare from Jenny. "And this is Larry and Jennifer."

Jill smiled. "Well, it's nice to meet all of you. Please, let me show you around. I'll go get my keys."

She walked out of the room and back through the door she had come in through. When she was out of earshot, Jenny turned and punched me in the arm.

"*Lying* in *Church!*" she said in an excited whisper. "And you guys get fake names but I have to use my *real* one?"

"Well, you seemed upset when I said we were joining a new church. I didn't think you'd want to be involved with anymore lying in church."

Jenny rolled her eyes and let out an exhaustive sigh. "Whatever."

"So, *Kevin*, what's the plan?" Hyatt asked. "Do you think Mee-Maw is going to tell us who killed Haynes?"

"Didn't they teach you anything in investigations? Observe, look, and listen. We may find something. We may not. Don't forget, this place was *your* idea."

"Yeah, but-"

Before he could finish, Jill returned, jingling a set of keys as she closed and locked the door behind her. "Alright now, let's get started."

We followed Jill through a set of large double doors leading to a massive auditorium with theater seating. It looked like it could seat five thousand people. Our view from the road and outside gave no hint of the massive size and scope of the mega church we were standing in.

"This is our main worship area," Jill said, taking the role of tour guide as we walked toward the huge stage. "The auditorium typically seats 3000, but we can reconfigure it to seat up to 5000."

"That's amazing. Isn't this a small town? Do you have that many people?" Jenny asked.

Jill looked back with a wry smile. "We are a growing congregation, honey. Now, right this way and I'll show you our daycare facilities. Do you three have children together?"

"Oh, I'm just with Kevin," Jennifer replied. "We don't have kids."

"Larry is my brother," I added.

"It's okay, we don't judge here," Jill said. "But even if you don't have children yet, you'll want to see the facilities we offer for when the Lord blesses you with a little miracle."

Jenny gave me a look and I couldn't help but laugh. It wasn't something we had discussed, but with everything going on, there was no way we were ready to bring children into the world together.

We walked behind the stage past the choir's seating area and followed Jill through a door that led to a narrow hallway. She stopped at the first door on the left and pulled out the keys, fishing for the correct one before unlocking the door and opening it.

"Very spacious, lots of different educational toys and play stations, and the nursery has sound deadening material to keep the little ones from interrupting the service or from being awakened by music."

"This is pointless," Hyatt whispered in my ear as we stood in the doorway. "We're not getting anything out of this."

Jill made a lap around the room pointing out the various features for the children and then ushered us out into the hallway. As we exited out into the hallway, Jill suddenly turned and motioned to three men in suits approaching.

"Ah! What a treat! That's Dr. Houston. He will be happy to meet with you."

"Holy shit," Hyatt mumbled to me. "Never mind."

We stood in the hallway as the three men approached. As they neared, I noticed that the two men flanking him were wearing earpieces. I noticed the bulge in the closest bodyguard's jacket, indicating a handgun of some sort.

Dr. Houston was a small statured man, about 5'8" with salt and pepper hair. He was wearing a dark suit with a blue tie. His dark cowboy boots echoed on the marble floor as he approached.

"Mrs. Bowers, thank you so much for your hospitality toward our guests," Dr. Houston said as the two exchanged a quick hug and peck on the cheek. "They have certainly come a long way to visit us."

The hair on the back of my neck stood straight up as he made eye contact with me.

"You're living in Texas now aren't you, Mr. Shepherd?" he asked, seemingly staring into my soul.

Jenny clutched my arm as Hyatt mumbled an obscenity not fit for our current location.

"I'm not sure what you mean," I said as I attempted to regain my composure.

"Oh, Alex, don't feel you have to hide your identity. This is the house of the Lord. We take in everyone, regardless of background or sins."

I looked down at Jenny. She looked like she had just seen a ghost, which wasn't that far from the truth, considering the man before us was speaking the name of a dead man.

"Mrs. Bowers, if you don't mind, I will kindly take over the tour from here," he said to Jill. "I will rejoin you for lunch soon."

"Thank you, Dr. Houston," she replied as she excused herself and headed back to the auditorium.

"Now, as I am sure you didn't just come here solely to seek information on joining our fine congregation, let's go to my office. I will answer any questions you might have. The same goes for you, Detective Hyatt."

I could see confusion and a hint of panic in Hyatt's face as his eyes darted back and forth between me and Dr. Houston.

"Thank you for meeting with us," I said. It was the only thing I could come up with. He had caught me so off guard that I felt like a new recruit highlighted by an instructor on day one of the academy. My mind was racing.

"It is no trouble at all," Houston said, flashing a smile that sent chills down my spine. "But before we go any further, there is one more small thing."

"What's that?"

"I noticed all three of you were carrying weapons when you entered earlier. And while I do support the Second Amendment and your God-given right to keep and bear arms, this is a place of worship. If you wish to go further, I must insist that Brother Clarence relieve you of your weapons."

I hesitated as the near guard stepped toward us.

"Don't worry, you'll get them back once our business is concluded. It is for your safety as well, of course."

"Yeah, that's not going to happen," Hyatt said.

"I'm sorry, but those are the rules here," Dr. Houston replied calmly. "If you wish to continue, I must insist."

"If you think I'm going to follow you down to your evil lair unarmed, you're smoking dope."

"It's okay," I interjected, holding up my hand for Hyatt to stop before he said anything else. "You and Jenny should go back to the car. I'll go."

"Troy, no," Jenny protested in a hushed tone.

"You can't be serious," Hyatt said.

I looked Dr. Houston straight in the eye, ignoring Hyatt. "Will that be okay, Dr. Houston? Just a chat between the two of us?"

"That will be fine," Houston replied, flashing the creepy smile once more. "But, please, I have an appointment soon so we must hurry."

I turned to Hyatt and Jenny and whispered, "Go back to the car and wait. If you don't hear from me in an hour, you know what to do."

"*An hour*?" Jenny asked. "You could be *dead* in an hour."

"I'll be fine," I said as I pulled my Glock from its in-the-waistband holster and handed it to Hyatt.

"No need for your men to hold it for me," I said. "The detective here will take it with him."

"Very well," Houston said with a nod of approval. "Shall we?"

CHAPTER THIRTY-TWO

The inner sanctum of the church looked a lot less like one of Saddam's palaces and more like an executive office suite. There were at least a half dozen lavish offices guarded by receptionists sitting out front. I still couldn't quite understand where all the money had come from to build a facility like this. There was just no way the little community could afford one, much less two, mega churches.

Dr. Houston led the way with his goons bracketing me as we walked to his office. A few receptionists looked up and waved to him as we walked by. If I didn't know better from interrogating his goons, I would've thought he was just another charismatic televangelist with a cult following.

We walked into Houston's office and one of his bodyguards closed the door behind us. He walked around a large wooden desk and took a seat in his plush leather chair.

"Please, sit," he said, indicating one of the two leather chairs across from his desk. "Let's chat. Would you like anything to drink?"

"I'm fine, thank you," I said as I made myself comfortable.

"Very well," Houston replied. He leaned forward and smiled, placing both hands on his desk. "What's on your mind, Mr. Shepherd?"

I paused to take in my surroundings. The office was at least 500 square feet. There was a fireplace off to the right of Houston with a poker that could be used for a weapon. To my left, there was another sitting area with a coffee table and two couches and dark curtains covering what I assumed to be a window to something – maybe a courtyard.

As far as potential weapons went, I noticed an engraved letter opener by Houston's right hand, a sturdy-looking ashtray next to a humidor against the wall, and, of course, the firearms from the guards that were watching over the proceedings. One had remained by the door while the other was standing behind Dr. Houston, opposite the fireplace. It wasn't ideal, but it was at least a workable situation.

"Well, for starters, let's cut the bullshit," I said. "If you know who I am, then you know why I'm here. I'm guessing those cameras outside and in the lobby had facial recognition software and at least one of the entrances had body scanners, which is how you knew we were armed and our real identities. Right?"

"Security is paramount here."

"What exactly are you protecting?"

Houston grinned. "The flock, of course. Is that not the job of your namesake, Mr. *Shepherd*?"

"About that," I said. "What makes you think that's my name?"

"Our security methods are privileged information, I'm afraid. I am not at liberty to discuss them with an outsider."

My jaw clenched as I eyed the letter opener and considered the various ways I would take care of the smug son of a bitch across from me and his two lap dogs. I had grown tired of the façade, knowing full well that he was likely responsible for the death of Cynthia Haynes, framing me, and possibly more.

I leaned forward, resting both forearms on my knees as I put my hands together.

"If you know who I am, then you know what I'm capable of," I growled. "Now, let's cut the bullshit. Why did you kill Cynthia Haynes?"

The guard behind Houston started to step forward, but Houston raised his hand to stop him. I glanced over my shoulder to see that the other guard had also tensed. The letter opener was still on the desk, away from Houston's reach as he leaned back in his chair. I was certain I could take him and possibly the guard behind him before the other guard had a chance to draw his weapon.

"Ah, yes. Very unfortunate. I didn't kill Ms. Haynes. You did."

"Bullshit. NOPD and the FBI have already pulled the forensic evidence. Your lies didn't stick."

Houston belted a derisive laugh. "No, Mr. Shepherd, not by your hands, but by your actions. Cynthia Haynes was on her way here when you intervened. She would have been safe and well-cared for. *You* caused her death and the deaths of those two men who were trying to help her. Did you know they were both also former law enforcement?"

"I didn't kill them."

"No, but they obviously couldn't be trusted. Without your actions, I never would have known."

"You just admitted to murdering three people in front of me."

"You're right. But who's going to do something about it? Alex Shepherd? Troy Wilson? Some third identity you're hiding in there? Besides, dead men tell no tales."

I glanced over my right shoulder and noticed the guard behind me had slowly moved to within arm's reach of me.

"So, why didn't you just kill me already? You know my friend is a detective and waiting outside, right?"

Houston smirked and turned the LCD monitor on his desk around to face me. It had four security cameras playing in real time. The top left camera showed Jenny and Hyatt in handcuffs sitting on the ground next to the marked unit.

"Mr. Hyatt is a disgraced, corrupt detective who accepted bribes in exchange for confidential information. He won't be arresting anyone anytime soon."

"Let Jenny go," I growled.

"That depends on you, Mr. Shepherd," Houston replied as he turned the monitor back around to its original position on his desk. "If you answer my questions, you have my word that she will be released unharmed. Unfortunately, I can't promise the same for Mr. Hyatt. He will have to answer for his crimes, of course."

"So, I guess we're doing this the hard way."

"That is your choice, Mr. Shepherd."

"What do you want from me?"

Houston picked up the letter opener and held it up in front of me. "Cooperation, of course. You have proven your capacity for extreme violence, which will not be tolerated in this house. Come peacefully with me, and you have my word that your friends will not be harmed."

I shifted uneasily in my seat. I had underestimated Houston and he had seen right through me. He obviously knew more about me than I did about him. He was very much in control of the situation.

"Well?" he asked as my eyes darted between the letter opener and the video feed of Jenny and Hyatt in the parking lot.

"Let them go," I said slowly.

Houston waved the letter opener in the air dismissively. "I simply cannot do that. You have my word that they will not be harmed, so long as you come along peacefully."

"If you're just going to kill me, why should I believe you won't kill them, also?"

Houston smiled.

"Whether or not you die is actually not up to me. My associate wishes to speak to you. For what purpose, I'm not sure, but I would assume it's to find out what you know. Your friends are of no use to us beyond a simple assurance that you will not cause trouble. I have no qualms with letting them go about their business once we are done with you."

"Who is your boss?"

"I did not say, *boss*, now did I?"

"You didn't have to. Now, who is it?"

"That's something you will have to wait to find out."

"Okay, then where are we going?"

"I cannot tell you that either, but you will be taking a ride on my private jet. I hope you don't get airsick."

"Don't worry about that."

"Do we have a deal?"

Houston placed the letter opener on the desk in front of him with the handle toward me. It was almost as if he was tempting me to take it and attempt and escape. I calculated my odds, given the known locations of his two henchmen and the escape route I had planned on the way in. I knew I could take them both down, but I couldn't get to Houston in time. And there was no way of knowing if he had a panic button under the desk.

Any action at that point risked the lives of Hyatt and Jenny. It was a risk I just couldn't take. Besides, I also needed to dig deeper into this conspiracy, and having Houston take me to his boss was a big development.

"On one condition," I said.

"You realize that you are in no position to be making demands at this point, don't you Mr. Shepherd?"

"Humor me."

Houston gestured for me to continue.

"I want proof of life updates every thirty minutes."

Houston seemed to consider my requirement for a second.

"That is a bit much, but I believe we can accommodate hourly updates."

"Deal," I said.

Houston stood and motioned to his bodyguard. "Clyde, please prepare Mr. Shepherd for transport and alert Joe and Archie that we will be wheels up in an hour."

CHAPTER THIRTY-THREE

We drove to the airport without incident. Houston's bodyguards had been fairly civil and treated me well as they escorted me from the church to the New Orleans Lakefront airport on the other side of Lake Pontchartrain. They didn't even put hand or leg restraints on me for the hour-long drive.

Hyatt and Jenny had been released from their restraints and moved into a waiting area inside the church. I had been allowed to Facetime with them prior to leaving. Jenny pleaded with me not to go while Hyatt promised that they would be okay. They both seemed to be in good health.

Upon boarding the luxurious private jet, I asked once more to check in on Jenny and Hyatt and the guards once again connected me via Facetime. To their credit, they were at least holding up that end of the bargain.

Houston and his personal bodyguards were in another vehicle about twenty minutes behind us. As we waited on the plane for Houston to arrive, an attractive young flight attendant offered me a sandwich and the non-alcoholic beverage of my choice. I picked a bottle of water and an Italian BMT, finishing just as Houston's SUV pulled up in front of the plane.

I had no idea when I might eat again or what would happen when we landed at whatever airport Houston was taking me. I had learned in my time with SWAT, fighting with the Kurdish YPG in Syria, and even as an operator with Odin to never pass up food or water because you just never knew when you'd get another opportunity on the battlefield.

And despite sitting in the lap of luxury on the lavish business jet, I knew I was most definitely in a battle. To what end, I wasn't sure, but there was no doubt in my mind that Houston intended to carry out his promise to silence me permanently.

To that end, I had no real plan. Fighting it out with Houston's guards and then interrogating Houston at the church was a nonstarter. There was just too great a risk of Jenny and Hyatt getting hurt, or the sheriff's department showing up – something that would've blown my cover and very likely permanently ended Hyatt's career.

I needed to know how far and deep this conspiracy went, and as long as Houston was willing to take me to the next level, I decided that going along was the best option. I would just do what I always did and come up with a plan on the fly.

I watched as Houston and his two body men boarded the aircraft. The flight attendant greeted him with a hot beverage in hand. He smiled at her as he accepted it and headed for the large leather seat across from me.

"I see you've made yourself at home," he said as he placed the drink on the table next to him. "Don't worry, it'll be a short flight."

"I guess you won't tell me where we're going?" I asked before finishing my bottle of water.

"Nashville," Houston replied.

"Oh, I get it. You're kickstarting my country music career. That's what all of this has been about, right?"

Houston leaned in close as the engines spooled. His three bodyguards seemed to take interest as he came within arm's reach of me.

"Make no mistake, the only reason you're alive right now is that you have not yet outlived your usefulness."

The plane started to taxi, and I looked out the window, seeing Houston's motorcade drive away. The amount of money involved in his operation was staggering. But despite the lavish amenities and relatively humane treatment, my situation felt eerily similar to my time in captivity in Syria with ISIS.

I thought about the deaths of Cindy, her husband, and Jacobson and the senseless murder of Cynthia Haynes as I turned back to see Houston's dead eyes still staring at me. I leaned in close so that his bodyguards couldn't hear me.

"Likewise," I said, staring him straight in the eyes.

Houston laughed dismissively and leaned back in his chair. He took a sip from his drink and then carefully placed it back in the table's cupholder. He appeared to be sizing me up as crossed his right leg over his left.

He started to say something but was interrupted by the engines throttling up as we took the runway and started accelerating. Houston briefly looked out the window and then closed the shade before looking back at me.

"I know everything about you, Mr. Shepherd. Do you think that just because you survived in the Middle East that you are invincible? That you are exempt from atonement for your sins?"

"How is it that you think you know so much about me?"

"For a dead man, you're not very careful. Even with that ridiculous beard, facial recognition software was able to determine your identities."

"Identities?"

"The one you claim and the one you are."

I looked out my window as we climbed away from the city over Lake Pontchartrain. To the best of my knowledge, Coolio had wiped all traces of Alex Shepherd from any facial recognition databases.

Or he had changed it so that facial recognition wouldn't recognize me as Alex Shepherd. I could never remember. I zoned out through most of his explanation, but it was clear to me that someone recognizing me as anything but Troy Wilson through such software was unlikely. At least not without help.

"You know a lot less than you think," I said.

I was bluffing, hoping his arrogance would lead him to reveal more without me having to beat it out of him. As appealing as that sounded, my odds of success just weren't that high in such a confined space surrounded by his bodyguards.

"We'll find out soon enough," Houston said before looking at his watch. "We have about forty minutes until we touchdown in Nashville. You might want to use that time to get some rest instead of running your mouth to make your situation worse."

"I'll take my chances," I said. "But I just don't get how a deeply religious man like yourself can have no issues with killing an innocent woman like Cynthia Haynes. Isn't that how you end up in hell?"

Houston closed his eyes and leaned his head against the headrest. "You are my hammer and weapon of war: with you I break nations in pieces; with you, I destroy kingdoms. *Jeremiah 51:20.*"

"What the fuck are you talking about? That woman was not at war with anyone. She was murdered in cold blood."

Houston suddenly sat up and leaned toward me. His eyes flashed a wild rage I hadn't seen since dealing with ISIS in Syria and Iraq.

"You will never get it! This war is bigger than you or me. This is about saving the soul of our country. Everything I've done – every action I've taken, has been to destroy this kingdom. So that we may build it back up on the path of righteousness."

"You didn't just kill Haynes, did you? You've done a lot more than that."

"I've done what I've been called to do."

"What did you do? Answer me, you sick fuck! Are you behind all of these cop killings? Did you kill my friends?"

Houston waved his hand dismissively without even looking at me. "Casualties of war. It's nothing personal."

"The fuck it isn't!" I yelled.

I stood and lunged toward him, aiming to grab him by the throat and choke the life out of him. Before my hand could connect, one of the bodyguards hip-checked me and knocked me off balance.

"Taser!" I heard just before I heard a pop and felt the prongs imbed in my shoulder and left thigh. The voltage caused my entire body to contract as I fell face first into the carpet.

They let me ride the lightning for what seemed like an eternity. If their tasers were anything like the ones I had been trained on, it was probably closer to the five-second max that the X26 I had carried was programmed for, but it felt like I was flopping around on the ground for minutes.

"Restrain him, gag him, and get a hood over his head," I heard Houston order his guards. "It seems our guest has decided against remaining civil. Treat him accordingly."

CHAPTER THIRTY-FOUR

It was raining when we landed in Nashville. The cloth hood they had put on me was soaked as they stuffed me into the back of the vehicle that met us at the plane. The flexcuffs they had put on me were starting to dig into my wrists as they buckled me into the backseat of what I assumed was an SUV.

We drove for about thirty minutes before reaching our destination. No one said anything to me from the time they put me in the SUV to the time they pulled me out. I assumed Houston was in another vehicle because I didn't hear his voice on the entire ride.

"I need to pee," I said as someone pushed me to start walking.

"Too bad," he replied. "Keep walking."

"I'm serious," I said. It wasn't a lie or a ploy. It had been several hours and downing that bottle of water on the plane had pushed me over the edge. I *really* had to go.

"Go," the man said as he shoved me forward.

"Alright, man, but if I piss my pants in the next few minutes, that's on you. Well, mostly it'll be on me, but the blame will be on you, pal."

I heard another man mumble something, presumably to the guard walking me, as we walked through what sounded like a parking garage. The hood over my head was still damp and heavy from the rain shower, but I could see painted lines on the ground and heard the echo of a car making its way up the ramp.

"Fine, but you're going in there with him," I heard the guard holding my arm say.

They walked me into a building. I could feel the cold air conditioning as they opened the door. We walked a few paces and then another door opened. I felt a second hand grab my right arm and then the first released his grip.

The new guard walked me through another door and then removed my hood. I was in a restroom with three urinals and a couple of stalls.

"Look at me," he said as he held up an opened switchblade knife. "I'm going to cut your restraints and then re-secure your hands in front of you so you can do your business. If you try anything at all, I will kill you. Do you understand?"

It was hard not to laugh in his face. He was holding the knife just inches from my face, and I could see a Glock holstered under his left arm concealed by his suit jacket. I was still sore and hurting from being shot and everything that had happened since the hospital, but I was confident I could disarm the man, take his weapon, and make an escape.

But I didn't. Escaping would get me no further along than I was before meeting Houston. Obviously, Houston needed to die, but first I needed to see who was pulling his strings. It was clear that someone else was either financing or directing his operation.

"You have my word," I said, looking the man in the eyes. "I really just have to pee."

The guard stepped behind me and cut the plastic restraints, firmly holding my left wrist as he did. I could tell he had some level of training, but I was sure he had no idea how easy it would've been for me to reverse and use that knife against him. The training I had received from Odin had given me the confidence and ability to extract myself from just about any situation.

The man pulled out a new pair of flexcuffs and cinched them down over my wrists in front of me. The temporary relief I felt from the plastic digging into my wrists was short-lived as the new pair were just as tight.

Despite the snugness of my restraints, it was enough for me to step up to the urinal and take care of business. It was an incredible sense of relief for what seemed like minutes. The guard and I made awkward eye contact, causing him to look down at his watch as if to try to hurry me along.

When I was finished, I zipped up and walked over to the sink where I did my best to wash my hands and then turned to walk out with the guard.

The door suddenly swung open and the other guard appeared. "Jesus, what is taking you two so long? We're already late and they're waiting for us. Put the hood on him and let's go."

"Okay, okay, we're done," the guard said as he wrung out the water from the hood and then shook it. I appreciated the gesture as he placed it over my head. It was still damp, but slightly less miserable than before.

They took me out of the bathroom and into an elevator. By my count, we had gone up twelve floors by the time the doors opened. I had no idea what floor we started on since we entered through a parking garage, but I was trying to keep at least some idea of where we were going.

The guard holding my arm pushed me out of the elevator. We walked about twenty yards and then I heard a lock click open. It sounded like the lock on a hotel door. Someone held the door open and the guard nudged me to start walking again.

They walked me a few more feet and then made me sit down. One of the guards held my arms as the other cut off the Flexcuffs. The relief was short lived, as his next step was to secure my wrists to the arms of the chair.

"Remove the hood," I heard from across the room. It was Houston's voice. The more I heard his smarmy tone, the more I wanted to make the man suffer for everything he had done.

The guard did as instructed and ripped the hood from my head. It took a second for my eyes to adjust and to take in my surroundings.

I was sitting in what appeared to be a hotel room suite. The curtains were drawn, and all the lights were on. We were in a sitting area and across from me were Houston, two bodyguards, and a woman.

The woman appeared to be younger – mid to late 20s. She had jet black hair and sky-blue eyes. She was conservatively dressed in business attire, legs crossed as she appeared to study me.

"Welcome, Mr. Shepherd," she said. "Thank you for coming."

"I didn't really have a choice," I said and then looked at Houston. "I'd like to see my friends now."

"They are fine," Houston replied tersely.

"That wasn't the deal."

Houston shrugged. "You're here now. What difference does it make?"

I tensed against my restraints. They were tight enough that I knew I could break them with enough force but chose to continue the illusion that I was trapped in the chair instead.

"If you hurt them, I swear to God-"

"Now, now," the woman said. "There's no reason we can't be civil."

Houston laughed. "Mr. Shepherd had every opportunity to be civil. Instead, he chose to attempt violence on my aircraft. Such behavior is certainly not *civil.*"

I took in a deep breath and exhaled slowly. Houston was trying to get under my skin and rattle me. He wanted me to be angry and hostile. He was doing a good job of it, but giving in wasn't going to get me anywhere. I was definitely going to enjoy killing him later, however.

"I'm sorry, I didn't catch your name, ma'am," I said.

"My name is Veronica Carver. Do you prefer to be called Alex or Troy?"

"How about we stick with my actual name and go with Troy?"

Veronica smiled and then turned to Houston.

"Dr. Houston, you've been very kind to bring *Troy* here to meet with me. But you're very busy. Don't you think you should return to oversee the next phase?"

"It is already in motion. Besides, I want to enjoy this."

"Mom, Dad, I hate it when you fight," I interjected. "Can I go now? I'm hungry."

"See?" Houston asked, gesturing to me.

Veronica stood and offered her hand for Houston to shake.

"It was very nice seeing you, Dr. Houston. I will be in touch very soon."

"You're serious?" Houston asked. He looked a bit surprised that she was forcing him out.

"I am," she said with a polite smile. "I must insist you return to continue our work. It cannot happen without you there."

Houston begrudgingly stood and shook her hand. He looked back at me in disgust.

"It's a shame I won't get to watch you die."

"Oh, I'm sure we'll meet again," I said, and winked.

His face reddened as he turned and stormed out of the hotel suite. Veronica waited for him and his men to clear the room and then turned to what I assumed was the head of her security detail.

"Leave us alone for a bit, please."

"Are you sure, ma'am?" the very serious-looking bodyguard in a black suit and red tie asked.

"If I need you, you will hear me."

"Yes, ma'am," the guard said. He motioned for the other two remaining men to follow him and they all left.

Veronica sat back down in her chair and crossed her legs.

"Alone at last?" I asked.

She looked around to make sure no one was listening and then leaned in.

"Let's talk about your time with Odin, shall we?"

CHAPTER THIRTY-FIVE

Odin had saved my life. It had also nearly killed me. It was an organization I never truly understood, and I had been more than happy to leave. Some things about it just never sat well with me.

I had first encountered them in Syria after I had flown there to join the Kurdish YPG to fight ISIS. My friends and I had been captured and tortured. A team that I thought had been U.S. Special Forces had rescued me. After a few days of recovering, I had learned the truth.

That was when I first met Kruger. He was the team leader and despite his harsh demeanor, he was an all-around great human being. He felt personally responsible for the death of my family – by failing to stop the terror cell that had hijacked the school bus my wife and daughter were on. He wanted to make amends and eventually invited me to join the team.

What the team was never really made sense. For the most part, we were mercenaries. We were paid by a billionaire named Jeffrey Lyons and given missions around the world to take out really bad people who, we were told, the world governments couldn't or wouldn't deal with.

It was on such a mission that things started to fall apart. A former British SAS operator who went by the codename "Cowboy" and I were compromised in Libya and barely made it out alive. We later discovered that Lyons had supposedly been killed and we were wanted dead by pretty much everyone.

It was then that I learned roughly what Odin was about. Named after the Norse god, Odin was a group of billionaires whose families had come together behind the scenes to right the wrongs of the world. What started as revenge for the sinking of the *Lusitania* eventually became a group of four powerful billionaires who used their wealth to not only fund covert special operations teams, but also to influence politics, monetary policy, and a whole list of other things that just made me uncomfortable.

The final straw was the advanced artificial intelligence computer *Helios*. It was too dangerous for any government to have, much less a group of billionaires that were accountable to no one. And ironically, it was their demise. They trusted a Russian operative that was a double agent for the Bratva who ended up killing them and stealing it for an oligarch.

So, we destroyed it and killed the oligarch. And that was the end of my association with Odin, or so I thought. I was given a new identity and moved to Texas. An errant social media post by an enthusiastic student at the school I worked for brought the Bratva's attention back to me, but after we handled it, there was no further mention of the Odin billionaires – they were all dead and Kruger had taken over. He was the only person I trusted with such power and responsibility.

Of course, with Kruger now dead, that meant Odin was dead too, so there was no real reason the woman across from me should be asking such questions.

"Odin? Father of Thor? Yeah, I like Marvel movies. What about him?" I asked.

"Funny," she said, obviously not amused by my diversion. "No, Troy, I'm talking about the group you used to work for. With Jeff Lyons."

"The guy on YouTube?" I asked. It wasn't a lie. Lyons had used a fairly successful gun-related YouTube channel as a cover for some of his activities.

"The man you worked for until his unfortunate demise. Are we really going to play these games?"

"I'd like to see my friends now. Your buddy doesn't seem to be a man of his word."

"I assure you they will not be harmed, nor will you. That's not why you are here."

"Why am I here? I can't imagine a woman of your means would have time for a poor deputy like myself."

"The truth is, I've been looking for you."

"Me?"

"Well, not you per se, but people who were associated with Odin. And when your alias showed up on Houston's facial recognition, I just had to talk to you."

"Why?"

"I need to find Mr. Mack," she said.

"Never heard of him."

"I find it odd that you would take such a position. What does such a denial gain you? You stand to lose far more by continuing this charade."

"What is that supposed to mean?" I asked.

"You know what it means. Of course, I don't want to hurt your friends, but with the training that I know you have, it may be the only way to get the answers I need," she replied as she pulled her cell phone from her pocket and unlocked it.

"Let them go," I growled.

She swiped the screen of her phone a few times and then turned it for me to see. My heart sank as I saw Jenny sitting on the floor in the corner of a room with barren walls and a concrete floor. Her knees were tucked up to her chest with her arms wrapped around them and her head buried.

"I said let them go," trying to project anger instead of the absolute terror and dread I was feeling.

"You shouldn't be mad at me. You dragged them into this."

"What do you want from me?"

"The truth."

"Fine. Odin is dead. It died with Kruger."

"Who is Kruger?" she asked.

"Mack. The guy you're looking for. He's dead, and as far as I know, Odin died with him. What else do you want to know?"

"He can't be dead," she replied softly.

"I don't know what else to tell you, lady. What's it to you?"

"He holds the key."

"Key to what?"

"The Odin files."

I cocked my head. "Look, lady, I am being one hundred percent honest with you when I say I have no idea what you're talking about. For the longest time, I thought Odin was just the one guy. Then when we had to track down Helios, I found out about the rest. But I never knew or cared about the inner workings of the rich guys running it."

"And I don't expect you to, but you can tell me where to find Mack."

I shrugged. "As far as I know, he's dead. I just found out recently, but apparently, he died a few months ago. Why do you need these files, anyway? Wasn't Odin just a few billionaires with a computer system that we ended up destroying? Kruger was the last one alive and now he's dead. So, Odin is dead too, right?"

"Odin was not rightfully his. He had no bloodline to any of the founders."

"Again, none of my business and I really don't care, but from what I understood, all the others had no legitimate heirs. Besides, you're obviously already rich. Do you really need any of that to do the shady shit they were doing? You seem to be doing just fine without it."

"I am the rightful heir to Odin!" she snapped. Her eyes flashed wild with rage.

"Okay, okay, I'm sorry," I replied. "Like I said, I really don't care either way."

"You will care…*or else.*"

"I'm not sure what you want me to do. I haven't seen him for months, even before he died."

"If you want your friends to go free, you will find him."

I considered her offer for a moment. Despite the large amounts of crazy going on behind her bright blue eyes, I knew she seriously believed Kruger was alive and held the key – whether figuratively or literally – to whatever it was she thought she needed. I also knew that refusing to help meant an instant death sentence for me and, more importantly, Jenny and Hyatt.

Agreeing to help seemed like the only answer to buy some time to figure out a way to out of our predicament. And if Kruger really were alive, he'd be the best person to help take down whatever evil empire she was trying to rebuild.

"If I do this, will you let my friends go?" I asked.

"If you find him."

"What if he's dead?"

"He's not."

"But what if he is?"

"Then you and your friends will be free to go."

"Just like that?" I asked, making no effort to hide my skepticism.

"Excuse me?"

"You'll let us go, no questions asked? Knowing we could go to the police?"

Veronica laughed. "You'll be free to try."

I could tell she was serious. She knew she was untouchable. Whatever operation she had built here had perfectly insulated her from fear of consequences. I promised myself I would change that when it was all said and done.

"Okay," I said. "I'll do it. But if he really is alive, I'm just warning you now, that's a genie you can't put back in the bottle. Be very careful what you wish for."

CHAPTER THIRTY-SIX

Veronica left me alone in the room for at least an hour before someone finally came in. She had left shortly after I reluctantly agreed to help, promising that Jenny and Hyatt would be moved to more suitable accommodations while I upheld my end of the agreement.

A man in a dark suit and blue tie walked in and freed me from my restraints. He sat down in the chair Veronica had been in and crossed his left leg over his right as I stood and stretched.

"Take your time," he said. "I know you've been in a rather uncomfortable position for a while."

"Have my friends been moved yet?" I asked.

"They have. You will be able to video chat with them in about an hour, as promised."

"Okay," I said, still standing as I scanned the room for potential weapons or exit strategies. "Next question. Who are you?"

"Please, have a seat when you're ready. I'll explain everything," he said. He was clean cut and professional-looking. His tight haircut and clean shave suggested military or law enforcement background. He appeared to have a fairly muscular build and looked to be in his mid to late thirties.

I sat, curious to hear what his story was in the seemingly endless barrage of meeting new sociopaths I had experienced in the last twenty-four hours.

"Would you prefer I called you Troy or Alex?" he asked.

"Troy is fine."

"Very well, Troy. You can call me George."

"George?"

"George."

"First name or last name?"

"It doesn't matter. That is what you will call me during our time together."

"And what will we be doing together?"

"Think of me as your partner in finding Mr. Mack. I will be with you to ensure you have all of the tools you need to succeed, and to prevent you from making any poor choices that might negatively affect the continued comfort of your friends."

"So, you're a chaperone."

"Something like that. Now, where should we begin?"

I held up my hands. "Easy there, guy. Skipping the foreplay and going straight into it never works, believe me. How about we get to know each other a little first. You know, since we're going to be *partners* and all."

"What would you like to know?"

"You seem like a squared away guy. I'm guessing military? LEO?"

George smiled. "If you're trying to size me up, rest assured anything you try to do to back out of your deal will not end well for you. If you're wondering if I can handle myself in the field, the answer is yes."

"I'm just wondering how anyone gets suckered into working for a group like this. One that kidnaps innocent people and kills them. Or kills cops in cold blood. You good with that?"

"Sometimes the end justifies the means. That's above my paygrade. Ours is not to question why, ours is just to do or die."

"What is it with you people and your cryptic bullshit? Do any of you know how to give straight answers?"

"We've wasted enough time on your foreplay. Let's talk about how we're going to find Mr. Mack so you and your friends can go back to your lives in Texas. That's what you want, isn't it, Troy?"

"I want justice for the deputies that your boss's friend killed."

"Revenge is such a waste of time and energy. Do you really think that will work out well for you? Of course not. But the sooner you work with me to find Mack, the sooner you can move on with your life."

"Will you at least explain why Kruger is so important? Your boss was vague about it."

George seemed to consider my question for a moment. He knew he had to build some level of trust with me if we were to work together effectively, despite the looming threat he held over my head. But I could tell he was also worried about telling me too much.

"Mrs. Carver requires access to certain files that Mack….*Kruger*… would have held as the assumed sole person to inherit Odin."

"See, that's what I don't get. Wasn't Odin just an idea? A bunch of billionaires doing things together for whatever agenda they had?"

"Odin was much more than that."

"Okay, but Veronica Carver is obviously very wealthy. Why can't she just do whatever crazy shit she's doing without it and why does it piss her off so much that Kruger was the only heir?"

"Because Odin was rightfully hers."

"How? All of the other billionaires died and had appointed no heirs."

"Oscar Stevens was murdered. His will was forged by Helios."

"Let me guess, Carver was to inherit his share of Odin."

"Correct."

"And the Odin files contain what? The original will?"

"Among other things."

"Okay, but what does having a share of a nonexistent organization do for her? Without the other billionaires at the table, isn't it pretty pointless?"

George uncrossed his legs and leaned forward, putting his elbows on his knees.

"Look, man, I've told you way more than I should have. I'm trying to get you to trust me by being honest with you, but that's really as much as I can tell you. Do you understand? You need to be worried about how we're going to find Kruger and not how it all works."

"I understand."

"Good," George said, leaning back in the chair. "Now, where would you like to start?"

I thought about his question. It was clear that Veronica believed the Odin files would give her more power, and that seemed like a very dangerous proposition. I still didn't know what her end game was with New Orleans and that piece of shit televangelist that had dragged me to Nashville to meet her. The thought of helping them made me sick.

But I needed to cooperate as best I could to ensure the safety of Jenny and Hyatt – at least until I could come up with a better plan or actually find Kruger and unleash the wrath of the angry bearded ginger on the unsuspecting trust fund baby. If he really was still alive, it was truly a case of *be careful what you wish for.*

I suppressed a smile thinking about what he would do to them if he found out what they were up to and said, "We need to go to Washington, D.C."

"What's there?"

"Special Agent Madison Tanner."

CHAPTER THIRTY-SEVEN

We landed at Manassas Regional Airport in Virginia just after 7 a.m. the next morning. The private jet was much smaller than the one that had taken me to Nashville but was still very comfortable and still had the "new car smell."

I had been given my own room in the hotel the night before. It wasn't as nice as the suite where I met Veronica, but it wasn't a dump either. There were cameras everywhere, including the bathroom and they warned me that any attempt to escape would result in the deaths of Hyatt and Jenny.

Other than the constant threat of their execution, they were both doing well. They had both been move to guest quarters at the church, which appeared to be in good condition. Hyatt had even been given the opportunity to talk to his family, explaining that he had been called away to help with a law enforcement special task force that was needed for the unrest in New Orleans. That excuse would maybe buy him two or three days.

I was given twenty minutes to talk to them each via video chat. George gave me strict instructions not to talk about Veronica or anything I had learned. I was only allowed to tell them that we had worked out a deal and that I would be home and we would all be free as soon as we finished.

I could tell Jenny wanted to know more, but she was cooperative and seemed to understand that it wasn't my decision to keep them in the dark. She only told me to be careful and that she couldn't wait to see me again.

Contacting Special Agent Tanner would have been the next step, but George said that it wouldn't be necessary. More specifically – he said don't even think about it. I assumed he was worried that I might tip her off.

"She will be home," he said with a knowing grin. "Don't worry."

An Audi A8 was waiting for us at the airport. An attendant at the FBO handed George the key fob and we began our drive. The GPS said it would take a little over an hour with traffic. George already had the address in his phone as he plugged it into the USB and selected maps.

"If you already know this much, why do you even need me? You seem like a sharp enough guy. I'm sure you could find out what happened to Kruger without me."

George raised an eyebrow behind his mirror-tinted aviators as he merged into traffic. "I'm not sure you really want that."

"What do you mean?"

"Do you think you would have been flown to Nashville if that were the case? You and your friends are quite the liability and Dr. Houston was more than happy to take care of it himself."

"So, when this is over, you're going to try to kill us, then, right?"

"Try?"

"Yes. *Try*. I may be broken, bruised, and shot up, but I'm not just going to roll over. You're going to have to get through me first before you hurt them."

George held up his right hand. "Easy, there, Dirty Harry. I think we need to get something straight before we go any further."

"Yeah? What's that?"

"I need to be able to trust you, and you need to be able to trust me. That's the only way we're both going to get what we want here."

"You just called me a liability. How can I trust someone that has my friends held hostage saying shit like that?"

"Because I am being honest with you. You were a liability. You still are. But my employer and I will uphold our end of the bargain if you uphold yours. It's quite simple. This is not personal."

"It's fucking personal to me!"

"Then you're going to have to compartmentalize that and keep your emotions in check," he said calmly. "This will go much more smoothly if you just do what we ask. You and your friends will be able to move on after."

"What's stopping that Houston asshole from *taking care of it himself*, as you said?"

George laughed. It was the first time I had seen him break his serious demeanor.

"Dr. Houston won't step out of line, I assure you. He knows better."

"So, I'm just supposed to trust you then."

"Precisely. It is your only option."

"For now," I replied.

George said nothing the rest of the drive as we continued to Tanner's house. I wasn't quite sure how I felt about the man. His no-nonsense approach appealed to me. I knew exactly where I stood at all times and he seemed to genuinely believe what he was saying.

That still didn't mean I liked him or would let my guard down around him. As far as I was concerned, he was the enemy. And if I had to end him to get to Jenny and Hyatt, I would without thinking twice. He was a willing accomplice to whatever Veronica and Dr. Houston were doing and was therefore just as guilty.

We arrived at Tanner's suburban townhouse just before 9 a.m. Her government-issued sedan was sitting in the shared driveway in front of the one-car garage. George parked on the street in front of her address, and I followed him to her front door.

"Nice place," I said as George hit the button on her doorbell camera and it started chiming.

George didn't respond as we waited for Tanner to answer. The chiming stopped and the door opened.

Tanner was wearing dark sweatpants, a gray t-shirt, and her hair was up in a bun. She had bags under her eyes and looked slightly hung over or sleep deprived. She looked at George first and didn't seem to recognize him before turning to me.

"Troy? What are you doing here?" she asked. Her voice cracked slightly. She sounded tired and depressed.

"Can we talk?" I asked. "Maybe over coffee?"

"Who's your friend?"

"This is George," I said. "I'll explain everything inside."

"Okay," she said as she held the door open and turned to walk inside. "Come on in."

We followed her inside. The place was a mess. There were moving boxes and clothes everywhere. A black cat hissed at me as I nearly stepped on it trying to navigate through the clutter. It was far from what I had expected from someone as squared away as Tanner had been.

She cleared off a high table in the kitchen and we sat down.

"I'll put on a pot of coffee," she said.

George and I waited as she walked back into the kitchen and started making coffee. Once the coffeemaker was started, she came back and sat down at the table with us.

"So, what's going on?"

"Are you okay?" I asked.

"I'm fine. It's been a rough couple of days. Why are you here now? Where's Jenny?" she asked.

"She's fine," George responded. "We just have some questions for you if you have time."

"Who are you?" Tanner snapped.

"My name is George."

"George *who?*"

"It's just George," I said, intervening before Tanner ended up in a confrontation with him and ruining my chances of getting Jenny and Hyatt back peacefully. "It's okay. He knows everything."

"Everything about what?"

"Odin, Kruger…all of it."

"I don't know what you're talking about," Tanner replied. I could tell by her body language that she knew George wasn't a good guy and didn't trust the situation.

"We just have a few questions, and we'll let you get to work," I said.

"I'm off today," Tanner said.

"I can help you get your job back," George said.

"Job back?" I asked. "What happened?"

Tanner shot me a look and then stood up from the table as the coffeemaker chimed. She said nothing as she walked into the kitchen and opened a cabinet, retrieving three cups.

"Her job back?" I whispered to George.

George nodded. As I turned back to the kitchen, I saw Tanner reach into a drawer and spin around, leveling a Glock 19 at George's head.

"Alright, asshole, who are you?"

CHAPTER THIRTY-EIGHT

"Keep your hands on the table and don't move," Tanner barked as she aimed her weapon at George. "Don't even think about reaching for your weapon."

"Maddie, please," I said, holding up my hands. "Let's all take a deep breath and calm down."

"Are you law enforcement?" Tanner asked.

"I am not," George replied calmly.

"Troy, please disarm him," she said and then turned her attention back to George. "If you even think about reaching for it, I'll shoot you. Do you understand?"

"I do," George replied.

"Don't do this, Maddie. It's not what you think," I pleaded, knowing that the lives of Hyatt and Jenny were at stake.

"We will sort that out later. For now, please relieve this man of his weapon."

George looked at me and nodded. "Go ahead. Do as she says."

"This is a mistake," I said as I reached under George's suit coat and withdrew the handgun from his shoulder holster. "You don't have the whole picture here."

I removed the weapon, dropped the magazine, and cleared it. It was a custom Staccato 2011 chambered in 9MM. I caught the hollow-point round as it ejected from the chamber and placed it on the table with the gun and magazine.

"My handcuffs are on that end table," she said, indicating a table to my left in the living room. "Go get them please."

"Seriously?"

"Yes," she snapped.

George once again nodded for me to comply. I was torn between wanting to see him in custody where I would no longer be under his thumb, and knowing that everything Tanner was doing directly put Jenny's life in danger.

I reluctantly complied, walking over to the end table, and removing the handcuffs from their leather pouch. I returned to the table where George was still sitting calmly with his hands in plain view.

"In front or behind the back?" I asked.

"Behind the back," she replied.

I shrugged and grabbed George's right arm to control him. "Please stand up."

A knowing grin flashed across George's face as he stood. He put his left arm behind his back as I placed the handcuffs around his wrist and tightened them to one-finger spacing.

Tanner lowered her weapon and sat back down at the table. "Have a seat. Both of you."

I helped George sit and then returned to my seat at the table.

"Am I under arrest?" George asked.

"You're being detained for now," Tanner replied before turning to me. "Now, just what the hell is going on?"

"I think you might be overreacting slightly," I said, knowing full-well it was a lie and she was doing exactly what she should be doing. "We're just here hoping you might be able to help us find Kruger."

"Cut the bullshit, Troy," Tanner replied.

"I like your spunk," George said to Tanner. "Fine, I will tell you what you want to know. Where would you like for me to begin?"

"What is your name?" Tanner asked.

"George Brady."

"Who do you work-"

"Let me stop you right there and help you get to the meat of the matter. Can we be honest with each other?"

Tanner nodded.

"Good, because, you see, Mr. Shepherd or Troy or whatever you choose to call him today doesn't have much time. He and I have an arrangement with my employer – the identity of whom is none of your concern. And if he fails to uphold his end of the agreement within the prescribed amount of time, his closest friends will no longer be cared for, sadly. Do you understand?"

"You realize you're confessing to kidnapping to a federal agent? Perhaps now is the time to Mirandize you."

George laughed. "That won't be necessary."

"Why is that?"

"Because you are suspended, are you not?"

"I'm still an agent."

"That's neither here nor there. Do you believe your suspension is simply a coincidence? Come on, now. How do you think I knew you would be home?"

I could see Tanner becoming visibly upset by the realization that George was somehow behind her recall to D.C. I tried to make eye contact with her to get her to snap out of the building rage, but she remained locked onto George.

"Then maybe I should just shoot you instead," she said, putting her hand back on her weapon she had placed on the table.

"You could, but as soon as I fail to check in, Troy's friends will be awfully disappointed. By the way, what time is it, anyway?"

"Where is your handcuff key?" I asked. I couldn't risk it. I had already resigned myself to working with him and figuring it out once I had a better handle on what I was dealing with.

"I'm not letting him go," Tanner replied. "He just confessed to kidnapping."

"They have Jenny and Hyatt, dammit," I said.

"And we will get them back, but I can't allow this man to just go free. You know that."

I stood and started looking around the room for her keys. "Where do you keep the key? I'm not risking it."

"It's not your call," Tanner replied and then turned to George. "Mr. Brady, you are under arrest."

She rattled off George's rights per Miranda as I went back to where I had retrieved the handcuffs.

"Do you have any questions about your rights?"

"None," George replied.

"Do you wish to answer my questions at this time?"

"Certainly," I heard him say. I looked back to see him still sporting that same smug grin he had since first being handcuffed. He knew he had the upper hand in all of this.

"Where are the hostages being held?" Tanner asked.

"They are at a safe location in Covington, Louisiana."

"What's that location?"

"You're asking the wrong questions."

"What questions should I be asked?"

I stopped looking for the key and turned, knowing he was baiting Tanner. She was either somehow playing him or severely underestimating him and the situation we were in.

George turned around and looked at me to make sure I was listening and then turned back to Tanner. "The question you should be asking is what happens next."

"And what's that?" Tanner replied.

"Well, despite your friend's objections, let's assume for the sake of argument you do arrest me and take me in on alleged kidnapping charges."

"Go on…"

"You're currently suspended for operating outside of your authority down in New Orleans, is that correct?"

"I'm on administrative leave. I doubt it will go beyond that."

"Fair enough. So, you take me in for kidnapping. Do you know what happens next?"

Tanner raised her eyebrows, waiting for him to continue.

"Well, for starters, in about fifteen minutes when I don't check in, our guests in Louisiana will see an end to our very generous hospitality."

"You son of a bitch!" I yelled. I wanted to rip his throat out right there, but somehow managed to hold back as he continued.

"After that, you'll take me in for processing. It'll waste the better part of the morning for both of us. By noon, I'll be released and you will be called back into the Special Agent In Charge's office. This time, you'll be facing your own kidnapping charges for unlawfully detaining an innocent man. Meanwhile, Mr. Shepherd over there will be taken in for murder – assuming he doesn't flee of course. I haven't ruled that out, and quite frankly, I wouldn't blame him."

Tanner laughed. "I like your confidence, but you know how I see this playing out?"

"Please, enlighten me."

"I take you in. An HRT team rescues Troy's friends. You spend the rest of your life in a prison in a cell next to the people who hired you."

George nodded. "I really like you, Agent Tanner. I can see why you were picked for this assignment. You've got spunk. Unfortunately, your youth brings with it a childish naiveté, and it appears you've watched too many movies."

"Maddie, can I talk to you for a second? Privately."

"That's a good idea, Agent Tanner. The clock is obviously ticking. And if you think I'm bluffing, why don't you ask yourself why you were recalled back to D.C. in the first place. Was it really because you overstepped your bounds? Or perhaps there's someone pulling the strings behind the curtain."

Tanner stared at George as she stood and walked to me. We walked into the living room out of earshot.

"We can't risk it," I whispered. "I don't think he's bluffing."

"Just what the fuck have you gotten yourself into this time, Troy?"

"We went to look into a megachurch that we thought was behind the killing of Cynthia Haynes. The guy's name is Dr. Houston, and he brought me to Nashville to meet his partner in all this. Her name is Veronica Carver, and she thinks she's the heir to Odin. I think she's trying to pick up where they left off with that Helios thing and trying to start a civil war and reset the country."

"How?"

"I think she's behind some of the unrest going on in New Orleans. I heard her tell Houston to go back to start a new phase. I think he's funneling money to them."

"Tick-tock, tick-tock," George yelled over his shoulder.

"So why did you drag me into this?" Tanner whispered.

"First of all, I thought you would want to help, considering all we've been through. Second, Veronica Carver made a deal with me. If I help George over there find Kruger, or at least find out what happened to him, she'll let me go free with Hyatt and Jenny."

"And you believe them?"

"No, but I need breathing room. I figured I could come up with a plan while working with this guy. It's too bad Kruger's dead because if I really could find him, they would wish they had never looked."

Tanner looked back at George and then whispered, "Well, he *might* be."

"He might be what?"

"Alive," she whispered.

"What?"

"Officially, his body was found and he was buried in China."

"China? What the fuck was he doing there?"

"It's a long story."

"So why do you think he's alive?"

"I said he *might* be. Apparently, people have seen his gravesite, so it's been confirmed. But there's never been an autopsy or official report."

"What people?"

"Tuna."

"Where the hell is that guy? And how come no one answered when I called?"

Tanner shrugged. "I haven't seen him since he took over Kruger's assets. He was at the estate when I got called about an arson investigation."

"Arson?"

"Yeah, someone burned down the entire mansion."

"Was anyone living there? How do you know it was arson?"

"Because someone left a message that could only be seen under UV light."

"What did it say?"

"Stamus Contra Mallum."

My eyes widened as I realized what that meant. It was something I had seen in the Middle East over dead warlords before I had joined Odin.

"We stand against evil," I mumbled. "Holy shit."

"And that's not all."

"What?"

"Whoever did this had access to the vault inside the house. They took some of your special armor, night vision, a few guns, and an optical camouflage suit Kruger had been working on with MIT."

"Excuse me, but if I don't make that call soon, your friends will be very upset," George said.

"Maddie, listen to me. You know the kind of shit these billionaires can do. If Veronica is sniffing around trying to reboot Odin, there's no telling what access she's had and who's been paid off. George could be telling the truth and could walk away if you burn him. Let's cut him loose. Help me find Kruger. He's the only one that can stop this."

Tanner hesitated.

"Please," I said. "It's our only option right now."

"Fine," she said with a sigh. "But if he even looks at me sideways, I'm shooting him."

"Fair enough."

CHAPTER THIRTY-NINE

Kruger's estate was a husk of its former glory. What had been a luxurious property with colonial architecture mixed with modern finishes had been reduced to burnt frames, rubble, and debris. Every building had been burned to the ground, and the only identifiable structures that remained of the mega-mansion that once stood prominently at the center of the property were two massive walls and the concrete safe room.

Tanner led the way, holding a UV light as she carefully stepped through the debris. I walked behind her with George bringing up the rear. He hadn't said much since Tanner had freed him from his handcuffs and agreed to help.

The steel door to the panic room was open. The drywall used to conceal it had been burned and the door showed signs of scarring from the flames, but it was still intact. Tanner walked in, holding up the light.

"You said Tuna was here when you got the call?" I asked.

"Yeah, he was here with the arson investigator," Tanner replied. She held up the light against the wall.

Stamus Contra Mallum covered the wall in big block letters.

"What did he say when he saw this?" I asked.

Tanner turned the UV light off as George searched the room with his flashlight.

"At first, he said the same thing you did. He didn't outright say Kruger was alive, but I could tell he thought it. He thought Kruger might be sending us a message."

Tanner turned the UV light back on and turned toward the back wall. *Quidquid Victor Ero* had been written the same way as the other wall.

"What's that one mean?"

"Come what may, I shall be victorious. That's why he thought it had to be Kruger."

"Why?"

"It was the motto of a disbanded military group and Kruger was one of only a handful of people who had been in both – Tuna being another."

"So, why didn't you go find him?"

"Tuna did. There were rumors of high-value targets being killed in various hotspots across the world. Tuna did everything he could to find Kruger because he thought Kruger might need help. He spent weeks looking for him."

"And he couldn't find him?"

"He found Kruger's grave. He had the body exhumed and DNA testing was done."

"Where's the body now?"

Tanner shrugged as she flicked off the UV light and stepped over some of the debris to walk out. "I'm assuming they just reburied him."

"I thought you said there was no official report?"

"Because there is no official report. Tuna did everything privately and the State Department went along with it."

"Why?"

"Tensions with China. No one wanted to rock the boat over a covert operative turned billionaire murdered in China. Officially, Kruger died of natural causes while vacationing in Shanghai."

"Naturally."

As we reached the door, we turned and watched George sift through the rubble. At some point, he had put on a pair of gloves and was digging through the ashes.

"Find anything useful, George?" I asked.

"I would like to take a look at the armory that you mentioned, if you don't mind," George replied.

"No problem," I said as I turned to Tanner. "Shall we?"

We made our way through the rubble and out of what used to be the mansion. About a hundred yards away was the armory, which sat next to an advanced shooting range that was still intact.

Of all the structures on the property, the armory was in perhaps the best shape. Despite the obvious fire damage, its concrete walls were still standing and the roof was mostly intact. Like the panic room, the door was open. The windows had been blown out from the heat of the flames, but the security bars were still in place.

We didn't need flashlights as we walked into the armory. The steel cages and safes that had housed most of Odin's weapons were all still in place, and open.

"Were all the weapons taken?" I asked.

"Not all, but most of the advanced stuff was taken. Tuna cleared out the rest, I'm guessing," Tanner replied.

George looked around the armory and then asked, "Were there any messages on these walls or any other buildings?"

Tanner held up the UV light against the wall. "Not that we could find."

"This *Tuna* person. What is his real name?" George asked, pulling out a small notebook from his suit pocket and flipping it open.

"Ty Turner," Tanner replied.

George thumbed through his notes, using a beam of light from one of the windows to help him see. "Ah, yes, here he is. Of course."

"I'm not sure how much more help we can be," I said. "This is as far as I can help you."

George scribbled something on his notepad and then put it back in his pocket before waving his hand dismissively. "Nonsense, you are doing great. I still need your help."

"I have told you everything I know," Tanner replied. "I can't help you anymore either."

"Agent Tanner, I actually agree with you," he said, flashing the same knowing grin as he had when he was handcuffed. "You have been a great help."

The hair on the back of my neck was standing up and alarm bells were going off in my head. I could feel something bad was about to happen – the same feeling I got on a traffic stop when things were about to go sideways and the suspect was about to run or fight.

I glanced at Tanner standing off to my right momentarily and then back at George. He was about fifteen feet from me at the corner of the armory as we stood near the door. As I looked back, I saw the glint of the light from the window reflecting off his handgun as he drew it from his holster.

Time seemed to stand still as I watched him level the gun at Tanner. She was too far away for me to move her, and I had no weapon to use to return fire. The only thing I could think to do was run toward her and shield her with my own body.

I looked away as I took two steps and then dove toward her. We connected just as I heard the gun go off, landing in a pile of soot and rubble as I took her down with me.

CHAPTER FORTY

It took me a second to regain my senses as we lay on the charred floor. I was on top of Tanner but unsure if the bullet had hit me, her, or nothing at all. My left hip had landed on something pretty hard and was throbbing, but other than that, I didn't feel like I had been shot.

My adrenaline was still surging as I turned around to look for George. If he had missed us the first time, he wouldn't the second. I looked back to find no one standing where I had expected him to be, and as the ringing in my ears subsided, I heard a gurgling sound.

I pushed myself up and onto my knees, quickly looking over Tanner before getting to my feet to square off with George. It took me a second to realize that he was not standing anywhere in the room, and the figure on the floor where he had been was actually him lying face down in the rubble.

I quickly looked back to see Tanner getting back up. "Are you okay?" I asked.

"Yeah," she said, still catching her breath.

I moved toward George as fast as I could through the debris. His handgun was a few feet from his outstretched arm. I picked it up and trained it on him as I closed in on him. The sound of gurgling became more pronounced.

I walked up to him and rolled him over with my foot. His face was black from the soot and blood was pouring from his neck as he struggled to breathe.

"Fuck! There's a sniper!" I said, ducking down as I realized what had just happened. "Someone else is here! Get down!"

"What the hell?" Tanner replied as she took cover behind an armorer's table.

"Wolf!" I heard someone yell in the distance. "Don't fucking shoot me, we're friendlies."

"Tuna?" I called out as I recognized his voice. It was the first time anyone had called me Wolf – a nickname I had been given while fighting with the Kurds in Syria – in a long time.

"Yeah, it's me, so don't shoot us," he replied. "We're coming in."

I lowered my weapon to the low-ready position against my abdomen and stood. Tuna walked in with his rifle slung across his chest. He was in the full Odin kit with modified Dragonsilk full coverage body armor, lightweight helmet, and comms gear.

Tanner stood and stepped away from the armorer's table as Tuna walked in. I could see two other people in similar gear outside, but I couldn't recognize their faces. They appeared to set up a perimeter outside while Tuna came in alone.

"Are you two okay?" Tuna asked as he took off his helmet and ran his gloved hand through his hair. "I let it go as long as I could, but when I saw him draw, I really didn't have a choice."

"Goddammit!" I hissed as the realization hit me that George would no longer be checking in with his superiors. I darted over to his body and started digging through his pockets. I first found the notepad he had just written on and then retrieved his cell phone. He had no wallet or identification on him at all.

"Shit! What are we going to do?" I asked. I felt completely helpless knowing that Jenny and Hyatt were so far away and there was nothing I could do to get to them before George failed to check in. "What have you done?"

"I saved your life. You're welcome," Tuna said. "Calm down and tell me what's going on?"

"They've got my girlfriend and a good friend as hostages down in New Orleans. George gave them instructions to kill them if he didn't check in with them regularly. There's no way to get there in time!"

Tuna walked up to me and put his hands on my shoulders. "This is not like you. I'm gonna need you to just slow down and breathe, buddy. First off, who's George?"

I wrestled free from his grip and pointed at the man lying in a pool of his own blood. "That asshole right there."

"I don't know where you got that name, but that guy's name is Wade Carver," Tuna said.

"No! Bullshit! He said his name is George Brady," I said. "He works for Veronica Carver."

"How did you find us?" Tanner asked.

"Well," Tuna replied. "Long story."

I shoved the notepad and phone in my pockets and pushed past Tuna. I was starting to get claustrophobic in that armory as I realized what was about to happen to Jenny. My stomach turned as I thought of the same helpless feeling that I had watching my wife and daughter die or learning that the Kurdish fighter Asmin had been killed in Syria. I refused to let another woman in my life be killed because of me.

"Where are you going?" Tuna asked as he turned to give chase. "Wolf, you need to stop and talk this out with us. We can help you."

I walked out into the open where three other men dressed in the same Odin gear had set up a perimeter. "Who are these guys?"

"They're part of my team," Tuna said.

"I thought you left that business," Tanner said.

"It's complicated and I can't really talk about it right now. I'm just here to help you. Why did Wade Carver go to your house?"

"How did you know that? And how did you find us?" Tanner asked.

"When we set up your doorbell camera as part of your security package, we set up a backdoor that runs everyone through facial recognition. Coolio set it up so that anyone in any of our databases would flag, including former members. When Shepherd here showed up, it flagged both of them and Coolio called me. He tracked Carver's car here."

"We don't have time for this shit," I said. "We have to get on a plane right now and get to New Orleans."

"Not necessarily," Tanner said before turning to me. "I saw you pull a phone off George or Carver or whatever his name is. Give it to me."

I slowly pulled out the phone and handed it to her. She took it and showed it to Tuna. He took it from her as she said, "If Coolio is still working with you, he can figure out who Carver was calling to check in. Maybe get a location?"

"Well, I can tell you where they were," I said.

"So, he can confirm. Either way, if we can nail down a location, I can get a tactical team from the FBI to get them."

"But you're suspended. How are you going to get the FBI to do that?" I asked.

"She won't have to. I can get a team in place and we can get down there and get them."

I shook my head. "They'll be dead by then. He checks in every hour."

Tuna smiled. "You'd be amazed what technology can do these days."

"Helios?" I asked.

"No, Helios was destroyed. But that doesn't mean some of its capabilities don't still exist."

"I don't know," I said.

Tuna looked me right in the eyes and said, "I'm going to need you to trust me, buddy. We are going to win. There are no other options. Copy?"

I looked at Tanner who nodded and then turned back to Tuna. "She's all I have in this world, man."

"I know. And that's why we're going to win," Tuna said before turning to one of his teammates. "Hey, Paco, uplink this phone to Coolio, will ya? And get a chopper here ASAP."

"I'm on it, boss," the grizzled operator said before Tuna tossed the phone to him.

"We'll get a helo to take us to the airport and be on a jet to New Orleans within the hour," Tuna said. "If we need to, I've got access to federal tac teams, but I'd rather do this one ourselves."

"Thank you," I said. "I really appreciate it."

"While we wait, want to tell me what you were doing with this prick?" Tuna asked.

I gave Tuna the rundown on why I had travelled back to my hometown and how we had ended up George's prisoner as a result of Veronica Carver's search for the Odin files.

"Wade Carver is her brother," Tuna said. "He actually washed out of BUD/S and tried to start his own paramilitary group just like Lyons. He ran a few government contracts with the DEA in South America but it was mostly high value asset security stuff. And then he started doing gun for hire stuff for the cartels before the Odin billionaires put a stop to it. Those kids were both nutjobs who were obsessed with taking over Odin.

There's a reason Oscar Stevens specifically wrote them out of his Odin will."

"Is that why he's on your list?" I asked. "The one that pinged with the camera?"

"No. *You* were in our database. Coolio just ran Carver's info as well. I knew it wasn't good if he was with you. With everything Kruger and Lyons had told me about them, I figured you were in trouble and Maddie wasn't far behind."

"So, is that what this is about? Brother and sister trying to reboot Odin?" Tanner asked.

"That's my guess," Tuna replied.

"When I was talking to Carver, she told the guy who had captured me to go back to New Orleans to oversee the next phase of their operation. Do you think it has something to do with the riots?" I asked.

"I guess you haven't been watching or listening to the news," Tuna said as I started hearing our arriving helicopter in the distance.

"What news?" Tanner asked.

"Most of the city has fallen," Tuna said, shaking his head. "A group of armed protestors flooded the streets and created an exclusion zone. They're calling it the *Crescent City New Republic.* New Orleans PD has abandoned it."

"Holy hell," I said. "But why? What is the point of all this?"

"You'd have to ask your friend, Veronica Carver," Tuna answered, raising his voice as the helicopter slowed to land on the helipad a few hundred yards away.

"Oh, I will," I said. "But first, let's go get Jenny back."

CHAPTER FORTY-ONE

We were wheels up in Tuna's private jet within an hour of the helicopter picking us up at the estate. It was the longest hour of my life as I waited for Coolio to report back.

The aircraft was just as nice as Dr. Houston's and had been fully stocked. I suspected it was the same jet we had flown on with Jeff Lyons while doing missions for Odin, but I didn't ask. The only thing I really wanted to know was whether Coolio had been successful getting the info off the phone and somehow faking the check in phone calls with whomever George had to call.

Tuna's team had joined us on the flight. He introduced them only by their callsigns – Paco, Butch, and Casper. They didn't say much to me – I guessed that they were all the same flavor of former special operators as I had worked with in Odin, possibly even from other countries.

"Do you want something to eat?" Tanner asked as she returned from the galley with a sandwich and a bottle of water. We were at cruising altitude and she had been the first to get up as soon as the seatbelt light had been turned off. "There's a lot of food up there."

"I'm not hungry," I said.

Tuna overheard me as he sat on the other side of the aisle getting the video chat with Coolio setup. "We taught you better than that," he said between bites of his own sandwich. "Get some food and drink some water. You never know when you'll be able to eat again."

"You're right," I said. We hit a pocket of turbulence as I got up. I steadied myself and helped Tanner to her seat before heading to the front of the aircraft. I picked out a roast beef sandwich, heated it up, and returned to my seat with a bottle of water.

"Happy now?" I asked, showing off the spoils of my quest to Tuna.

"Good. You're just in time. Coolio is about to brief us on what he's found."

I sat back down in my chair and watched the large screen TV above Tuna's head. The other operators seemed uninterested as we waited for Coolio to appear on the screen.

The loading screen was replaced by video of Coolio working on his computer before he turned to look at the webcam. "Hey, Agent Tanner and Wolf. It's good to see you two again. Glad you're okay."

"Thanks, Coolio," Tanner said.

"What did you find, Coolio?" Tuna asked.

"Okay, well, first, I was able to fully access Wade Carver's phone and using a few videos I found of him on YouTube, I was able to reasonably replicate his voice. I also ran a search through his call history and found that the only number he called was a burner phone with a New Orleans area code. I ran a voice analysis on it, and I think it's Dr. Michael Houston."

"I could've told you that much, Coolio, but where are they?" I asked impatiently. "Can you find where they're being held?"

Tanner glanced over at me as if to scold me for interrupting. I didn't acknowledge her glare. We were running out of time and lives were at stake. As much as I liked Coolio, he often tended to geek out on the little details while delaying the important information.

"When I checked in, Houston said they were moving forward with their plan on schedule and hung up. I'm still tracking the phone and it's currently heading south on the Lake Pontchartrain Causeway Bridge. I tried using the cameras at the toll to see if there was anyone with them, but the windows were too dark. It appeared to be a three-vehicle convoy."

"So, you've got nothing?" I asked.

"I will keep tracking the convoy, but there are no guarantees that the hostages are with them."

"They have names," I growled.

"Easy, buddy," Tuna said. "Coolio, can you get eyes on the church?"

"They're using old school closed-circuit cameras. They don't have much of a digital footprint."

"Shit!" I said, slamming my fist on the table. "We don't have time for this."

"I can get a SEAL team to clear the church within the hour," Tuna said. "Don't worry."

"SEAL Team? How the hell are you going to do that?"

"SEAL Team 3 is training with SWCC at Stennis just across the border in Mississippi."

"They're already pre-briefed and ready, boss," Coolio replied. "Just give me the word."

"Using the military on U.S. soil?" Tanner asked. "Let me call the agency and get an FBI tac team to do this the right way."

"Coolio, what's the status of the FBI's SWAT team in New Orleans?" Tuna asked.

"One second," Coolio said before returning his attention back to one of his many computer monitors. "Looks like they're currently deployed just outside the CCNR boundary to assist with evacuations of city leaders."

"CCNR?" I asked.

"That's the Crescent City New Republic," Coolio replied. "It's what they're calling the area the armed groups have taken over."

"Oh, right, Tuna mentioned that earlier," I said. "So, it sounds like the SEAL Team is the only option? I agree that we can't wait for Houston to get wherever he's going. It may already be too late, but we have to try."

"What about the local SWAT team?" Tanner asked. "City or Sheriff."

"City doesn't have a SWAT team and Hyatt works for the St. Tammany Parish Sheriff's Office. He was taken into custody by a sheriff detail at the church."

"You think they're in on it?" Tanner asked.

"No," I replied. "But if there's even a chance someone is, I don't want them to get tipped off. And I don't want to put our SWAT team at risk. We've already lost too many good people."

"Doesn't sound like we have any other options," Tuna said to Tanner.

"That SWAT team is also deployed to New Orleans right now, boss," Coolio added. "Or at least some of them. That's what their system is showing."

"Fine," Tanner said. "But nonlethal to the max extent possible. Don't make it a bloodbath."

"Make it happen, please, Coolio," Tuna said. "Weapons tight. Let them know our ETA and to hold everyone until we can get there."

"On it," Coolio said. "And now about those pages you sent me from that notepad."

I pulled the notepad from my pocket. On the helicopter ride to the airport, I had given it to Paco to take pictures and send to Coolio for analysis.

"What did you find?" Tuna asked.

"It's mostly just personal notes and reminders without a lot of context, but I did find several references to Odin and its members. Somehow, they've managed to get names, locations, and other pieces of information."

"Anything that might help us find Jenny and Hyatt?" I asked.

"Not that I could find. He wrote *Phoenix* in several places, but I can't find any holdings in Phoenix by them or Dr. Houston's church. It could be something else. There's also a date on it."

"What's the date?" Tanner asked.

"Tomorrow," Coolio replied.

"Coolio, check the CIA and NSA databases. See if there are any relevant operations named Phoenix," Tuna said.

"One sec," Coolio replied, returning to one of his other monitors as he started typing.

"There are three operations in the last ten years – *Operation Dark Phoenix*, *Project Blue Phoenix*, and *Operation Alpha Phoenix*," Coolio said.

"What are the highlights?" Tuna asked.

"*Dark Phoenix* was a weapons program to arm the Syrian rebels," Coolio replied as he scrolled through the files. "*Blue Phoenix* was a study on the effectiveness of a bioweapon to create a regional pandemic. And it looks like *Alpha Phoenix* was an operation in Venezuela to force a regime change through civil unrest. The only one that appears to have been executed was *Dark Phoenix*."

"*Alpha Phoenix* - what was the plan with that one?" Tuna asked.

"What are you thinking, Tuna?" I asked, trying to understand what CIA operations had to do with a couple of rich civilians. "Is the CIA involved?"

"No," Tuna said. "But Carver worked as a defense contractor in Venezuela. I'm sure he worked with the CIA too."

"The plan was to cultivate an insurgency by funneling money and weapons to separatist groups friendly to the U.S. Phase One was to stage a government overreach of some sort that could be used to influence public support and fuel the unrest. Phase Two was to destabilize and take control of one major city. And Phase Three would support the government retaking the city."

"Wait, what? Why?" I asked, interrupting Coolio.

"Just wait a second," Tuna said. "Go on, Coolio."

"Okay. Phase Four involved the assassination of a high-ranking insurgency member. And Phase Five funneled the rest of the money and weapons to support the uprising and overthrow of the government."

Tanner was a lot smarter than I was and put the pieces together immediately. "It's all about optics and emotion. Start a small fire, put it out, and then start an even bigger fire to topple a regime."

"So, you think that's what's happening here?" I asked.

"I'm just thinking out loud here, but isn't that what happened? State Trooper kills an unarmed man on a traffic stop and kicks all of this off, right? Now they've taken control of the city. It sounds like we're operating from a playbook."

"But what about my friends? They were ambushed!" I said.

"It makes sense," Tanner interjected. "We found that a lot of the gangs involved either had no prior history of working together or were from out of state entirely – same for the protestors. In fact, most of the protestors were from the northeast."

"So, you're saying they used the Terry Haynes shooting as the catalyst for the others?"

"Hoping to cause even more government intervention," Tuna added.

"Which would lead to more violence and unrest," Tanner replied.

"And that's what Carver meant when she told Houston to be there for the next phase. Do you think they're on Phase Three now?" I asked.

"If this is their playbook, then yes," Tuna replied. "Coolio, send me the entire document please."

"Wait, if it works so well, why didn't they do it?" I asked.

"Says here it was deemed unfeasible due to high civilian casualties," Coolio answered. "Especially during the final phases."

"Shit," Tanner hissed. "There's about to be a bloodbath in New Orleans."

"How long until we land?" I asked.

"Looks like thirty-five minutes," Tuna replied, looking at the display next to his left hand.

"And how long until that team is in place to get Jenny and Hyatt, Coolio?"

"On station in twenty minutes, sir," Coolio replied.

"Are you still tracking Houston?" I asked.

"Affirm," Coolio said. "Just cleared the bridge and headed toward I-10."

"We need to divert to Lakefront Airport," I told Tuna.

"Why?" Tuna asked. "I thought you wanted to get Jenny and Hyatt out first."

"Let the SEALs clear the church, but my gut is telling me they're with Houston."

"That doesn't make sense," Tanner said. "Why would he do that?"

"Because they're going to use them as bait. Think about it. They become hostages of this uprising and get killed when the government retakes it. Maybe they pin it on the government and use it to show how brutal the government is. Or maybe they tie it to the insurgents and hope that the government uses more force. Either way, I've got a bad feeling about this."

"Jesus Christ," Tuna said. "I think you might be right."

CHAPTER FORTY-TWO

There was no satisfaction in being right. The SEAL Team raided the church just as we were touching down at the New Orleans Lakefront Airport just after sunset. We watched the raid from their body cameras as we taxied in, and watched silently as they went from room to room, securing workers and armed guards without firing a shot.

As they confirmed that the last room in their search was clear, we reconnected with Coolio to get an update on the status of Dr. Houston. We still couldn't confirm that Jenny and Hyatt were in the vehicle with him, but my gut was telling me that this was absolutely the case.

Tuna's team was busy kitting up and checking their weapons as we waited for Coolio to give us a status update on Houston's convoy. They showed no emotion as they went through their pregame routine in preparation for going into a war zone to rescue two hostages and capture an evil asshole. I had no doubt it was something they had done many times before, both as a team and in their former lives.

"It was a little harder to track them once they neared the city," Coolio said. "The power is out around and in the exclusion zone, and the street cameras are all offline."

"Did you find them or not?" I snapped. Tuna and Tanner each shot looks my way as Coolio looked like a kicked puppy.

As much as I liked Coolio, my patience with everything had run thin. We simply didn't have time to wait for him to explain his processes. All we needed to know was where they had been taken so we could plan a rescue mission.

"Sorry, Coolio, go on," Tuna said. "We're just all a little on edge right now."

"Right, sorry, I'll get to the point faster. I think they're in a suite at the Hyatt Regency next to the Mercedes-Benz Superdome," Coolio said. "It looks like they have their own generator that's up and running, so I should be able to get into their security feed shortly."

"Okay, we will need schematics of the hotel and nearby buildings. What's the status of law enforcement in the area?" Tuna asked.

"The hotel is next to the two sports arenas which are at the southern edge of the exclusion zone. There is a perimeter set up by NOPD with CCFR checkpoints two blocks northwest and two blocks south."

"Can you pull up a map of the occupied area?" Tuna asked.

The image of Coolio on screen was replaced by a map of New Orleans. The CCFR exclusion zone was shaded in red. It stretched from I-10 to the Mississippi River and from the Business 90 Pontchartrain Expressway northeast to Canal St. There was a second shaded area in the French Quarter, but there were segmented lines going through it.

"What's this second area in the French Quarter?" I asked.

"It's an area occupied by protestors deemed to be peaceful. The threat assessment is moderate but they are believed to be unarmed. The City of New Orleans has withdrawn law enforcement from the area, although they have not officially created a zone like the CCFR."

"Do they have a command and control structure?" Tuna asked. "Where are they sleeping?"

"There's a tent city and field hospital in both Lafayette Square and Duncan Plaza. They've allowed medics to go in and out," Coolio replied. "The command structure is still relatively unknown. Law enforcement hasn't been able to determine who is calling the shots, if anyone. There have been no attempts to negotiate yet."

"How many dead so far?"

"None, yet," Coolio replied. "Three officers were injured by rioters early on. There have been a few violent crimes committed within the exclusion zone that required medics to remove the victims, but it's unclear on what their injuries were."

"How many armed insurgents are we expecting?" Tuna asked.

"Unclear," Coolio answered. "Police estimates are anywhere from 3,000 to 5,000 people are involved. They are assuming everyone is armed, but they don't have an accurate number. They also believe the Superdome will soon be taken over as another housing area as a tribute to Hurricane Katrina."

"Why Katrina?" Tuna asked.

"It was a shelter during Hurricane Katrina, but in the aftermath, the city and state failed to get people adequate food, medical attention, and maintain security."

"Intelligence reports suggest that they may use it to show the inadequacies of a government that doesn't care about its people. They've cited it as another example of the government's systemic racism," Coolio said.

"And that's right next door to the hotel?" Tuna asked.

"That's correct," Coolio said as he pulled the map back up and highlighted the area. "It's not very far at all."

"What's our ingress method?" I asked. "Street level?"

"The State Police have blocked off all exit ramps into that part of the city," Coolio reported. "The river has no significant presence, but it's a long way on foot."

"We have darkness on our side. We need to get real time thermal imagery and airborne surveillance before we do anything."

"How are we going to do that?" I asked. "Do you have a drone?"

Tuna tapped the control station next to him. "I guess you didn't notice the sensor suite under the jet."

"I don't even know what that is," I answered.

"This jet is equipped with infrared, electro-optical, and thermal imaging. We'll get a better look when they finish fueling and we're back airborne."

"There's no time for that! If we're going in on foot, we're going to have to get moving as soon as possible!"

Tuna smiled. "Who said anything about going in on foot?"

My eyes widened as I realized what that meant. "Oh, fuck me!"

CHAPTER FORTY-THREE

During my time with Odin, I always hated jumping out of airplanes. I had never even been skydiving before meeting Kruger and his team, but it seemed like every mission involved some form of jumping out of a perfectly good airplane, so they taught me how to do it safely.

Luckily, we weren't doing a HALO jump or anything complex for this mission. It was just a simple jump from ten thousand feet, parachuting right to the rooftop underneath the rotating VIP lounge and observation deck on the top floor.

Tanner had been given a crash course in how to use the surveillance equipment of the aircraft and would be on comms with Coolio to help give us threat awareness until we were safely on the rooftop. She had also coordinated with the FAA to give the aircraft priority access as a law enforcement mission through the Temporary Flight Restriction that had been placed over the city.

Tuna checked my gear one last time as I waited behind the other three near the modified jump door. They had fitted me with spare gear they brought with them on missions. It was mostly the same gear I had used with Odin. It just wasn't custom fit and was either tight in some places or a little loose in others.

The latest addition to the gear actually seemed like a huge improvement. The traditional panoramic four-tube night vision goggles had been replaced by a headset that almost looked like a virtual reality system. Tuna explained that it was a head-up display called the Integrated Visual Augmentation system – a mixed reality headset that combined simulated imagery from sensors on the suit with the real world. It provided color night vision, infrared, and thermal imagery. I had never felt so much like the Predator in my life.

The best part about it was that it was lighter than the old quad-tube system. I didn't feel like I had to keep adjusting my lightweight ballistic helmet to keep it in place. I had no idea who Tuna was working for now or if he had just gone his own way and started his own team, but they were definitely on the cutting edge of technology.

"If the display in the helmet fails, switch to the one on your wrist immediately. Don't fuck around trying to get it working. Got it?" Tuna warned as Paco jumped and was followed immediately by Casper.

"Got it," I said.

"Good," Tuna said and then pointed to the door. "You're up."

I tucked in close behind Butch as he moved up to the door. The aircraft had a modified baggage door that was certified for jump operations. We were technically in the baggage compartment as we duck-walked to the door.

I checked Butch's chute, tapped him on the shoulder and gave him a thumbs up. He nodded and then exited the aircraft. I followed, pausing at the door to reconsider my life choices before jumping out into the darkness.

It took me a second to get my bearings as I stabilized into a freefall position. The city was mostly dark, with glowing fires on the streets throughout. My HUD displayed a green X over the Hyatt, which was one of few buildings with lights on it. Even the Superdome was completely dark. If the insurgents were going to take it over, they would have to figure out how to get the backup generator online or convince the city to restore power.

The altimeter in my display worked flawlessly. We had jumped from just over 12,000 feet and it gave me a countdown as I approached opening altitude. When the timer reached zero at three thousand feet, I pulled the ripcord and the chute opened without incident.

I switched on the color night vision feature of the visor. It took a second for my eyes to adjust, but it was almost like turning night into day. I was amazed at how clear the overlay was. Whoever had developed it had done an amazing job.

I looked up and verified my chute was in working order and then focused on gliding toward the landing zone. The HUD made it easy, giving me steering commands to account for wind drift as I approached the x-shaped roof. I could see the others already on the roof and rolling up their chutes.

"Drone is airborne," I heard Paco say as I started my flare over the roof. He had brought a backpack drone which would help us more precisely maintain situational awareness once inside the building since its thermal imaging would be much closer than the jet orbiting overhead.

I landed successfully despite how long it had been since I had last jumped and went to work securing my chute. Tuna landed right after me and did the same. We were met by Butch and headed toward the stairwell while Paco and Casper went to the northwest corner of the roof to take down the generator.

I readied my suppressed HK 416 and followed Tuna to the northeast corner of the roof. There was a ten-foot drop from where we landed near the observation deck to the roof of the northeast wing of the building. As I waited for Tuna to descend the ladder, I stopped and looked out onto the city.

It was worse than I had seen while at the hospital. It didn't just look like a war zone – it was a war zone. It looked more like what I had seen in Syria than a city in the United States. Burning cars lined the streets. I saw people in masks roaming the streets carrying rifles on the street directly below us. And off in the distance, I could see blue lights indicating the border of the newly acquired sovereign territory. The city I had grown up loving had fallen.

I followed Tuna down the ladder, and we headed for the stairwell. I tried to shake off my awe at the carnage down below. I needed to focus on the mission at hand to ensure Jenny and Hyatt made it out of the war zone safely. What happened to the city wasn't my problem.

We stacked up on the door with Butch taking the role of breacher and me bringing up the rear. Switching to thermal, I scanned the rooftop to ensure there were no tangos we had missed in our surveillance.

"Drone feed is up. I've got eyes on Dorothy and Toto," Paco announced over our radios.

I looked at the display on my left forearm and switched it to the drone feed. Thermal imagery showed four people in the room – two sitting and two standing. As Paco switched from thermal to electro-optical, I could clearly see Jenny sitting in the chair, but Hyatt's back was turned away from the window.

"Midnight," Tuna replied, instructing Paco and Casper to kill the generator.

"3…2…1," Paco called over comms. "Light's out. Go!"

Butch pulled open the door and Tuna entered with his rifle up and ready. I followed close behind him and continued down the stairs as he peeled off right to cover down the stairwell. We used bounding movements as we descended the two floors to the level where Hyatt and Jenny were being held.

I opened the door as we reached the floor and Tuna entered followed by Butch. We moved quickly and quietly in a single file, scanning for threats as we made our way to the suite. Stopping at the corner of the hallway, Tuna directed me to continue.

I sliced the pie, arcing out into the next corridor to our right as I quickly and methodically looked for threats. The idea behind the movement was to allow me to see them around the corner before they would see me.

The hotel was setup as an atrium, with glass elevators at the center and rooms wrapping around the hollow center. The restaurant below was empty since the hotel had been evacuated a few days earlier. I could hear laughter echoing in the distance.

Across the atrium, I saw a man carrying a rifle with a weapon light. He was shining it away from me as he walked toward the elevators. I aimed my rifle at his head. The heads up display calculated the impact using a sensor from the rifle. Just to be safe, I used the traditional ACOG to line up my sights, noting that they matched as I squeezed the trigger.

The suppressed round hit the target, causing the man to crumple to the ground as I continued forward followed by Tuna and Butch. A diamond on my HUD indicated that the target room was just a few doors down to my right.

"Approaching the objective," Tuna announced over our radios.

"Delta Two in position," Paco replied. "Two tangos inside. Still no sign of Boss Hog."

I peeked at the display on my wrist as I took the far side of the door. Tuna and Butch lined up on the opposite side as we prepared to enter. The drone footage showed the two men walking around the suite, apparently confused by the loss of power. I could hear them talking to each other on the other side of the door, but couldn't make out what they were saying.

Tuna looked at me, and I gave him a thumbs up. He placed a device against the RFID reader on the door and the lock clicked open.

"Execute," he said over the radio.

I heard glass shattering as Tuna did a silent countdown with his hand to me. As he dropped his last finger, he opened the door and I bolted in the room, hooking left with my rifle up.

Paco and Casper had entered through the window, taking out the two armed guards on Tuna's command. We cleared the room with Tuna while Butch stayed in the hallway watching for more hostiles to show up.

As soon as we finished clearing the suite, I ran straight to Jenny and Hyatt. They had taken cover on the floor when the windows shattered and were still face down with their hands zip-tied behind their backs.

"It's me, sweetie," I said as I helped her up and cut her restraints.

"Troy?" she said, struggling to recognize me with all of my gear on. I pulled off the helmet and visor so she could see my face. "Oh, thank God you're okay!"

"Are you okay?" I asked, moving her hair from her face as I tried to get a good look at her in the dark room.

"I'm fine," she said. "But, Troy…"

"Hyatt, what about you?" I asked as Tuna helped him up. "You okay, buddy?"

"I'm good. We've got a problem," Hyatt said.

"Where's Houston?" I asked.

"Troy!" Jenny snapped, trying to get my attention.

"What is it, babe?"

"They're going to kill Aaliyah Jackson," she said. "You have to stop them!"

"What? Who is that?" I asked.

"That's the leader of the peaceful protestors in the French Quarter," Tanner chimed in over comms.

"That must be the next phase of their plan," Tuna said.

"That's not our problem right now," I said. "We need to get you two out of this city."

"Do you know where Houston is?" Tuna asked.

"He said he'd be back soon. Didn't say what his plans were," Hyatt answered.

"Troy, you can't let them kill that woman," Jenny insisted. "They want to make New Orleans a war zone."

"It already is," I said. "The whole city is burning. I can't save anyone but you right now."

"Troy!" she protested.

"We can talk about it when we're out of here," I said as I put my helmet back on and looked to Tuna. "Ready when you are, boss."

CHAPTER FORTY-FOUR

"Delta One, you've got a problem," Tanner called out over the radio. "Multiple armed hostiles are headed your way."

"Which direction are they coming from?" Tuna asked.

"I count at least ten coming from the Superdome," Tanner replied.

I looked at Jenny and said, "We've got enough problems trying to get ourselves out of here. We simply can't worry about the others. I won't risk it. I'm sorry."

"Alright, let's get moving," Tuna said. "Jenny, hold on to Wolf and stay close. Hyatt, you're with Paco. It's going to be dark, so stay close and watch your step going down the stairs."

"Snuggle up, big man," Paco said to Hyatt.

"The hotel has been evacuated," Casper added. "Call out anyone you see."

"Everyone ready?" Tuna asked.

"Let's move," he said before keying up his radio. "Butch, we're coming out."

"Clear," he replied.

Tuna took point with Casper close behind him. I followed with Jenny holding on to the carry handle on my body armor. Paco and Hyatt filed in behind us as we made our way back into the atrium toward the stairwell.

We entered the stairwell and started down. Tuna, Butch, and Casper alternated bounding movements to cover our descent while Paco and I maintained our relative positions in the formation. I was careful and deliberate with my steps as we went down each flight of stairs to ensure Jenny had no issues. Red emergency lighting barely illuminated the steps for her, and I knew she was likely exhausted from being held captive.

"Contact left," Casper called out as we made our way down. He dispatched the threat quickly with his rifle, hitting the armed man in the forehead. "Clear."

We continued moving down the stairs. As Tuna reached the recently dropped tango, he kicked away the rifle and continued to the next level.

"Be careful," I whispered to Jenny as we approached the lifeless body. We carefully stepped over him and then kept going. We had twenty more flights of stairs until we reached the street level exit for our egress out of hostile territory.

"What's the status of the approaching threats?" Tuna asked over the radio.

"I count six in the lobby and six still outside," Tanner replied.

"Keep us updated," Tuna said. "What about our exfil?"

"Still clear for now," she replied.

"Copy."

We kept moving down the stairs, unimpeded as we quietly moved toward the street level exit. I checked on Jenny as we stopped at each floor. She was hanging on and doing a great job staying right on my heels. Hyatt was struggling a bit with Paco, but had made no complaints so far.

"Four contacts moving up your stairwell," Tanner announced.

"Contact," Casper replied before firing.

Casper dropped the first tango, but the second was just out of his field of fire. The two men that were behind him took cover and began blindfiring toward us. The sound of the rifles in the confined space was deafening, causing Jenny to let go of the carry handle on my armor and cover hear ears as she squatted down and took cover behind me.

Tuna returned fire along with Casper, but the steep angle to the lower floor made it tough to get a clean shot amidst the relatively effective suppressive fire from the tangos below.

"We're moving back into the atrium," Tuna announced over the radio.

Butch laid down suppressive fire as Casper moved to the breacher position. He opened the door toward him and Tuna moved in. I grabbed Jenny's arm with my left hand and held my rifle up with my right and followed.

We stopped in the hallway by the drink machines and icemaker that led to the atrium. I checked Jenny over to make sure she hadn't been hit and then pointed to the carry handle for her to hold on again. Casper covered the stairwell as we stacked up.

"I don't see any hostiles on this floor, but there are more making their way up the stairwell you were just in. Recommend you go to the northwest stairs and take that exit," Tanner said.

"Copy," Tuna replied.

We moved out into the atrium and turned right. Down below at the restaurant level, I could see hostiles with weapon-mounted flashlights. I heard one of them yelling commands at the other, but couldn't quite make out what he was saying.

Tuna pointed to the northwest corner of the atrium and tapped his helmet with his left hand as he moved out. Jenny and

I were right behind him. I reminded myself to not let my guard down, especially from above and the room doors to our right. Even though the hotel had been evacuated, there was still a chance a hostile or even a noncombatant could spring out at us. I made a point to check every room window as we passed them while Tuna focused on what was in front of us.

Casper dispatched two hostiles in the stairwell before joining us as we continued down the narrow walkway. I switched to infrared on my helmet mounted display and saw no threats between us and the current objective.

As we reached the end of the corridor and started to make the left turn toward the other side of the atrium, a loud explosion suddenly rocked the building. The floor shook beneath us and I heard glass shattering. I grabbed Jenny and took cover with her against one of the room doors as a secondary explosion shook the building.

"Jesus! What the fuck was that?" Paco yelled.

"Is everyone okay?" Tuna asked.

Everyone gave a thumbs up after taking a quick inventory. I looked Jenny over and she nodded before whispering, "I'm fine, Troy."

"Overwatch, what the hell was that?" Tuna asked over the radio.

"Car bomb two blocks from you near the exfil point," Tanner replied. "Looks like it was targeting NOPD SWAT that was staging."

Goddammit. More good officers killed for this phony war. It made me so angry, knowing that it was all just a ploy to create chaos by people with no real worries in the world.

"Your exfil point is no longer viable," Tanner said. "Recommend you go to the secondary."

"The place where the hostiles are now staging?" I asked, chiming in even though I knew I shouldn't.

"There's no time to debate it," Tuna said as he stood. "We're moving to the secondary exfil site."

And with that, our quick exit had just turned into a trip right into the hornet's nest. We were headed to the Superdome – the place where all of the hostiles that were trying to kill us had just come from, and potentially where thousands more were staging.

I didn't like it.

CHAPTER FORTY-FIVE

The New Orleans Centre Shopping Mall had once connected the Superdome to the Hyatt Regency hotel. Growing up, my dad used to take me to night games for the New Orleans Saints and we would stay at the hotel and walk through the mall to get to the Superdome. I always loved going to the comic book and toy stores if we had time. It was one of my fondest memories with my dad.

But in 2005, Hurricane Katrina flooded the mall and it was never reopened. Saints owner Tom Benson purchased the complex in 2009 and eventually tore it down, creating Champions Square for outdoor events instead.

Aside from missing out on the nostalgia and a trip down memory lane, the mall would have been a much better tactical option than our current plan. It was a direct, indoor route to the Superdome with plenty of cover and concealment. It would have given us the best chance of making it to the Superdome in the shortest amount of time.

As it stood, our window for extraction was incredibly small now that our primary option was gone. We were originally going to head out on foot and out of the exclusion zone where two SUVs were waiting to take us back to the airport. We had calculated that it would have taken eighteen minutes from the time we hit the street to reaching the pickup site, assuming minimal resistance.

But the car bomb had changed that. Our new plan involved a complicated routing through the hotel to get to the Superdome parking garage. On the northwest corner of the top level of the garage was an abandoned heliport. That's where an Army Blackhawk helicopter would land to pick us up.

A helicopter exfil made the most sense. In the days of Odin, an AH-6 Little Bird would swoop in, pick us up almost anywhere, and we'd be in and out in seconds. I still didn't quite understand what agency or group Tuna was working for or with, but during the planning of our mission, he told me that wasn't an option.

The best we could do, he said, was to convince an external agency to come in and get us, and that would have to be coordinated in real time by Coolio. There was a good chance it wouldn't happen at all, so it could only be a backup plan at best.

"I've contacted the Louisiana Army National Guard out of Hammond," Coolio reported as we made our way down the stairs. He had been relatively quiet for the mission, allowing Tanner to pick up overall control from the aircraft. "They're doing supply runs for law enforcement and will meet you at the rendezvous point in twenty-six minutes."

"Copy," Tuna said. "Thanks, Coolio."

Twenty-six minutes. It was barely enough time, even if we encountered no resistance. It would have been tough to do with just the team, but adding Jenny and Hyatt to the mix made it a daunting task. I wasn't sure they could keep up that much longer, and carrying either or both of them would double or triple the required transit time.

We exited the stairwell on the fifth floor. Tuna confirmed with Tanner that there were no hostiles in the rooftop pool area and we exited the hotel. The hotel had been warm without the generator to power the air conditioner, and the hot, sticky Louisiana summer air offered no relief. I was sweating profusely as we made our way around the pool to the adjacent parking garage.

"Parking garage is also clear," Tanner announced.

So far, so good. We approached the concrete wall of the parking garage and stopped. I helped Jenny over it and then climbed over the three-foot barrier myself before turning to help Hyatt.

The parking garage was mostly empty except for a few cars that had been left prior to the evacuation. With everyone safely in, we continued toward the far stairwell and descended to the third level.

We exited the stairwell and quickly moved to the entrance of Benson Tower. The keypad was disabled due to the power outage, so Butch broke the lock and held the door open for us to enter. I followed Tuna as Jenny did her best to keep up.

Jenny had been a cheerleader for the San Antonio Spurs and was still in twice the shape I was in, but without sleep and minimal food and water in the last couple of days, I could tell she was struggling. I did my best to keep up with Tuna while trying not to push her too hard as we moved into the office building.

We were careful to minimize noise as we walked on the polished marble floors. With the high ceilings, the acoustics were favorable for giving away our position. Hyatt's shoes made the most noise, clicking along the floor as he tried to keep up.

Tuna sliced the pie and rounded the corner into the upper lobby. There were no signs of anyone around and if the building had a generator, it had either been shut down or never started. It was almost pitch black, making it even more difficult for Jenny and Hyatt.

The lighting improved as we reached the entrance to the pedestrian bridge that crossed over Lasalle Street to Garage 1A at the Superdome. Cars on the street below were burning, creating an orange glow through the windows.

I checked my watch as we waited for Tanner to clear the route ahead with the drone. We had burned ten minutes getting to the pedestrian bridge. Now, we had just sixteen minutes to get to the other side of the Superdome. There were few options for cover and concealment in between, and the Dome was still a hotbed of activity.

"There are four armed hostiles as you exit the pedestrian bridge. They are standing near the entrance of the stadium at Champion's Square," Tanner advised. "There's some movement on the street level below the bridge and on Poydras Street to the north, but your route is clear."

"I concur," Tuna said, looking at the display on his wrist. "We're moving. Coolio, what's the status of our helo?"

"On time, boss," Coolio replied. "They are unarmed, so they will only wait three minutes before leaving. They've listed it as a high-risk mission."

"Copy that," Tuna said as he waved his finger in a circle for us to keep moving.

Butch once again broke the lock on the door. This time he went out first since the door opened outward. Tuna followed and Jenny and I stayed behind them. We tried to stay low as we crossed the bridge. There were rioters casually walking by the burning cars. They were armed and carrying bottles in their free hand. I wasn't sure if they were drinking or using it for Molotov cocktails or both.

A metal gate blocked the exit as we reached the other side. Butch pulled out a pair of collapsible bolt cutters, extended the handles and locked them into place. He cut the chain that had been padlocked to secure the gate and then continued through.

Once through, we turned left and exited onto the top floor of the parking garage. Like the one we had just gone through, it was mostly empty except for a few abandoned cars. We dropped to a knee and paused as we waited for the drone to reposition.

I kept my scan focused in the area of the hostiles by the Superdome entrance. They had the high ground, but I could still see them from the waist up. As Tanner gave the go ahead to continue to the next checkpoint, I saw a group exiting the stadium.

"Standby," I said.

I switched from infrared to EO and selected the daytime mode. The camera in the helmet didn't have much of an optical zoom, but it was enough to make out light blue shirts exiting the building.

"What's going on?" Tuna asked.

"Exiting the Dome at Champions Square," I said. "Overwatch, can you get eyes on?"

"No problem," Tanner replied.

"Talk to me," Tuna said. "We don't have time to sit here."

Four men wearing what appeared to be New Orleans Police Department uniforms walked out and met the armed hostiles. They stood there, appearing very cordial as they shook hands and laughed.

"Four hostiles wearing NOPD uniforms just exited," I said as I looked at the drone feed on my wrist display.

Tanner zoomed in, clearly showing the duty belts, uniforms, and hats from the overhead black and white view.

"Shit," Tuna hissed.

"What does that mean?" Jenny whispered.

"It means either these are cops that are in on it too, or they're impersonating cops to start the next phase of their plan," I replied.

I looked at the countdown timer. *Nine minutes.*

CHAPTER FORTY-SIX

"Let's move," Tuna said as I watched the men dressed in police uniforms move away from the hostiles toward Champion's Square. "Overwatch, get the drone back on our exfil route if you can and watch these officers with the jet's sensors if you can."

"I'm on it…I think," Tanner replied.

"I'll help," Coolio chimed in over the radio.

"Thanks," Tuna said. "We're on the move."

I looked back at Jenny who frowned at me before grabbing the carry handle on my armor. I could tell she wasn't happy about our decision to press on, knowing that something much bigger was in the works that would kill more innocent people.

But Tuna was right. We were running out of time until the helicopter arrived and there was no time to worry about what they planned to do next. Our only concern needed to be getting Hyatt and Jenny to safety.

"We've got eyes back on," Coolio reported. "I'm running their faces through my databases now."

"Copy," Tuna replied.

"Your path is clear to the helipad. Street level activity only," Tanner added.

We moved through the open lot and used the car ramp to get to the next level. We had a quarter mile left to go and it was all open with limited options for cover and concealment. It was the most dangerous part of our route, and with less than ten minutes left, we had no time to waste.

We stopped briefly as we reached the stairs from the parking garage to the gate level. Hyatt and Jenny tried to catch their breath as we waited for Tanner to clear the next five hundred feet.

"Still clear," Tanner said.

"We're almost there," Tuna said. "Stay low, move quickly. Keep your scan up. Watch the street. Everybody ready?"

Jenny and Hyatt nodded as the rest of us responded with a thumbs up.

"Let's move."

We moved at a fast jog after going up the stairs to the gate level. I could see lights on inside the Super Dome, but saw no people through the glass doors. The street level below and to our right was clear except for a few people walking and talking with each other on Poydras. I couldn't tell if they were armed, but I assumed they were.

"Facial recognition has come back on two of the people wearing police uniforms," Coolio reported. "They both have significant criminal histories and no record of working for NOPD. One resides in Memphis, Tennessee and the other in Baltimore, Maryland."

"Copy that," Tuna said, still leading the pack as we jogged across the open area.

"There's a vehicle stopped at the steps of Champion's Square. Three people are out and heading to the impersonators," Coolio added.

"Keep me updated," Tuna replied.

As we reached the other side of the Superdome gate level, I heard a helicopter off in the distance. I looked at the timer and saw that we were down to two minutes left. *Right on time.*

Tuna led us down the pedestrian ramp to the garage, and we stopped momentarily to take cover and let everyone catch their breath. I looked off to my right and switched to infrared view in my helmet-mounted display, finding the white-hot exhaust of the Blackhawk's engines as it approached from the north.

As we started moving across the garage, Coolio keyed up once more.

"I still can't get facial recognition on the other two, but I was able to get an ID on the men that just exited the vehicle. They're all walking down the steps now. Two of the men are local with only minor criminal histories, but the other man is pretty well known."

"Who is it, Coolio?" Tuna asked. We weren't quite jogging, but we were still moving quickly enough that he was still breathing heavily as he asked.

"His name is Jeremiah Sharp. I did a quick search and it appears he's a well-known reverend in New Orleans, and his church is associated with the same church Hyatt and Jenny were held captive in Covington, boss."

I nearly froze as I heard the name. *Reverend Jeremiah Sharp.* He was the one that led me to Cynthia Haynes. I knew he wasn't innocent in any of this.

"We have to stop that son of a bitch," I said. "Especially if they're impersonating cops."

"Standby," Tuna said.

The Blackhawk started its final approach, coming in low and fast with its lights off. We picked up the pace, crossing the empty parking lot and going up the ramp to the abandoned heliport.

The Blackhawk touched down and the crew chief got out to help everyone get in. Butch, Casper and Paco set up a perimeter while Tuna and I helped Hyatt and Jenny get in first.

"Get in," Tuna ordered me as he pointed to the helicopter.

"Contact left!" Casper shouted as he started firing at a group approaching from the street with rifles.

"What are you going to do?" I asked, realizing none of the others were getting on the helicopter.

"What we need to," Tuna said. "Now get on the chopper and get out of here."

"More hostiles approaching from Poydras Street," Tanner announced. "You've stirred the hornet's nest."

"Get going!" Tuna said.

"Troy, what's going on?" Jenny asked.

I took off my helmet and reached for her. She moved from her seat to her knees to get close to me.

"They're going to stay and put an end to this, I-"

Before I could finish, Jenny cut me off. "Go. Don't let them get away with this and hurt more innocent people."

"I love you," I said as I put her face in my hands and kissed her.

"I love you too," she said. "Please be safe."

"I will," I said before nodding to the crew chief to get in.

"I know this city better than anyone. I'm coming with you," I said to Tuna after putting my helmet back on.

Tuna nodded as we stepped away from the helicopter and it powered up to take off.

"Let's end this," he said to me as the helicopter took off and made a hard right turn away from the occupied zone.

CHAPTER FORTY-SEVEN

With Jenny and Hyatt safely airborne and out of harm's way, we took cover at a building next to the helipad. It was a double-wide mobile home that had once served as the control station for the New Orleans Downtown Heliport but was now just an abandoned building.

"You've got half a dozen hostiles approaching from the south end of the Superdome," Tanner reported.

"What's the status of Reverend Sharp and the uniformed hostiles?" I asked.

"They went into the Superdome together," Coolio answered. "His vehicle is still out front."

"Focus on what's in front of us," Tuna warned. "We will deal with the others soon enough."

Casper and Paco picked off four of the six hostiles approaching. The other two took cover behind the concrete barrier on the gate level of the Superdome. Tuna pointed toward the stairs and then tapped his helmet with his left hand, signaling, "On me."

We moved from the cover of the building to the stairs and descended onto the top level of the parking garage. There was very little ambient lighting and there was no moon, giving us some concealment in the darkness. It was the best we could hope for while traversing the wide-open area with no other options for cover or concealment.

The two hostiles on the gate level above and in front of us took potshots in our general direction, but it was clear they didn't see us. The software in the helmet had an interesting feature that located where the shots were coming from and put a marker over the estimated enemy position, correlated with their heat signature. I was still getting used to all the fancy gadgetry, but so far, I was extremely impressed with the toys Tuna had brought to the fight. They were game-changers.

One of the hostiles stood from cover to try to find us and Butch immediately picked him off. Seeing his friend drop, the remaining hostile dropped his rifle and took off running. He headed north toward Poydras Street and disappeared as he ran down the stairs toward the street level. *Smart man.*

"Clear to the gate entrance," Tanner announced as we reached the stairs from the parking garage to the gate level.

We moved up the stairs and headed straight for the nearest entrance. Casper checked the door and found it was locked. Butch broke the lock and then opened the door for us to enter.

Tuna took point and I followed close behind. We hopped over the entry turnstiles and headed toward the concession area. The lobby area was completely dark, except for a few red emergency lights, but I could see that there were a few lights on the field as we moved closer toward the center of the building.

"A marked NOPD unit just pulled up next to Sharp's vehicle. The man who exited was not in uniform," Tanner reported.

"We're moving to that side now," Tuna answered.

As we moved past the escalators, I heard what sounded like a baby crying echoing in the distance. I wasn't sure if I was actually hearing it or just imagining things, but it was followed by a man's voice yelling something.

"There's someone on the field," I said. "We need to check it out."

"On you," Tuna said as he took position on my right and Casper to my left.

We turned left toward the stands. As I reached the nearest entrance to the seating area, I could see people sitting in the middle of the football field. I stopped and took cover against the concrete wall as the others took up positions across from me at the entrance of the seating area.

"Jesus Christ," I said as I used the helmet's optical zoom. "There must be two hundred people here."

"I count six armed hostiles," Paco reported. He and Butch had moved to the next entrance over to survey the field.

There appeared to be mostly women and children sitting at the fifty-yard line with a few older males. It reminded me of what ISIS had done in Syria with rounding up women and children after taking over cities to use as slaves. I could only see three of the six guards. They were wearing civilian clothes and carrying M4-style rifles, possibly patrol rifles they had stolen from NOPD.

"Overwatch, are you seeing this?" Tuna asked over comms. The cameras in our helmets were linked to Tanner's displays on the aircraft orbiting overhead.

"I do. Would you like me to advise FBI HRT?" Tanner asked.

"Standby on that," Tuna said.

"Boss, not to pile on or anything, but two of the hostiles wearing NOPD uniforms are heading to the marked unit parked out front," Coolio added.

"Is Reverend Sharp with them?" I asked.

"He doesn't appear to be."

"Okay, Overwatch, advise local law enforcement of a possible impersonator attack. Get their faces to the authorities so they can issue a BOLO."

"Copy that," Tanner replied.

"What's the plan, boss?" Paco asked.

"We're going to clear this building. Neutralize any threats. Capture Reverend Sharp if we can, but the priority is to get these people to safety," Tuna replied.

"That's a lot of people down there," I said. "They might be safest in here once we take out their captors. I think we should focus on putting an end to this and getting Sharp."

"The people come first," Tuna replied. "Overwatch, start working on an exfil plan for approximately two hundred women and children."

"Are you sure you don't want me to alert HRT or the authorities?" Tanner asked.

"Not yet," Tuna said. "Is everyone ready?"

We all went down the line, answering in the affirmative. I wasn't happy with the plan, but Tuna had a lot more experience with this than I did, even when considering my time with SWAT. I trusted his leadership and had to have faith that he knew what he was doing.

"Let's roll," he said, moving back out toward the concession area and escalators.

CHAPTER FORTY-EIGHT

Our best chance at saving the hostages was to split up. Paco and I drew the proverbial short straw and were sent to the stairs to make our way to the suite level where we would cover the others from sniping positions.

As much as it sucked, sending the two of us made the most sense. I found out Paco had been a U.S. Army 1st Special Forces Operational Detachment-Delta Sniper prior to joining Tuna's group. At least, I thought that's what he meant when he said, "Relax, bro, I was a sniper with Delta."

I had spent most of my time with SWAT as a sniper, and had also been tasked with sniper duties with Odin. It wasn't a new role for me either, but doing it with this rifle and helmet-mounted display would take some getting used to.

Paco and I split up when we hit the suite level. From a tactical sniper perspective, the stadium gave us the best possible vantage points. The bottom box seating also gave us the best concealment and cover, using the concrete for protection.

For the team on the ground, however, the stadium was less than optimal. Their cover options were limited and the hostages were out in the open. If Paco and I missed our targets, the team would be exposed without the element of surprise.

The biggest help for them was the darkness. Whether by choice or by virtue of being on generator power, the only lighting was one spotlight shining on the hostages at mid-field and red lighting throughout the stands and concession areas. The cover of darkness was on our side for the most part.

I located the suite that Tanner had told me to use based on the map she pulled up. The door was unlocked, so I quickly entered and cleared the room before heading to the box seats. Based on the banner behind the bar, it was apparently a suite rented by a local accounting firm.

I made my way down to the lowest section of the seating area and set up behind the concrete barrier. I set up my shooting position between the railing and the concrete and lined up my sights on the guard nearest to me on the field.

The symbols in the HUD changed as I aimed. I thought it would be tough to get used to for a longer shot, but it seemed to adapt to the stable shooting position. The helmet displayed wind information and appeared to automatically correct for the distance and bullet drop. It took some of the fun out of it, breaking down what took years to learn and perfect to nothing more than putting the green thing on the bad guy's forehead.

"Bravo One in position," Paco announced.

"Bravo Two in position," I replied.

"Thirty seconds," Tuna replied. He and the others had gone down to the locker level on the lowest floor. He planned to access the field through the players' tunnel and exfil them to the street the same way.

"A second NOPD vehicle has arrived," Tanner reported. "Reverend Sharp and the remaining impersonators are walking out to the three vehicles out front."

"Keep an eye on the NOPD vehicles. Get their unit numbers if you can and send it to the on-scene commander," Tuna replied.

"I can't cover you and these vehicles," Tanner said.

"Prioritize the NOPD vehicles. We have a drone. We will be fine."

"What about Sharp? He's getting in the lead vehicle."

"We know where to find him. Are the authorities ready for these hostages?"

"SWAT will meet you at the entry control point on Poydras with medics."

"Alright, we're in position," Tuna said.

I steadied the crosshairs on my target. My display put indicators above the three other hostiles, indicating who was targeting them. I had no idea how it knew, but the amount of information it gave me was crazy. As Tuna and the team reached the tunnel exit, four indicators populated my display in addition to mine.

"3...2...1....Execute!" Tuna ordered.

I squeezed the trigger. The modified suppressor barely allowed a sound as the bolt cycled and the hostile collapsed onto the turf. The other four hostiles dropped simultaneously as Tuna and his team moved toward the hostages.

A woman screamed as she saw the guard next to her collapse. Tuna and the others spread out and quickly covered the distance between the tunnel and the hostages.

As the team secured the hostages and made sure they were unarmed, a flash of light blue caught my eye at one of the lower - level fan entrances to my right. I took aim with my rifle and saw a man in an NOPD uniform standing there watching Tuna and the rest of the team.

Placing the crosshairs on him, I hesitated. His uniform was convincing and I couldn't bring myself to squeeze the trigger on a cop, even knowing that he most likely was an imposter.

Before I could shake it off, the round hit the imposter in the forehead and he collapsed, tumbling down the stairs.

"What the hell are you doing, Bravo Two?" Paco asked. He had likely seen my targeting indicator over the NOPD officer and watched my hesitation in real time.

"I couldn't confirm he was hostile," I replied.

"If they're armed and in this AO, they're hostile. Knock that shit off before it gets one of us killed," Paco warned.

"Is there a problem up there?" Tuna asked.

"None, boss," I replied.

"Good. The hostages are all mobile. We're moving to extraction. Once we're in the tunnel, you can move to the secondary overwatch positions."

"Copy," Paco answered for us.

Tuna and the team rounded up the hostages and started toward the tunnel. Tuna took point while Casper took the left side and Butch brought up the rear. Without optical zoom from my vantage point, it almost looked like shepherds herding a flock.

The entire group of nearly two hundred people made it into the tunnel without incident. When Butch made it into the tunnel and called, "Clear," I started back up into the suite to egress and move to our secondary position. Paco remained in position to cover the tunnel and prevent any pop-up threats from following since he had a better angle from his perch.

"Bravo Two is on the move," I announced over comms.

As I reached the exit to the suite, I heard Tuna yell over comms, "Everybody hold position!"

"Casper, get up here," he added.

"What's going on, Alpha One?" Paco asked.

"Standby," Tuna replied.

It seemed like an eternity as we waited for them to sort out whatever they had found.

"Alright, all teams, we're going to have to find a secondary extraction," Tuna said finally. "These doors are all wired with explosives. We don't have time to disarm them all."

"Copy that," Paco replied. "Bravo Two, get back to your previous position."

"Overwatch, start working on a new exfil route for us," Tuna ordered.

"I'm on it," Tanner replied. "Also, heads up, Sharp and the NOPD vehicles are on the move."

"Copy."

I moved quickly back to my previous perch and hurried to get set up again. Our mission had just become even more complicated.

CHAPTER FORTY-NINE

The hostages flooded back onto the field from the same tunnel they had entered moments before. My suite had an excellent vantage point to their new destination on the other end of the field, so I resumed my previous position to cover them.

"The Blackhawk just landed at Lakefront Airport," Tanner reported. "Your friends are safe, Bravo Two."

"Thanks," I replied over the radio, breathing a small sigh of relief. It was good that at least that part of the mission had been successful so far.

I turned my focus back to covering Tuna and the hostages. Paco held his position until all of them were out of the tunnel.

"Bravo Two, you got'em?" he asked over comms.

"10-4," I replied.

"Roger. I'm moving ahead to find a new overwatch position to cover them out of the building."

"Take Bravo Two with you," Tuna directed.

"Negative," Paco replied. "I'll do better solo. Bravo Two needs to cover you on the field."

"Copy," Tuna said. "Keep us updated on your status."

"You got it, boss," Paco answered.

The herd of hostages moved more quickly than I expected across the field. Except for a few stragglers, they all moved with a sense of urgency as Butch led them to the opposite end. A lone hostile carrying a rifle emerged from the entrance to lower level stands across from me.

I quickly took aim as the helmet-mounted display did all the work and squeezed the trigger. He crumpled and rolled down the concrete stairs as I scanned for more threats behind him.

"Tango down, your nine o'clock," I called out.

"Tracking," Tuna replied. "Good kill."

There was no way to tell what threats were lurking in the concessions areas, but the seating area remained clear as the hostages crossed the field. As they reached the opposite tunnel, Paco radioed Tuna.

"Boss, I've got good news and bad news."

"What's up?"

"The good news is, there are no more hostiles on this side of the stadium or in Champion's Square. I just took out the last two standing watch out front."

"And the bad news?"

"Your secondary exit is also rigged with explosives."

"Okay, once we get through the tunnel, we'll take the stairs up to the plaza level and move exit through our infil on the west entrance. Overwatch, any chance you can get us a heavy lift helo?"

"I can try," Tanner replied.

"I'll start scouting the new route," Paco announced.

"Alpha One, where do you want me?" I asked.

"Cover our exit and then move to meet us at the west entrance," Tuna replied.

"10-4," I said.

I continued scanning for threats as the last of the hostages made it into the tunnel. Tuna lagged behind momentarily and then continued behind them.

"Clear," he called.

I waited a few seconds, looking for any sign that someone else might be in the stands or near the field. When I was satisfied that they were clear of all threats, I got up and headed back up the stairs to the suite.

"Bravo Two is on the move," I said over comms.

"Bad news," Tanner said. "The best I can get is two Blackhawks from the unit that picked up our friends. No heavy lift helos available."

"That won't work. We will have to get them to safety on foot."

I moved out of the suite and headed toward the stairwell. As I reached the door, I thought I heard something. The helmet had the ability to not only cancel noise and muffle gunshots, but also had a microphone to hear sounds far away.

Fumbling through the menu on my wrist controller, I found the feature and turned it on. The microphone picked up what sounded like a woman crying followed by, "Somebody please help me."

The display indicated that the isolated sound was just over thirty meters away and to my right, away from the suite I had just been in.

"Alpha One, Bravo One," I said over comms.

"Go," Tuna replied.

"I'm hearing a woman crying saying '*Help me*' on this floor. Possibly another hostage. I'm going to go check it out and meet you downstairs."

"Do it."

I turned toward the arrow and headed toward it with my rifle up and ready. As I moved closer, the pleas for help stopped and turned to sobbing. The indicator showed that the sound was coming from inside one of the suites.

"Louisiana State Police stopped one of the marked units and apprehended two of the imposters," Coolio announced over comms. "I'm still working on getting them to the other one."

"What about the reverend?" Tuna asked.

"I lost them while tracking the NOPD units," Tanner replied. "Can I send your video feed footage to the Joint Terrorism Taskforce so they can get a bomb team to the Superdome?"

"Have Coolio scrub the data from it and then send it," Tuna answered. "Let them know we're still bringing the hostages to them."

"Got it," Tanner replied.

As I approached the door, I tried switching to the thermal mode of the visor, but the concrete walls were too thick to see through. I stopped at the edge of the door and listened, hoping to get a fix on any other people in the room.

The only sound that could be heard was that of the woman sobbing. If there were others in the room with her, the microphone in my gear wasn't picking them up.

"I've reached the location of the voice," I said. "I'm going to breach."

"Keep me updated," Tuna replied coolly. I half expected him to tell me to wait for back up or, at the very least, to be careful. But that wasn't how this team operated. He trusted his people and expected us to make smart decisions. It was vastly different from my experience in law enforcement.

I stood off to the side and tried the handle on the door. I could feel the lock disengage as I pushed down. *Unlocked.*

I took a deep breath and gave myself a silent countdown as I readied my weapon. *Three…Two…One.*

As I hit one, I pushed the handle down and opened the door. *Don't get caught in the fatal funnel*, I reminded myself as I moved through the doorway. As I moved forward, I quickly checked left behind the door and then sidestepped right to clear the room.

The lights were off, but the night vision visor perfectly illuminated the suite. It was completely empty with no sign of the woman.

"Help me," I heard the woman mumble.

I continued clearing the suite. I checked behind the bar and found a woman with her hands and feet bound. Her mouth had been taped, but she had managed to remove it enough to speak as it hung loosely on her face.

I signaled for her to be quiet as I continued toward the box seats. Reaching the plexiglass divider before the stairs, I found a dead man and a rifle a few feet from her. I guessed that Paco had taken him out at some point while we were covering the hostages on the field. Either he didn't call it or I didn't hear him.

I removed the rifle and then returned to the woman. I slung my own rifle as I pulled out my knife to cut the duct tape around her wrists and feet.

"Oh thank God," she said. "Are you with the police?"

"No, ma'am," I said. "But it's going to be okay. You're safe now."

"You have to stop them. They're going to kill him."

"Stop who?"

She looked away, tears rolling down her cheeks.

"Stop *who?*"

"Reverend Sharp," she said.

"We're already working on it," I said. "Let's get you out of here."

"No, no. You don't understand."

"Understand what?"

"He's going to kill the mayor. You have to stop him."

CHAPTER FIFTY

"My name is Eloise Parker," the woman said as she grabbed on to the carry handle on my body armor. "I'm the Mayor's chief of staff."

"Bravo Two, status?" Tuna asked.

"Standby," I said as I stopped and turned around to face Eloise.

"You're what now?" I asked her.

"I'm the Mayor's chief of staff. She's at the rally in the French Quarter. They're going to kill her!"

"Who's going to kill her?" I asked.

"Reverend Sharp. I don't know how. I just know I overheard him talking about some plan to take her out."

"Don't worry, she'll be fine," I said. "We'll stop it. Let's get moving."

"I just don't understand why he did all of this. We all go to his church. This ain't like him. They told us we were protesting police brutality then they rounded us up and made us come here. He must've seen y'all coming because he took off from here fast and in a hurry. Then somebody shot that guard."

"Don't worry," I said as I placed her hand back on the carry handle on my armor. "You will be okay and so will the mayor."

"Overwatch, are you getting this?" I asked over comms, hoping they had been watching my video feed and heard the whole thing.

"I'm working on it, boss," Coolio responded. "Sharp's vehicle just stopped at the tent city. I do not have eyes on him."

"Bravo Two, get down here," Tuna barked. "We need to finish extracting these people."

"Good news on that front," Tanner interjected. "FBI tactical teams are repositioning to Poydras Street to help evacuate the hostages. They're about five minutes from the exclusion zone's entry control point."

Eloise wasn't nearly as fast or in shape as Jenny had been. She put a lot of her weight into holding onto the carry handle, adding heavy resistance if I tried to do anything more than a brisk walk. I tried to pick up the pace a bit, but each time I did, she let go of the carry handle, so I had to stop and wait for her.

"We don't have time to wait any longer," Tuna said. "Catch up when you can, Bravo Two."

"Copy," I said.

We reached the stairwell and had to stop as Eloise caught her breath. I guessed that she was in her early sixties, but it was hard to tell.

"I'm sorry, ma'am, but we have to keep moving," I said.

"Okay," she said as she put her hand on her chest. "I can do it."

"We're going downstairs, so that shouldn't be too bad," I said. "Just hold on and stay close."

"Okay."

The stairs proved to be more of a challenge for Eloise than I anticipated. Every few steps, she stumbled and started to fall. She used the carry handle to catch her fall, nearly bringing me down with her several times. A few times, I also had to turn and outright catch her as she fell forward. She was either really weak from whatever they had done to her in captivity, or in really bad shape or both.

"Two hostiles fifty meters ahead of you," I heard Paco call out over comms.

It was followed shortly with, "Hostiles neutralized."

"Copy," Tuna replied. "We've reached the pedestrian ramp and are heading to the street level."

We were making terrible time. Based on our glacial progress down the stairs, I had a feeling the herd of hostages would be gone by the time we reached the exit. It was entirely possible that we would be on our own the entire way to the safe zone. There was no way I would be able to face any threats with her dragging me down. We had to pick up the pace.

"We need to keep moving," I said as she stumbled again. "We're almost there. Don't give up on me."

"I'm trying, honey," she said. "But these legs ain't what they used to be."

"Bravo Two, what's your status?" Tuna asked over the radio.

"We're five minutes to the exit," I replied. It was an optimistic timeline, but for the last few steps, Eloise had seemed to pick up the pace slightly.

"Bravo One will stay behind with you," Tuna replied. "We're about to link up with the FBI team."

"10-4," I replied.

As we reached the final flight of stairs, Eloise stopped and tried to catch her breath. "Oh lawd, you are working me today. I've got to rest."

"Ma'am, we don't have that option right now," I said. "This place is rigged with explosives and is not safe."

"You go ahead, sugar. The Lord will provide for me."

"I appreciate that, but right now I'm the one providing a way out for you. And we have to keep moving."

I cleared down the stairs and back up behind us and then gently took her hand. "Just a few more steps. You can do this."

"Alright, honey," she said as she clenched my hand. "Let's go."

I helped her down one step at a time, doing my best to clear for threats as we made our way down the stairs. Helping her directly seemed to pick up the pace slightly, but I hated how vulnerable it made us. We were completely screwed if a popup threat emerged above or below us.

Reaching the bottom of the stairs, I stopped and motioned for her to stay there. I opened the door and cleared left and then right on the plaza level. Satisfied there were no threats, I motioned for her to join me and then we moved toward the doors.

"Bravo Two has reached the exit," I announced over comms.

"Copy," Tuna replied. "Once we get all of the hostages to safety, we'll link back up with you. Bravo One, status?"

"Moving to rendezvous with Bravo Two," Paco replied.

I helped Eloise get through the turnstiles and then on through the doors. Once outside, I saw Paco heading toward us. He motioned for us to come toward him as he spun around and dropped to a knee.

"Okay, it's not that far. No more stairs this time. It's a ramp to the street level," I told her reassuringly. "We're going to get you through this."

She nodded as she grabbed the carry handle one more time. We started toward Paco and Eloise finally picked up the pace. As we reached him, he fell in behind us to cover our rear as we moved toward the pedestrian ramp in front of the exit that had been rigged with explosives.

As we started down the ramp, I saw the tail end of the hostages and Butch about an eighth of a mile away on Poydras Street. The first of the hostages should have been just reaching the entry control point to the safe area outside the exclusion zone under the I-10 Overpass.

A bullet zipped by as we reached the bottom of the ramp on the street level. The helmet display located the shooter and marked it with an arrow. I pushed Eloise behind the concrete ramp and took aim. Before I could fire, Paco fired two shots, neutralizing the shooter.

"That was close," he said. "Keep your head on a swivel."

Paco covered me as I helped Eloise back up and helped brush the street grime off her. "Are you okay?" I asked.

"I think so," she said. "But I fell on my bad knee."

"We don't have much farther to go. Just past that overpass," I said, pointing to the I-10 overpass to my left.

"Okay, I can do it," she said. "Let's do this."

I held on to her arm as she limped forward, nearly falling against the concrete wall of the pedestrian ramp. I looked at Paco and shook my head.

"Shit," he hissed.

"The last of the hostages are in the exclusion zone," Tuna announced. "Bravo One, we're heading to you. Where are you?"

"Still at the stadium. We're not going to be able to move very fast," Paco replied.

"We're heading to you and will cover you. Keep moving," Tuna replied.

"I'll help her," I said. "You watch our ass."

Paco nodded as I slung my rifle and put her left arm over my shoulders. I considered doing a fireman carry, but she was far too large and unwieldy for that. There was no way I could carry her that far. I tried my best to support her weight with her injured left knee tapping the ground as we moved forward.

We made it to Poydras Street and rendezvoused with Tuna and company without incident. With three others to help cover us, Paco slung his rifle and put Eloise's other arm over his shoulder. Despite her girth, the two of us were able to nearly lift her off the ground and forced her to move faster.

There were no threats as we carried her to the exclusion zone. Once we made it through the entry control point, medics helped put Eloise on a stretcher.

"Thank you so much, boys," she said. "But y'all need to go make sure the good reverend don't do nothing stupid."

"We're on it, ma'am," I said. "Don't worry."

CHAPTER FIFTY-ONE

The tent city was a tactical nightmare. The occupiers had set up two entry control points with armed guards, plus roving patrols around the perimeter. It was not an amateur operation.

A frontal assault was out of the question. There were too many unarmed people milling about the area. There was a high risk of them being used as human shields or taking up arms themselves. We had no idea who the rioters were and how many, if any, were hostages like the people in the Superdome. We simply didn't have the manpower to pull it off, and we weren't going to get any help from official channels.

We had considered sending Casper and Paco in to blend in as rioters. As long as no one challenged them, they could get in and find Reverend Sharp so we could extract him without any bloodshed.

But despite Casper's persistence, Tuna wasn't on board with that idea. There was too much risk that they would be discovered, captured, or killed. As much as he wanted to stop Sharp, he argued, he wasn't willing to risk any member of his team. Our primary mission had been accomplished by rescuing Hyatt and Jenny. Anything beyond that was secondary and therefore had a lower acceptable risk threshold.

So, instead of taking down the camp, we watched and waited. I took up position atop the parking garage of Tulane Medical Center. It was directly across the street from Duncan Plaza, one of two parks where rioters had set up tent cities. It was right next to City Hall and appeared to serve a command and control function as well as some medical care for the injured.

Paco perched on the roof of the parking garage across the street from us while Tuna, Butch, and Casper stayed at street level in the Suburban we borrowed from the FBI. Our mission was only to watch the camp and wait for Sharp to make his next move, but I was set up with my rifle to make the shot should the opportunity present itself. I wasn't going to let him slip away again.

I scanned the camp for any signs of Sharp from my vantage point. Paco also relaunched the micro-drone with a new battery and Tanner was still overhead with the sensors on the aircraft. As we left the FBI's staging area, she reported that Louisiana State Police had apprehended the second marked unit with the imposter NOPD officers. As far as we knew, Sharp was the last link to stopping whatever they were planning.

"I've got sensors on Judas," Paco announced over comms, indicating he had found Reverend Sharp. "West side of the compound, exiting what appears to be a command tent. Four hostiles with rifles with him."

"Copy," Tuna replied. "Overwatch, run facial recognition to confirm that's him."

"Working it," Coolio replied.

I checked the display on my forearm and accessed Paco's drone feed. Sharp's face was clearly visible as he walked toward an SUV. I looked up in my display and tried to find him with my helmet-mounted display. The green arrow in my visor pointed to his location relative to my position. I found him and took aim with my rifle.

The aiming reticle compensated for the distance, target movement, and environmental conditions as I placed it on Sharp's head.

"Bravo Two, stand down," Tuna said, apparently seeing that I had targeted Sharp. "Do not take the shot. We need him alive."

I hesitated as I tracked Sharp across the park. He was pure evil and needed to die, but Tuna made a good point - killing Sharp wouldn't lead us to Houston or stopping whatever was next in their plan. He was more valuable alive.

"Don't do it!" Tuna added.

"Copy," I said. "Judas is heading to his vehicle."

"We'll move to intercept. Standby."

There were only two ways to exit the park. The street to the east had been blockaded with a burned out car and the south side was lined with police barricades from when the park served as protest grounds in front of City Hall across the street. We had both routes covered with our vantage points atop the two parking garages.

I watched Sharp get into the SUV through the right rear passenger door while three of his goons joined him and the other stayed behind. They pulled out of the row of SUVs and headed toward me. I adjusted my targeting reticle on the driver, waiting for Tuna to give the order.

When it reached the street, the SUV turned left toward Paco's position and where Tuna and the others were parked.

"Bravo One, tracking," Paco called out. "Bravo Two, you're cleared to reposition."

"Moving," I replied as I stood and started running to the other side of the parking garage to get a better shot.

Sharp and his goons didn't seem to be in a big hurry. They were still only going twenty or twenty five miles per hour by the time I reached the other side of the garage.

"Send it," Tuna ordered.

Paco fired his rifle, striking the driver and causing the SUV to veer off to the left and strike a parked car. Tuna and company sped toward them in the SUV and stopped in front of them.

I had a clear shot to the occupants on the right side. I dispatched the armed front passenger as he got out and tried to raise his rifle. The round struck him in the back of the head, causing him to crumple back into the vehicle.

Paco took out the remaining armed gunman on the other side as Tuna and Butch reached the SUV. Reverend Sharp attempted to exit, but Butch grabbed him and lifted him up off his feet by his collar as he slammed him back into the asphalt.

He quickly flipped him over and flexcuffed his hands behind his back before they dragged him back to the SUV.

"Move to extraction," Tuna ordered over the radio as they reached the Suburban.

I looked back toward the camp to ensure no hostiles were responding. When I was satisfied it was clear, I ran to the stairs and headed to the ground level.

The Suburban was waiting for me outside by the time I got there. Somehow Paco had beaten me to it as I got in and saw Sharp hogtied and gagged in the cargo area.

"Overwatch, we'll meet you shortly."

"Your route is clear to the exclusion zone," Tanner replied.

As we sped away, I looked back at Sharp squirming in the back. After everything he had done, I was looking forward to watching him break.

I only wished Kruger could be there to interrogate him. He was an expert at breaking evil assholes like Sharp.

CHAPTER FIFTY-TWO

I wasn't allowed to watch the interrogation of Reverend Sharp in the back of Tuna's business jet. Despite my objections, he believed I was too emotionally invested and would only hinder the time-critical progress.

Instead, I was reunited with Hyatt and, most importantly, Jenny in the pilot lounge of the New Orleans Lakefront Airport's fixed-base operator. Although I had really wanted to be a part of breaking Sharp, taking a shower, getting some food, and hanging out with Jenny in the FBO's big, comfortable leather chairs felt amazing. It was good to finally be out of that gear and having her safe by my side.

Jenny didn't want to talk about her time with Houston, and I didn't press the issue. After eating, Hyatt had fallen asleep in the lounger across from us. It was clear they both had been through a lot in the last forty-eight hours.

Agent Tanner walked in carrying a folder. She saw Hyatt sleeping and made an exaggerated effort to stay quiet as she walked up to our chair and squatted down next to us.

"The agents working the case will want a debrief with them and then everyone is free to go home," Tanner whispered. "We'll have Houston on kidnapping and conspiracy charges."

"How's it going with Reverend Sharp?" I whispered back.

Tanner shrugged. "I'm not allowed in there either."

"And the FBI is okay with that?"

"They don't have a choice. Tuna calls the shots."

"What exactly is he doing now, anyway?"

"I can't say."

"Because you don't know or you can't tell me?"

"Does it matter?"

"I guess not."

Before I could ask a follow up question, Tuna appeared in the doorway and nodded for me and Tanner to join him.

"I'll be right back," I told Jenny as I gently pulled my arm from under her and got up. "Get some rest."

"Don't be gone too long," Jenny replied as I bent down and kissed her.

"I won't," I said before turning to follow Tanner and Tuna.

We walked out into the hallway. To my left, I saw Tuna's business jet sitting parked out front and a few SUVs parked next to it. Two serious-looking men in suits walked in escorting Reverend Sharp. He was wearing leg and hand restraints as he shuffled into the lobby and then turned to the exit before reaching us.

"Where's he going?" I asked as I stopped to watch.

"Federal custody," Tuna replied.

"So, he can lawyer up and the feds can eventually cut him loose?"

"What did you expect, Troy? He has to answer for his crimes," Tanner interjected. "He'll have his day in court."

"I wish I could believe that," I said.

"Not out here," Tuna growled as he motioned for us to follow him.

We walked down the hall and into room labeled *Mission Planning* with maps and charts everywhere. Tuna closed the door as we sat down at a small table and he joined us.

"Are you ever going to tell me who you're working for?" I asked.

"It's not important right now," Tuna replied.

"And what is important? You're letting a cop killer walk."

"He will face justice."

"You really believe that?" I asked. "With his connections and how much this city loves him? Who's going to convict him?"

"You're not thinking clearly, Troy," Tanner said. "Don't let your frustration get the best of you."

"Frustration? Is that what you call this? That asshole killed an innocent woman and good cops – my friends! I'm not frustrated. I'm fucking *pissed*. And you and I both know that there's no chance that piece of shit will get the justice he *deserves*."

Tanner leaned in close and lowered her voice. "So, you want to kill him? Is that it? Do you realize what that would do? He's the *leader* of the Crescent City New Republic. We're just now finding this out. If we would have killed him, it would have made him a martyr. That mob would've killed twice as many cops. Instead, we're going to publicly bring him in and the governor intends to take back the city."

"People are going to die either way. They're not going to go down without fight."

"The fake cops weren't the only part of the plan," Tuna said. "He wasn't going to be the one to kill the Mayor."

"Then who was?"

"White supremacists," Tuna answered. "Or at least, people posing as white supremacists."

"What?"

Tanner pulled out her phone and showed me a mug shot of a man with tattoos on his face and neck. "This is Walter Carey. Leader of a local militant Marxist group called The NOLA 5. Reverend Sharp was supplying them money and weapons."

"Sharp wasn't going to kill the Mayor," Tuna added. "*They* were. He was just giving them the means, opportunity, and access to the Mayor."

"To what end?" I asked.

"War," Tanner answered. "New Orleans isn't isolated. It's ground zero for something bigger."

"So, they create the riots, destabilize law enforcement, and then add a third party?"

"Pretty much," Tanner said. "Their goal is to get people to join in. And with how divided the country is politically already, it's not hard to imagine their plan working."

"Remember the IEDs at the stadium?" Tuna asked, referring to the explosives on the entrances.

"Yeah," I said.

"They were going to pin that on the right-wing groups for killing innocent women and children who took shelter to get away from the riots."

"That is fucking sick," I said. "And you're going to let that evil little bastard live?"

"He's just a pawn," Tuna said. "And to deescalate the situation here, as I said, we need him alive. He will answer for what he's done."

"It's cute that you think arresting him will do any of that."

"The FBI is handling it," Tanner reassured me. "Whatever corruption you saw at the local level won't be a factor."

"Oh, like *they're* any better?"

"Hey!" Tanner protested. "That's not fair."

"What's your deal right now, dude?" Tuna asked.

"That piece of shit is directly responsible for the murder of good cops – *my friends*. After all the bullshit I've been through, I have zero confidence than anything short of a bullet will put a stop to this. It's naïve to think otherwise."

"You're entitled to your opinion, but this is the way it's going to be," Tuna said.

"What about Houston?" I asked. "Did you find him?"

"Sharp gave us a location. Coolio is working on verifying it right now."

"And you're going to *arrest* him too?"

"We're going to do what's necessary to stop the threat. How that plays out will be up to him."

"Okay," I said. "When do we leave?"

"As soon as the FBI is finished debriefing your friends, we'll take you home on the jet and you can go back to living your life. I've even arranged for a replacement truck to be delivered to your house."

"Fuck that, I'm going with you," I said. "It's time to finish this – with Houston and that Veronica Carver chick who's pulling his strings."

Tuna laughed as he stood. "Dude, you're in the wrong mindset for an operation like this. That's not something I can have on my team."

"It wasn't a problem rescuing the hostages or grabbing Sharp, was it?" I argued.

"No, but had you made the same comments before, I would've had you sit that out too. You've been in this business long enough to know that there's no place for emotions. If you let your anger get the best of you out there, people will die. I'm not willing to risk it."

"I know it's not what you want to hear," Tanner interjected. "But it's for the best. You and Jenny need to go home and let us take care of it."

Tuna stepped around the table and put his hand on my shoulder. "I know you've been through a lot, man. You're like a brother to me, but your head is not in the game right now. I promise I will follow up with you and let you know what happens, and that the people responsible for this will answer for what they've done. But it's time for you to go home."

I stood as the anger started to build. "Sending me home after all of this. Yeah, sounds real brotherly alright. Thanks for nothing."

CHAPTER FIFTY-THREE

There wasn't much to say on the flight back to San Antonio. Jenny and I hung out in the back of the aircraft while Tuna and his team coordinated their next mission with Coolio using video teleconferencing.

After Jenny and Hyatt finished their chats with the FBI agents, we said goodbye to Hyatt. A sheriff's office helicopter picked him up and brought him back to the Northshore. He promised not to mention seeing me to anyone.

"No one would believe me anyway," he said as we hugged it out and said goodbye.

We both knew we would probably never see each other again, and as much as I hated it, I hoped that would be true. My return from the grave had brought him nothing but turmoil. The farther away I stayed, the better.

It was a short flight to the San Antonio International Airport. We landed and taxied to the general aviation side of the airport where a car was waiting for us.

"Thank you for helping us," I said to Tuna as we exited the aircraft.

"Anytime," Tuna replied with a smirk. "But don't make it a habit."

"Promise me you'll take those nut jobs down."

"They will answer for what they've done," Tuna replied. "Don't worry."

"I want video."

Tuna laughed. "I'll see what we can do."

Tanner followed us to the car and gave us both hugs. "I'm really glad you're both home safely now."

"Thank you for everything," I said. "You answered when we needed you. I really appreciate it."

"Well, like Tuna said, don't make a habit of it. But it's fine. You uncovered some really evil stuff that I'm glad we'll be able to put a stop to."

"A lot of people good people have died because of them," I said.

"And they will answer for it," Tanner replied. "But there is some good news."

"What's that?"

"After we landed and you were talking to Tuna, I got a call from the agents in New Orleans. Detective Jackson is awake and expected to make a full recovery."

"That's awesome!"

"It gets better. He's already agreed to testify."

"Testify for what?"

"Against Reverend Sharp and the bribes he and a few others were receiving to look the other way."

"Shit," I said. It pained me to hear that cops were on the take. Despite Jackson's distrust for me, I respected him and had thought he was one of the good ones. I was glad he was trying to atone for his sins, but the fact that he was corrupt in the first place was incredibly disappointing.

"I thought he was one of the good ones," I added.

"I haven't seen his statement yet, but from what I understand, it's complicated."

"What's complicated about being a corrupt cop?"

"Sharp was helping their families in low income areas – housing, food, medical bills, etc. They were working legitimate paid security details for the church. They were loyal to him, but it's not clear yet what those cops were doing for him. What Jackson is really giving us is a look into Sharp's operation. Don't be too hard on him."

"I hope you're right and it really just was loyalty versus outright corruption. Definitely keep me updated."

"Oh, you will be," Tanner said. "Don't be surprised if either of you are asked to testify before a grand jury."

I squirmed slightly. "I'm not so sure that's such a good idea."

"Relax," Tanner said. "It will be sealed and you will be treated the same as someone in witness protection."

"Okay," I reluctantly agreed. "Whatever you need."

Tanner hugged each of us again and we said our goodbyes before getting into the car. The driver took us to the long-term lot on the other side of the airport where Jenny's car was still parked.

We stopped for lunch and then headed to Jenny's parents' house to pick up her dog. After a brief visit, we continued our drive to our house outside of Fredericksburg. A brand new replacement pickup was waiting in my driveway with a note on the windshield.

Don't wreck this one

- *Tuna*

The keys were in the gas fill door, and I opened it up to find that he had spared no expense in the interior. I checked the underseat storage in the backseat, unlocked it, and found a brand new rifle similar to the ones Tuna's team used, magazines, the Dragonsilk body armor, and the fancy helmet that we had used on the last mission. A note was left on top of the lightweight armor.

Just in case.

I lowered the seat and locked the storage compartment before getting in and starting the truck. I drove to Deputy First Class Will Miller's house to pick up Kruger.

"Wilson!" Miller said as he answered the door. "You okay?"

Miller's seven-month-old K-9 in training stood next to him as he held his collar.

"I'm good, man," I said. "How's the new puppy?"

"Carter is a good dog, just a little skittish. We're working on that. Puppies are so much work. I still miss Freya."

Miller had lost Freya while trying to apprehend a kidnapper just before the school attack in Fredericksburg nearly a year ago. He had been sent back to patrol without a K-9 while the sheriff's department waited for grant money to train a new dog.

"Where's Kruger?"

"Sergeant Maclin wanted to keep her. If you would've called before just showing up, I could've saved you the drive."

"Maybe I just wanted to see you and Carter-pup, here," I replied with a grin.

"Yeah, yeah. Save it for your hot teacher. Do you want me to give you his number or do you think you can manage?"

I laughed. "I've got it."

"What the hell happened over there? You were in the news for a day about being a murder suspect and then it all just disappeared."

"It's a long story. Let's grab a beer sometime and I'll tell you about it," I said, knowing that what I'd tell him would only be a third of what actually happened.

"Sounds good, man."

I bent down and gave Carter a pat on the head before turning back to my truck.

"Sweet new ride. Doesn't that thing have like seven hundred horsepower?" Miller asked as he noticed my new truck.

"I guess so," I said. Honestly, I was clueless about it.

"Must be nice! Those things are super expensive."

I shrugged, again having no idea about it other than what Tuna's notes had said.

"You'll have to give me some investment advice if you're able to afford that kind of thing. Wow."

"Over beers," I said as I turned toward the truck. "Talk to you later."

I dialed Sgt. Maclin's cell as I backed out of Miller's driveway and headed that way.

"I don't have bail money. So, don't even ask," Maclin answered.

"Hey, sarge. Just got back to town and was wondering if I could swing by and pick up Kruger."

"What makes you think she's still assigned to you?"

"Hope?" I replied sheepishly.

"You're on your way?"

"Yes, sir."

"We'll talk when you get here," he said before abruptly ending the call.

That's not good.

It was a five minute drive to Maclin's house. When I arrived, he was sitting on a rocking chair on his front porch, smoking a cigar as Kruger lay next to him.

As soon as I exited the truck, she sprinted toward me, nearly barreling me over as she plowed into me and turned for me to scratch her wiggling butt. I squatted down and hugged her neck as she licked my face.

"Don't get too comfortable with her," Maclin warned from the porch.

I stood as Kruger took her place next to me. We walked up the three steps to the porch and met Maclin who stayed in the chair.

"Sit," he ordered.

I slowly sat down in the rocking chair next to him. Kruger sat next to me, nudging my hand for me to continue scratching her head.

"Look, I'm sorry about-"

"Stop," he said, letting out a cloud of smoke from his cigar. "I just want to know one thing from you."

"What's that?"

He looked at me and paused as he stared into my eyes. I could tell no matter what he said next, he was looking to gauge my reaction.

"Who's Alex Shepherd?"

"Me," I said without hesitation. I knew there was no way he was asking a question he didn't already know the answer to, and lying would just make things worse. I had no idea how he knew, but the fact that he was asking meant someone had tipped him off.

"Or at least, it used to be," I added as Maclin stared at me without reacting.

Maclin nodded as he took another hit from his cigar and exhaled a puff of smoke. He stared off into the distance as he considered his next words.

"Nice truck," he said without looking at me.

"Thanks," I replied.

"Horrible thing that happened to your family," Maclin said, still staring off into the distance. "Watched it live on TV after we put down a few assholes of our own. It could've easily been us too."

I said nothing, just trying not to think about it. Kruger licked my hand as she realized I was stressed.

"I don't blame you for wanting to start over. Wish you'd have told me, but I understand why you didn't."

"I'm sorry," I said, not knowing what else to say or where he was going with this conversation.

Maclin pulled out his phone and unlocked it, swiping to the photos before handing it to me.

"Recognize this fella?"

I took the phone from him. On the screen was a security camera photo of a man in a dark suit. As I zoomed in, I realized it was Wade Carver – the asshole that had nearly killed Tanner and me while looking for Kruger.

"Said his name was Special Agent George with the FBI. Showed up right after you were in the news for that murder charge. Said he thought you were really Alex Shepherd and mixed up in some kind of Russian mafia thing which was why the school was attacked last year."

"He's not with the FBI," I said.

Maclin laughed. "Oh, I know. As soon as he left, I called my buddy in San Antonio who runs that office. They had never heard of him and no such agent was in the area."

"I *was* Shepherd, but none of the other stuff is true, except the school attack. They were Russians, but they were coming after me. I'm not with them."

"So, what is the truth?"

I hesitated for a second and then decided to tell him. If I couldn't stay in Fredericksburg, I really had no other options. And with as much as he already knew, I figured the truth was my only shot.

So, over the next thirty minutes, I told him everything that happened from going to the Middle East to joining Odin. The only thing I left out was my path of vengeance between waking up from the coma and leaving for Iraq. I figured that part was better left untold. Not that I regretted doing it, but I didn't want to confess to something that was essentially its own series of crimes.

"And this George fellow is dead?" Maclin asked.

"After I was released, I went looking for the people responsible. I found the guy, but they took my friends hostage and me to Nashville. He wanted to find out what happened to one of the special ops guys I used to work with. He was killed by that team."

"So, this is over?"

I nodded. "The group that helped me rescue Jenny and Hyatt are seeing to that as we speak. Everyone will be brought to justice."

"What do you want to happen next?"

"Well, right now I'm starving. I'd like to take my dog and go home to my fiancée who's hopefully cooking something good. Then I'd like to get back to work at the school and go back to just being Deputy Troy Wilson, School Resource Officer."

Maclin considered it for a moment. "Like nothing ever happened, huh?"

"As much as possible, yes."

He killed the remainder of his cigar into the ashtray on the table next to him and stood, holding out his hand.

"Welcome back, Troy," he said as I stood and shook his hand.

"Good to be home," I replied. "And speaking of home, I better get back."

"Take a few days off, and then check in with me. I'll put you on a shift until it's time to go back to school."

"Ten-four," I replied. "Thanks, sarge."

I got back in my truck and headed for home. Less than a mile from my house, my phone rang. I still hadn't set up the truck's Bluetooth, so I pulled it out of my pocket and answered.

"Did you get that son of a bitch yet?" I asked after noticing that the caller ID belonged to Special Agent Tanner.

"Troy, I've got bad news," Tanner replied. "You're not going to like it."

"Is everyone okay? Is it Tuna?"

"Everyone is fine," Tanner replied. "But we lost Houston and Carver."

"What the fuck? How?"

"That's unclear right now," Tanner replied. "We think they might be together and on their way to Beijing."

"Why do you think that?"

"A jet registered to one of Carver's holding companies departed Fort Worth Alliance Airport not long after Houston was last seen. The flight plan showed it headed for Beijing."

"So, shoot his ass down."

"I wish it were that simple."

I pulled into my driveway and parked, leaving the engine running as we continued the conversation.

"So, you're headed to China?"

"We're headed back to Virginia, Troy. That's why I'm calling you. You need to be careful."

"You're not going to go get him?"

Tanner's voice dropped to a whisper. "We've been ordered to stand down. We can't do anything anymore, Troy."

"Stand down? I thought Tuna was his own boss. Who ordered it?"

"The President," Tanner whispered. "He doesn't want any further issues with the Chinese. They're off limits for now, Troy. I'm sorry. But you need to watch your back. Just in case."

"Thanks for nothing," I said angrily before hanging up.

CHAPTER FIFTY-FOUR

TWO WEEKS LATER

"Troy! Do you hear that?" Jenny asked frantically, waking me up from a dead sleep. "Someone's in the house!"

I was up, out of bed, and holding the Glock 17 from my nightstand before she even finished her sentence. Seeing the commotion, Kruger leapt from her bed and joined me as I headed for the bedroom door wearing nothing but my boxers.

"Go in the bathroom and lock the door," I whispered.

Jenny grabbed her handgun from the nightstand and carried her dog with her into the bathroom. When I heard the door lock, I unlocked our bedroom door and headed into the hallway with my handgun up and ready.

I cleared the guest room, shining the weapon-mounted light briefly as I checked all four corners before heading back into the hallway. Kruger followed, not alerting to the presence of anyone. I was too tired to consider what that meant as I moved toward the living room.

Kruger led the way this time as we entered the living room. She went straight for her Kong and tried to bring it to me as I swept for threats and then cleared the kitchen. There was no one in the house and she knew it.

I checked the garage and under our vehicles before heading out into the yard. Kruger followed me, taking the opportunity to use the bathroom as I checked the front yard and then walked around to the back. I heard a coyote in the distance, but there were no signs of humans anywhere around.

"C'mon, girl," I said as we went back into the house.

We walked back into the bedroom, and I put my weapon back on the nightstand. "It's clear, honey. You can come back out."

The door unlocked and Jenny emerged, holding her gun and dog. I looked at the clock and sighed. It was just after 4 a.m. My alarm would go off in an hour. There was no way I was getting back to sleep.

"We've got to stop doing this," I said as I sat on the bed and rubbed my eyes.

"I'm sorry," Jenny said softly as she holstered her gun and sat next to me.

She put her arm around me and rested her head on my shoulder. "This is miserable."

"Third time this week. At least we're getting better. Last week it was every night."

"I really thought I heard something," Jenny said.

"I know," I said, putting my hand on hers. "Better to be safe."

"Do you think they'll ever get Houston and that lady?"

"I don't know," I replied. I had only talked to Tanner once since she called me on the way home from Maclin's house. She didn't have anything to offer, other than they were still "monitoring" the situation and she had been reassigned to another case. She would let me know if she found out anything, but I should stay vigilant just in case.

Despite all they had done for us in New Orleans, I thought it was a shitty thing for friends to do to us. They had basically thrown in the towel and abandoned us, leaving us to fend for ourselves against a threat that may or may not even be coming.

"Ugh, it's 4:05," Jenny said as she looked at the clock and then collapsed onto the bed.

"Try to go back to sleep."

"You know I won't be able to sleep after that, but don't let me keep you up. You need your rest. I'll go watch TV in the living room or something."

"I guess we're up then, because there's no way I'm sleeping either."

"I'll go make coffee," Jenny said before yawning. "God, today is going to be so painful. In-service training all day before school starts in two weeks."

"I'll be right there with you," I said as I leaned down and kissed her.

"Didn't you say you were working the road until the kids come back?"

"I am. But the Sheriff wanted all the SROs to be there for in-service training with you. Let the new teachers get used to us and all that."

"You never told me that."

"I'm pretty sure I did."

"Really?"

"Yes, ma'am."

"Hmpf."

She got up and headed for the kitchen. Bear followed, causing Kruger to groan as he trotted by her bed and hopped over her outstretched paws.

"I know, girl," I said as I stood and stretched. "It's going to be a long day."

* * *

"You don't have to stay and wait for everyone to leave," Principal Lawrence said as I walked into her office with Kruger. "A few teachers are getting their classrooms ready. I'll lock up after them."

"Yeah, Jenny is one of them. I'll stick around," I said.

"Are you okay?" Lawrence asked. "Lots of crazy stuff about you in the news not too long ago."

"I'm fine," I said. "It was all a misunderstanding. Funny how that part never makes the news."

"Well, I'm just glad you're okay. That city is such a mess now. Those poor people," Lawrence said, shaking her head. "I'm just glad they arrested the guy behind it. How awful to be using a church for such things!"

If you only knew, lady.

I nodded and turned as Mr. Lerner waddled in. He was a portly science teacher with thick glasses and a ridiculous-looking bowtie.

"Deputy Wilson! Good, I'm glad you're here. There's something that needs your attention."

"What's up?" I asked.

"It might be nothing, but I've been seeing the same white van drive by at least five times today while working in the chemistry lab. It's parked out there now. The kids aren't here, so it's probably nothing, but you told us to let you know if we saw anything weird at any time."

"I'll check it out, thanks," I said as I clenched Kruger's leash and we headed out the door.

I walked out of the office and turned left toward Jenny's classroom. With no kids around, my first thought was her safety. We reached her room and I quickly opened the door.

"Stay in here. Lock the door," I said.

"What's going on?" Jenny asked, startled by my sudden entrance.

"I'm not sure, but stay here and don't open the door for anyone until I come back."

"Okay," Jenny said as she dropped what she was working on and walked to the door.

I turned and exited as she closed and locked the door behind me. We walked past the office and outside to my marked Chevrolet Tahoe. I opened the door for Kruger to hop in her specially made area in the back and then got in.

We drove around the block, out of sight of where the van was last seen. As we reached the street in front of Mr. Lerner's lab, I saw the white van parked next to a curb. It appeared to be running and its brake lights were illuminated.

I called in to central dispatch and advised them that I was initiating a traffic stop on a suspicious vehicle. A unit nearby keyed up that he was en route to back me up in response as I activated my overhead emergency lights and pulled behind the van.

"Driver, turn off the vehicle and step out," I ordered over the Tahoe's loudspeaker.

I exited my vehicle with my hand on my weapon, lowering the Level 3 self-locking hood and depressing the automatic locking retention button as I prepared to draw. I heard Kruger whining as she started to get excited, ready to take down the asshole if he did anything stupid.

The driver complied, putting the vehicle in park and then slowly stepped out with his hands raised slightly. "Easy, officer."

"Walk to the front of my vehicle and put your hands on the hood," I said.

"What's this about, sir?"

"Is there anyone else in the vehicle?" I asked.

"No, sir. Just me."

Kruger's whine had turned to barking as she saw the man approaching.

"You hear that dog? If you're lying to me, you won't like what she has to say."

"I promise you I'm not lying," he said as he reached the push bar on my Tahoe and put his hands on the hood. He was wearing jeans and a white t-shirt without any company logo or anything identifiable on it.

The backup unit arrived. It was Deputy Bader, a young rookie who had just finished the Field Training program and recently been road certified. He approached from the passenger side as I covered the vehicle and kept an eye on the man.

"Check the vehicle for other occupants," I told Bader before moving toward the man.

"You're not under arrest, but for your safety and mine, I'm placing you in handcuffs for the time being," I said as I grabbed his right wrist and placed it behind his back.

The man complied and offered his other arm as I cuffed him.

"Do you have any weapons on you? Anything that can poke me or stick me?"

"Just a pocket knife," the man said.

"Where?"

"Right front pocket."

"And that's it?"

"That's it."

I did a pat-down for weapons and found the knife. I removed it from his pocket and placed it on the hood.

Once I was satisfied that he didn't have anything on him, I walked him to the curb, made him cross his ankles and then sat him down.

"What's your name?"

"Eric Kline. Can you please tell me what this is about, sir?"

"Where's your ID?"

"In the center console of the van."

"Is there anything illegal in the vehicle?"

Kline sighed and then looked away. "I didn't do anything."

"Remember that dog I told you about? She'll find it if you don't tell me."

"Look, bro, it's just a bag of weed."

A bag of weed. Either Houston wasn't sending his best and brightest after us, or this guy had nothing to do with us.

"And that's it?"

"I swear to God."

"No weapons?"

"No, man, I'm on probation."

"For what?"

"Nothing."

"Nothing? They just threw you in jail for nothing?"

"Burglary," he said, staring at the ground. "But it was five years ago!"

Bader returned, shaking his head. "Vehicle is empty."

"There's a bag of weed in the center console. See if you can get his ID."

Bader nodded and headed back to the van.

"I can't go back to jail, man," Kline said.

"Do you have any warrants?"

"Naw, man, I'm clean."

"Why are you riding around a school and parking here? You know this is a drug free zone, right?"

"I couldn't find the address."

"Address for what?"

"A job."

"Burglary?"

"No, man, come on," Kline said, shaking his head. "I'm doing landscaping. Bossman gave me a new house to get started on and I couldn't find the address. I had just pulled over to call him and was waiting for him to call me back."

Bader returned with a small bag of marijuana and a wallet. "This is all I could find. Bunch of tools in the back but nothing else."

"Run him around the world," I said, asking Bader to check his information against any federal, state or local warrants.

"You got it."

"It's just a bag of weed, man," Kline protested.

"I'm not worried about the weed. Who do you work for?"

"His name is Carlos Vegas."

"And who does he work for?"

"Nobody, man. He owns the company. Vegas Lawncare."

"Dr. Houston?"

"Who?"

The reaction appeared genuine. He was either the best actor, or had no idea who the guy was and was not a threat to me or Jenny.

Bader returned a few minutes later holding Kline's ID. He turned away from Kline and told me he had a warrant in our county.

"You lied to me," I said as I walked to him and grabbed his arm.

"What do you mean?"

"You said you didn't have any warrants, but you have one right now."

"For what?"

"Failure to appear last month," Bader answered.

"Man! I took care of that!"

"Apparently not," I said.

"Dammit, man! Over a bag of weed?"

"You're going to jail for a warrant, not the weed," I said.

"Aw, damn!"

"I'll 10-5 him to County," Bader said, indicating he would transport him to the county jail.

"Thanks, man," I said. "Once I get the car inventoried and towed, I'll be on the way."

"No problem," Bader said as he took Kline to his unit.

I pulled my phone out of my pocket and dialed Jenny's number.

"Is everything okay?" she answered.

"It's fine. Just a guy in the wrong place at the wrong time. Listen, I'm going to be home late. I'll have to do some paperwork since we arrested him."

"Arrested him?"

"Yeah, he had a warrant."

"I really wish this would stop, Troy."

"Me too, sweetie."

"Maybe it's over. Maybe they've just moved on to whatever twisted plan they have next and Tanner was just being cautious."

"I don't know," I said.

"I'm so tired, Troy. We can't keep living like this. We're chasing ghosts."

I paused, letting her words hang as I watched Bader drive off with Kline. She was right. With no end in sight, at some point, we would either just have to accept the fact that this was the new normal or go on with our lives and hope that Houston and company had given up on us.

"I'll pick up dinner on the way home," I said. "I love you."

"I love you too, Troy," Jenny said before hanging up.

CHAPTER FIFTY-FIVE

After booking Kline and typing up the report, I stopped by a local barbecue place and picked up dinner before heading home. Kruger and I were both exhausted after the long day, and I was supremely jealous of her ability to sleep on the fifteen-minute drive home.

The garage door was open when we arrived home – something Jenny often did when she got home before me to be "more welcoming" as she called it. I backed the Tahoe in, leaving enough room that either her SUV or my truck could get out of the garage if necessary and killed the engine.

"You hungry, girl?" I asked as I grabbed the bag of food and opened Kruger's door.

She jumped out, sniffing the bag as I closed the door behind her. She trotted alongside me, eyeing the feast that I had brought home as we walked through the garage and closed its door.

"Honey, I brought food," I said as we walked in through the laundry room.

"I'm starving," Jenny said, meeting me in the kitchen and taking the bag. She kissed me and then went to work putting the food on plates as I unsnapped the belt keepers on my duty belt.

I snapped the belt keepers together and removed my duty belt as I headed to the bedroom to change. I put my duty weapon in the quick access biometric safe on the nightstand and changed into a t-shirt and shorts before heading to the living room.

Jenny had set up our meal on the coffee table as she turned on one of our favorite shows for a night of binge watching.

"Did you get a new phone?" Jenny asked as I sat down next to her.

"Huh? New phone?" I asked as I sat down and Kruger hopped up on the couch next to me. We were book-ended by dogs with Bear on the other side sitting next to Jenny.

Jenny leaned over and picked up a phone from the end table and handed it to me. "Doesn't look like your normal phone."

I cautiously took the phone from Jenny and studied it. It was a brand new smartphone.

"Where did you find this?"

"Care to explain?" Jenny asked suspiciously.

"Answer me," I said.

"It was on the coffee table. I saw it when I sat down and thought you dropped it off on your way to change clothes."

"This isn't my phone."

"Really?" Jenny asked incredulously with a raised eyebrow. "Is there something you want to tell me?"

"This isn't a joke," I said as I shot up from the couch, holding the phone. "You're telling me this was here when you got home?"

"I don't know," Jenny said as she stood with me. "I just saw it when I sat down and thought it was yours."

"Fuck! Someone's been in the house. Don't touch anything."

"Troy, what's going on?"

As I started to answer, the phone started ringing in my hand. The caller ID read *ANSWER TROY.*

"Oh my God," Jenny said as she picked up Bear and held him close.

I turned the screen to face her. "Definitely not my phone."

"Troy, answer it," she said.

I hesitated as I looked around the room. Whoever had put the phone there had obviously installed a camera somewhere. "Was the alarm still set when you got home?"

"Yes, I disarmed it," Jenny said. "Answer the phone."

I sighed, knowing that no good would come of whatever was about to happen.

"Who are you?" I asked as I answered the call and turned on the speakerphone.

"Your options are limited, Mr. Shepherd, so pay close attention."

"Houston," I replied. I immediately recognized his voice. "Why don't you come out and talk to me man to man instead of breaking into my house?"

"You couldn't leave well enough alone, could you? I should have killed you when I had the chance. But that's neither here nor there now. You have information that I need."

I looked around the room, trying to find something out of place that could be where they had hidden a camera.

"I already told your dead associate everything I know."

"Ah, yes, but now there's new information that I know you have that I need from you. About your associates with the Luna Group."

"I don't know what you're talking about."

"We'll see. For now, you will walk out into your driveway with your hands in the air. Turn around, face your house and get on your knees. Someone will be with you shortly."

"And if I don't?"

"That would be ill advised," Houston said. A round zipped by my head as it crashed through a front window and hit a picture of Bear hanging on the wall. I instinctively grabbed Jenny and brought her with me to the ground as I heard the glass shatter. She dropped Bear who yelped from being startled and ran off.

"I guess I should've mentioned that first, but there's a sniper outside. If you do anything I don't like, he will kill your dogs and your girlfriend."

I had dropped the phone in the commotion. I motioned for Jenny to stay down as I picked it up and calmly stood.

"Can I at least put some clothes on first?" I asked.

Jenny shot me a look. "Troy, no," she whispered.

"You have thirty minutes," Houston said. "If you're not out by then, my men will burn the house down with you in it after they kill your girlfriend and dogs. Don't test me."

Houston ended the call. I tossed the phone onto the couch and crouched down next to Jenny.

"Stay low," I said. "Let's get you and the pups to the bedroom."

I tried to stay between her and where I thought the bullet had come from as she squatted low and headed for the bedroom. I retrieved her gun from the nightstand safe and handed it to her.

"Get in the bath tub and lock the door," I said.

"Troy, you can't go out there," Jenny pleaded. "We can't do this again."

"We don't have a choice," I said as I dropped to one knee next to the bed. "It's time to end this."

"There has to be another way."

I stopped what I was doing and turned to her, standing as I held her face in my hands.

"I love you," I said before kissing her. "It's going to be okay."

CHAPTER FIFTY-SIX

There were three possible locations for the sniper around my property. At least, that's what I estimated based on my sniper and counter-sniper training when I was on the SWAT team at the St. Tammany Parish Sheriff's Office. They were where I would've been if I were in their shoes.

Our house sat on a little over an acre of land. The nearest house was an eighth of a mile away separated by open fields. We were on a small hill with higher hills about a quarter of a mile away on two sides. Judging by the angle of entry of the bullet, if there was only one shooter, he was perched on a hill to our northwest.

The good news, if that was true, was that our basement had an exit on the opposite side of the house in the back yard. It would give me an opportunity to get out undetected. But if there were more shooters or I was wrong, I'd be stepping right into a kill zone.

I geared up and headed into the basement, hoping that the access in the hallway was out of the line of sight of whatever cameras Houston's goons had installed in the living room. I grabbed my custom Remington 700 sniper rifle from the safe and Glock 17. Both were equipped with suppressors.

The helmet-mounted display powered up and I went through the setup. I entered the rifle's information, including caliber and scope type and it appeared to sync to the Leupold scope. I preferred to shoot the old-fashioned way, but it was interesting to me how advanced the artificial intelligence in the helmet was. Tuna or Kruger had obviously spent a whole bunch of money on developing this technology or they had gotten it from someone who had.

I chambered a round and then made my way to the stairs leading to the backyard. After taking a deep breath and clearing my head, I unlocked the door and slowly exited with my rifle up and ready. The helmet-mounted display aligned with the scope, giving me a real time assessment of where the bullets would hit at any time, even without aiming. Without anything connecting it to the scope, I had no idea how the system "knew" and I had no intention of testing it. Technology was nice but no replacement for the fundamentals of shooting.

It was quiet when I stepped out into the yard. I lowered to a crouch, hoping the six-foot privacy fence would be enough to conceal me from where I thought the sniper would be located. I took a second to listen for any signs of hostiles before moving to the gate on the southeast corner of the house.

I slung my rifle and drew my suppressed Glock 17 as I reached the fence. I switched the HUD from its color night vision mode to thermal and slowly opened the gate outward. Scanning for threats, I moved toward the edge of the garage to take cover from the location I thought the sniper might be.

Reaching the end of the house, I switched back to night vision mode and low crawled the rest of the way to get into position. Bushes near the driveway gave me some concealment as I moved to an opening where I could get a shot at the sniper.

I flipped back to thermal mode to look for hot spots on the hill about a quarter of a mile away. Each time I found a spot, I'd turn off the HUD completely and use the scope on my rifle to identify what I was looking at. After ten minutes, I realized he was either no longer on the hill or he had never been there in the first place.

As I started to move, I heard a round zip by and hit the house followed by the register of a rifle. The threat system in the helmet immediately pointed to my right and indicated it had located the threat.

I rolled onto my side and pivoted around. The HUD aligned with the scope and placed an indicator on the sniper's location along with a desired aiming cue. I left the night vision mode on and zoomed in, seeing a clear image of a man lying prone in some brush next to a spotter.

I watched him cycle the bolt on his rifle and chamber a round as I took aim. I cheated a little, using the helmet's cueing system to speed up the shot. It estimated the winds at two knots from the east and the distance to target at one thousand one hundred feet.

I squeezed the trigger. The round impacted the shooter in the forehead and he fell dead. The spotter didn't react initially and then bent down to check his partner when he realized what happened.

As I chambered another round, the AI in the helmet identified the spotter and gave me a shooting solution. I ignored it, instead opting to take my chances now that the threat had been reduced.

Instead of picking up the rifle and returning fire, the spotter stood to run away. I fired, hitting him in the left thigh and causing him to trip and roll a dozen or so yards down the hill.

With the threat neutralized, I stood and slung my rifle as I drew my Glock and headed to their location. I needed answers, and the spotter was going to give them to me.

CHAPTER FIFTY-SEVEN

"I'm sorry Troy, I really am," Agent Tanner said over the truck's Bluetooth speakers. "But there's nothing the team or the FBI can do to help right now. Even if we knew where they were."

"They were in my house! They disabled my alarm and broke in and out without a trace!" I shouted angrily.

"I know. I wish we could do more, but our hands are tied. Even the team's hands are tied right now. I wish I could tell you more. I'll fly down there in a couple of days and tell you everything in person, I promise. But right now, I can't. They are untouchable. I'm sorry."

"I'm sorry too," I said before mashing the button on the steering wheel to end the call.

I stepped out of the truck and opened the back door. I put on the custom body armor, helmet, and readied the modified suppressed H&K 416 rifle with custom digital sight that linked to the helmet's targeting system.

I closed the door and started up the hill into the woods. On the other side was the mansion overlooking Sandy Creek just northwest of Austin. The spotter had sworn Houston would be there.

He had been tough to break, but didn't require some of the more advanced techniques I had learned from Kruger. Between the interrogation and the gunshot wound to his leg, walking might be a challenge for the foreseeable future, but I expected him to make a full recovery in prison. The Sheriff promised to see to it personally.

I had only met Sheriff Gonzalez once before that night. He had given me an award for stopping the active shooter at the school a year earlier. He was a good man and great leader, but I preferred to stay off his radar.

Jenny called 911 after my interrogation, and deputies rushed to my house to secure the scene. They found the shooter and his weapon, and I gave them the spotter. I pointed out the round in my living room and the side of my house, and told Detective Murray that there had been a struggle when the spotter tried to finish the job.

They took my rifle for ballistics and released me. The preliminary evidence was enough to not pursue charges at this time. Sheriff Gonzalez said he had no doubt that it was a clear-cut case of self-defense, and said he was just glad we were okay.

As I crested the hill and approached the edge of the tree line near the compound, I stopped to do some surveillance. The other important bit of information that the spotter had given me was that he was part of a private security firm called *Wildfire Industries* – a defense contractor that had employed former special operations forces as mercenaries all over the world. He confirmed that Houston's private security detail was provided by a subsidiary of the same group.

Using the optical system in the helmet, I switched between infrared and thermal imaging as I scanned the perimeter. There was one guard standing watch near the edge of the massive detached garage at the edge of the property. He was the closest threat to me en route to the mansion. He was wearing a suit and smoking a cigarette as he leaned against the building and appeared to look out into the trees off to my left. He did not appear to be carrying a rifle, but I was sure he was armed with at least a handgun. I marked his position with the targeting system and continued scanning for more threats.

I found two more roving patrols. These two were much more serious, both wearing tactical clothing, plate carriers, and rifles. I had to assume that the closer I got to the mansion and the front of the estate, the more heavily fortified it would be.

As I prepared to move, I checked my watch. It was just after 1 a.m. I had driven straight to the address after the deputies cleared the scene at my house. I didn't want to drag this out any longer. I knew waking Tanner up was a waste of time, and I was surprised she had even answered, but I was hoping she might have some reassurance that the team had this handled. Instead, all she did was confirm the realization that I was on my own.

I readied my rifle and turned back to face the closest guard. He was still leaning against the detached garage, casually smoking a cigarette. As I took aim and placed the targeting system's computed reticle on his cranium, he flicked the cigarette into the ground, stepped on it, and turned back toward the house.

Looking back to the other two patrols, I planned a route out of their line of sight toward the lone smoker. The helmet mounted display did a good job of keeping tabs on their general position, updating each time I found them.

I stayed low as I moved out of the tree line and moved quickly toward the lone guard by the garage. With his back still to me, I let my rifle fall against its sling and drew my knife as I approached.

Sneaking up behind him, I grabbed his mouth with my left hand and jerked him down and back as I drove the blade into his throat. He struggled momentarily before I dragged his lifeless body behind the garage and out of sight. I disarmed him and cleared the weapon before tossing it aside.

I turned toward where the targeting system thought the other two were. They hadn't moved far from the two marked locations. When the system identified them, it put arrows over them indicating threats.

The nearest one was walking toward the tree line to my right while the far guard held his position near the fenced in pool area. There was no easy approach to either of them, so I took aim at the nearest guard and fired.

The suppressed subsonic round impacted the guard in the head. He crumpled to the ground as I turned to the second guard. I lined up the constantly computed targeting reticle on his forehead and squeezed the trigger.

Before his lifeless body hit the ground, I was up and moving toward the house. I could almost hear Kruger yelling at me for charging into an unknown tactical situation alone, but that ship had sailed. If he wanted me to do it right, he shouldn't have gone off and died or disappeared or whatever the hell had happened to him.

I entered the pool area through the open gate and headed to the nearest door. As I took cover against the stucco wall, the door opened and a guard exited. I dropped my rifle against its sling and unsheathed my knife, taking him down silently before moving into the house. I knew I had just been very lucky.

The kitchen was empty as I moved to the stairs. Reaching the bottom, I saw a guard rounding the first flight of stairs. I double-tapped him with a round to the chest and head and then caught him before he rolled down the stairs.

I went up the stairs to the second floor. Another guard was walking away from me toward a set of double-doors that I assumed led to the master bedroom. I used my knife to neutralize him before heading to the double-doors.

Stopping just short, I took a second to catch my breath and calm myself. I was exhausted from lack of sleep, and I was angry. With every kill, my bloodlust grew stronger. I couldn't stop thinking about Cynthia and Jacobs and all the good cops Houston had executed.

I readied my rifle and kicked the door in. I hooked right to clear the room and then turned back toward the bed when I was sure no one was behind the door. As I stepped toward the massive bed, I suddenly froze in horror.

"What? Who are you?" Houston screamed as he suddenly shot up in bed.

My brain couldn't process what I was seeing. Houston was naked at least from the waist up. There were naked children next to him on either side – two girls and a boy. They were preteens at best, probably younger. They screamed when they saw me standing at the foot of the bed.

Houston capitalized on my shock, grabbing his chrome 1911-style handgun from the dresser and firing. The .45 caliber round hit me in the chest, knocking the wind out of me as it caused me to take a step back.

The custom, lightweight armor did its job. The impact felt like the paint-filled *simunition* rounds we used in SWAT training and the police academy. It would probably leave a huge welt where it impacted, but it was otherwise harmless.

"Get out of here, kids," I growled. My blood was boiling. I didn't return fire, but instead moved quickly to the side of the bed where Houston had leaned to get the handgun.

The kids screamed and ran off. Houston followed up with two more shots. I heard them, but my adrenaline was pumping so hard and I was so angry that I didn't even feel them hit my body armor. I saw the completely naked children evacuate the bed out of the corner of my eye as I lunged toward Houston.

I don't know how many more times he fired, but the slide locked back. I snatched it from him and hit him with the butt of the pistol causing blood to gush as it broke his nose.

"You fucking pervert!" I yelled.

I turned to see the kids standing next to the bed crying and staring at me. "I said get out!" I shouted.

Startled, they complied, quickly grabbing their clothes off the floor and scurrying out the door.

"You can't kill me," Houston said defiantly as I turned my attention back to him. "They won't let you."

"Is that so?"

Houston smiled through the blood trickling down his mouth. "I don't know how you managed to escape, but if you kill me, they'll kill your family."

"The sniper? Yeah, he's not going to be a factor."

Houston laughed. "I have more men."

"I noticed."

"Fine," Houston said. "Take me in. Hand me over to the FBI. See how long that lasts. Where are the rest of your friends, by the way? They should've told you I'm untouchable."

"You killed a lot of good cops."

"For the greater good. You're such a small-minded man, Alex. So blinded by your own self-righteousness that you can't see the bigger picture."

"Does that picture involve molesting little kids, you sick fuck?" I asked, the rage inside me building.

"Perfectly consensual and legal within the eyes of the church. As someone who's okay with murder himself, you have no moral high ground here."

"You're right about that," I said as I hit him again with the butt of the handgun.

Only this time, I didn't stop. *I couldn't stop.* For everyone he'd killed, for the unrest he had caused, and for the children he had abused – I couldn't stop myself from bashing his face in. Blood splattered everywhere. Every crack was immensely satisfying. I pounded his face until there was nothing recognizable anymore and his body went limp.

I stood over his body, my chest heaving and clenching the bloodied gun.

"I'm not just okay with it. I *enjoyed* it. You piece of shit."

CHAPTER FIFTY-EIGHT

There were at least a dozen or more children in the basement from ages six to fifteen. Most of the younger ones didn't speak English. The oldest girl, Carlita, told me they were all from migrant caravans taken from their families in Central and South America.

I got them all upstairs where they reunited with the kids that had been in the bed with Houston. Carlita told me that they were part of a nightly rotation – where it was explained it was an honor to be selected to stay with him. Mostly he just used them for sex and housework. It was the most repulsive thing I had ever heard.

Carlita helped me get everyone food and water and then we escorted them out into the courtyard in the back. I dragged the bodies of the guards into the house and then Carlita joined me in the house.

I gave her very specific instructions on what to say to the dispatchers when she called 9-1-1. I made her repeat it to me several times and then I watched as she dialed.

"The house is on fire!" she said. "They have all died! We need help!"

I nodded my approval as she gave the address and disconnected. I then pointed for her to rejoin the others as I went upstairs with the can of gasoline I'd found in the garage. I drenched Houston's corpse and bed with gasoline and then tossed a lit match on it.

Satisfied that it was burning, I went downstairs and disconnected the gas line from the stove and then headed outside to join them. I made sure they were well clear of the fire and then checked one last time that Carlita would be able to handle them until firefighters arrived. She was barely a teenager, but already so mature – being subjected to such cruelty had made her grow up way too fast.

I headed back into the woods the same way I had come in as I heard sirens in the distance. As I made it to my truck, I heard the first gas explosion and felt it rock the ground. I removed my armor and stored it in the locked case along with my rifle before heading back home.

* * *

It was almost five a.m. when I pulled into my driveway. I was exhausted. The adrenaline dump from the night's events had just started to take its toll. Combined with the cumulative fatigue from constantly looking over my shoulder and waiting for Houston's next attack, I had nothing left in the tank.

Jenny was asleep on the couch when I walked in and disarmed the alarm. Kruger and Bear ran to greet me as I closed and locked the door behind me.

Hearing the commotion, Jenny got up and stretched. "Is it over?" she asked.

"I think so," I said as I put my arm around her and continued toward the bedroom. "I'm exhausted."

"Me too," she said. "I was worried and waiting for you. Must've fallen asleep on the couch."

"I should probably take a shower," I said as we shuffled into the bedroom.

As I stepped into the shower and the hot water hit me, I was suddenly and inexplicably overcome with guilt. Maybe it was delirium from the exhaustion or maybe it had just finally caught up to me, but the faces of every man I had killed in the last few years flooded my memories. From the Imams to the Russians, to Houston's men, they all flashed in my mind.

I didn't even recognize myself anymore, and I knew my girls wouldn't recognize me. It was a horribly unsettling feeling. The vengeance, rage, and despair from losing them had turned me into a monster – a monster with an unquenchable thirst for killing.

I tried to shake the feeling off – reminding myself that everyone I had killed had been an asshole that deserved to die. They had been terrorists, mafia thugs, child molesters, and killers themselves. None of them had been innocent.

But the more I tried to convince myself, the worse I felt. I had spent a career putting people in jail for breaking the law. The exercise in moral relativism didn't make it better. It was just wrong no matter how I tried to justify it. Vengeance was not justice.

"Baby, you okay in there?" Jenny asked.

I had gotten lost in my own thoughts and subsequently lost track of time. I finished cleaning up and then got out. After toweling off, I went straight to bed. The exhaustion finally caught up to me, and I fell asleep almost immediately.

I awoke to Jenny gently rubbing my shoulder and Kruger's nose just inches from my face as she stared at me. "Troy, you need to wake up."

Startled, I gasped. "What?"

"It's okay," she said. "I'm sorry to wake you, but Agent Tanner and Michelle Decker are here to see you. They said it's important."

I sat up and rubbed my eyes. "What time is it?"

"Just after noon," she said. "I didn't want to wake you but they said it's urgent."

"Okay."

I rolled out of bed and put a t-shirt and jeans on before walking into the living room. Decker and Tanner were sitting on the couch sipping coffee. They stood as I walked in.

"You guys got here fast," I said. "I'm guessing it's not good news."

Tanner frowned. "I told you to just be patient, Troy."

I sat down in the recliner next to them. Jenny joined me, sitting on the arm as we waited for Tanner and Decker to explain their presence.

"I'm guessing you being here means I need a lawyer," I said, looking at Decker before turning to Tanner. "You here to arrest me?"

"We're here to give you options," Decker replied. "And, yes, Maddie thought it would be best for you to have representation. They flew me here this morning."

"Are the kids safe?" I asked.

"Yes," Tanner replied. "Most were undocumented immigrants separated from their families at the border. Others were trafficked from South America. ICE is working that right now."

"Then that's really all that matters. Houston was a piece of shit and a pedophile. Case closed. What about the woman?"

"Veronica Carver had turned state's witness," Tanner said. "That's why I told you we couldn't do anything. She was going to give up Houston and a plot by the Chinese government in exchange for immunity."

"What kind of plot?" I asked.

"Chinese intelligence agents had been working with her and Houston to destabilize the United States – to create race riots, delegitimize law enforcement and government actions, and eventually start a civil war."

"And she gets a free pass for confessing?"

"This is big, Troy. She was directly involved in it and had paid off factions within our government. The Attorney General is more than willing to give her immunity in exchange for shedding light on the corruption within our own house. China has been a bad actor in the past with the attempt on the President at Midway Island. This is far beyond that."

"If they're so embedded in the government already, what good is prosecuting going to do? Who can you even trust?"

"We were working on that," Tanner said. "And that's why keeping Houston alive was so important. He was going to be the first high-profile domino to topple, hopefully leading to more investigations and a turn in public opinion. But you couldn't wait."

"Hey, you didn't tell me any of this shit on the phone."

"I couldn't," Tanner said. "Not over an open line. And I'm barely comfortable talking about it in person. I swept the living room and kitchen for bugs before Jenny woke you up – found the camera Houston had used to track you."

"Okay, so, now what? Houston is dead. Good riddance. Surely that doesn't mean it's over."

"If it were up to me, you're right," Tanner said. "I wish it were that easy. But someone tipped off the FBI that you were there, and to everyone but the AG and our task force, Houston was a high-profile philanthropist who was just murdered. They're going to come for you, Troy."

"And that's why you're here?" I asked Decker.

"They can't intervene without tipping off their investigation," Decker replied. "I'm here because I want to help you."

"What are you suggesting?" I asked Tanner. "Are you going to arrest me?"

"You need to disappear, Troy," Tanner answered. "Let Coolio do what he does and get you a new identity. Somewhere far from here."

"I'm not doing that," I said.

"What? Why not?" Tanner asked.

I looked at Jenny and put my hand on hers. "I've made a life here. I'm not running anymore."

"It's not a matter of running versus not running. It's prison versus freedom, Troy. Jenny can go with you. We can make that happen," Tanner said.

"What would that mean?" Jenny asked.

"It means you'd never see your family again. Or your students. Or your friends. They would have a funeral and mourn an empty casket – or a faked body. *Jenny* would cease to exist," I responded.

"Oh, wow," Jenny said, shaken by the response.

"Don't worry, I'm not asking you to do that."

"But I'd never see you again," Jenny said softly, holding back tears.

"I'm not doing this again," I said.

"Troy," Decker interjected.

"No, I've made up my mind," I said. "I've done some bad stuff over the last few years – stuff I should've answered for a long time ago. The reason all of this evil keeps haunting us is because I keep running away from it instead of answering for what I've done. Vengeance is no excuse."

"You won't survive prison, Troy," Tanner warned. "They'll make sure of it."

"That's fine," I said.

"You have to think this through rationally, Troy," Tanner pleaded.

I nodded as I looked her in the eye.

"Special Agent Tanner, I would like to confess to the murder of Dr. Houston last night."

EPILOGUE

Five months later

I had made a huge mistake. I didn't regret confessing to the murder of Houston and burning down his house. I had let my rage overcome my judgment and had hurt the chances of real justice in the process.

No, the mistake was in leaving Fredericksburg in the first place. It was dragging Jenny to Louisiana and risking her life yet again as my past collided with my new life. It was not heeding the warnings of Hyatt and Tanner and continuing to seek vengeance over justice.

No matter how much it hurt losing my former teammates, I should have listened to my own inner voice and stayed home. I thought the risk was having my real identity revealed and losing everything, but it turned out I was only half right.

I was still Troy Wilson, and incarcerated as Texas Department of Corrections Inmate #269301 at the Polunsky Unit maximum security prison in Livingston, Texas. I was serving month four of a life sentence for arson and nine counts of murder, but because of the guilty plea, I would be eligible for parole in twenty-five years with good behavior.

Despite the objections of Jenny, Decker, and Tanner, I felt it was the only option. As much as I loved her, I couldn't ask Jenny to leave her family and her life forever. It was not fair to make her pay for my mistakes like that.

And for me, running away again and starting another new life was equally unpalatable. It meant I would never see Jenny again and have to start over, pretending we had never met.

I was just tired. And with facing what I had done, I at least had the option of seeing Jenny again. Whether she stayed with me and visited or moved on, as I had asked her to before turning myself in, was another story. I hoped she would stick it out at least a little while, but deep down I knew it was better for her to move on with her life. She had yet to visit in the four months I had been in prison. If her choice had been to try to move on, I truly wished her the best. It wasn't her fault.

Despite the chance for parole, I knew I'd probably die in prison anyway. Someone would inevitably find out I was a cop – maybe even the Russian mafia would find me – and that would be the end of it. It was a fitting end to a tragic story.

So far, though, no one had taken interest in me. I started in G-3 Medium Security and eventually was able to work my way into working on the animal detail caring for security horses and canines three days per week. My background as a K-9 handler had helped me get the position, and although I didn't know much about horses, I found the work therapeutic and relaxing.

"Wilson, Sergeant Roland wants to see you in the stables," Corrections Officer Nayland said as I was cleaning the canine kennels. It was late in the evening on a Friday afternoon, just past sunset on a short winter day, on my last shift for the week.

"Do you want me to finish this first?" I asked, holding a shovel and bucket full of dog crap.

"He said he wants to see you now," Nayland said, motioning for me to come with him. "We'll get someone else to finish this for you."

"Okay," I said, putting the bucket down and leaning the shovel against the concrete wall.

I couldn't put my finger on it, but something seemed off about Nayland's demeanor. He usually supervised the animal detail as a K-9 handler himself. I had only been doing the detail a few weeks, and I still didn't know everyone's name, but I had never heard of a Sergeant Roland. Something just felt off about the entire request.

Nayland shackled my arms and legs per policy and escorted me out of the kennels toward the barn next door. We walked through the stables to the far end where Roland and two other corrections officers that I didn't recognize were standing in an empty stable.

"That will be all," Roland told Nayland. "Thank you."

"Do you want me to remove his restraints?" Nayland asked.

"No, we'll take care of it," Roland said. "And we'll sign him back in to his cell. You can clear him from your detail."

The hair on the back of my neck was standing straight up. My eyes darted around, looking for a weapon or means of defending myself. I knew this was about to get bad for me.

Roland waited for Nayland to leave. When the metallic click of the security door locking echoed through the barn, he turned and faced me. The other two guards stood on either side of me, waiting for his instruction.

"I'm guessing this isn't a social visit," I said, breaking the silence.

"Look, I don't want to do this either, but it is what it is at this point," Roland said. "You've got two options: you can make this easy for all of us or you can drag it out and make it painful. I'd really rather you just make this easy so we can go on with our day."

"What do you want?"

"Information," Roland said, pulling out his phone and hitting record on the voice recorder feature. "About Freddie Mack. If you tell us what we want to know, I promise this will be painless."

Painless. I looked at the guard to my left and saw a syringe sticking out of his shirt pocket. *Painless* to them meant some form of lethal injection. I was sure of it. They had no intention of letting me walk out of the stable alive.

"I thought your boss was working with the feds," I said, making sure the recorder could hear.

"Don't worry about who's doing what. You just need to answer the questions. Otherwise, things could get really violent for you very quickly."

"Fine," I said, defeatedly. "What are your questions?"

Before he could answer, the lights were suddenly killed. The stable went pitch black.

"What the fuck?" one of the guards said, pulling out his flashlight.

The other guard grabbed me as he and Roland took out their flashlights.

"Go find out what's going on," Roland said. "And what the fuck happened to the backup lighting?"

The two guards walked out of the stable with their flashlights searching for threats as Roland grabbed me. I heard what sounded like a suppressed round followed by the crack of something solid breaking bone. Roland nervously shined his flashlight toward the gate of the stable we were in.

"Mark! Jimmy! What the fuck is going on out there?" he yelled.

His light shined on something. It was a blur of movement, but there appeared to be nothing there, almost like looking through a distorted window.

I heard the unmistakable sound of a bolt cycling on a suppressed rifle and felt blood spray my face as Roland collapsed next to me, dropping his flashlight.

"Who's there?" I said, seeing nothing in the pitch black.

I heard keys jingle and then felt my shackles being removed.

I heard the low growl of a familiar voice as the infiltrator grabbed my arm.

"C'mon, bub, we've got work to do."

Thanks for reading!

If you enjoyed this book, please leave a review!

VISIT WWW.CWLEMOINE.COM FOR MORE INFORMATION ON NEW BOOK RELEASE DATES, BOOK SIGNINGS, AND EXCLUSIVE SPECIAL OFFERS.

ACKNOWLEDGMENTS

To all my readers, thank you for continuing on this journey with me. I appreciate the comments, feedback, and reviews. It has been an honor.

To **Dr. Doug Narby**, as always, thank you for your support, wisdom, and friendship. One of my favorite things in writing is discussing these chapters with you. Thank you for always being there for me.

Pat Byrnes, you've been there since the beginning. Thank you for being my first fan and beta reader. I appreciate your comments and reviews.

Thanks again to everyone who has supported me. I can't wait to see what the future will hold.

Thanks for reading!

C.W. Lemoine is the author of ***THE SPECTRE SERIES and THE ALEX SHEPHERD SERIES***. He graduated from the A.B. Freeman School of Business at Tulane University in 2005 and Air Force Officer Training School in 2006. He is a former military pilot that has flown the F-16 and F/A-18. He currently flies for a Legacy U.S. Airline. He is also a certified Survival Krav Maga Instructor and a sheriff's deputy.

www.cwlemoine.com

YouTube Channel

https://www.youtube.com/user/cwlemoine

Facebook

http://www.facebook.com/cwlemoine/

Twitter:

@CWLemoine

Made in United States
Troutdale, OR
06/18/2023

10660690R00217